SUSAN MALLERY

hold me

HQN™

HQN™

ISBN-13: 978-0-373-78900-9

Hold Me

www.HQNBooks.com

Printed in U.S.A.

This book is dedicated by one of my favorite readers:

To all Susan Mallery's readers, may you enjoy her stories
as much as I do.
—a devoted romance reader, Jan W.

CHAPTER ONE

No one woke up in the morning and thought to themselves, *Today I'm going to get lost in the woods*. But even without a plan, it happened.

Maybe it was simply that innate human need to explore. Maybe it was bad luck, or maybe it was just people being idiots. Grandma Nell had always loved to say, "Beauty is skin deep, but stupid goes clear down to the bone." Not that Destiny Mills was going to be judgmental either way. People got lost, and her job was to make sure they got found. It was kind of like being a superhero. Only instead of laser vision or invisibility, she had a brilliant computer software program and a finely honed search and rescue team.

Well, technically the team wasn't *hers*. It belonged to whatever town or county had hired her company. Her firm had created the software program, and she was one of three facilitators who helped those wanting to use it. She showed up, trained the search and rescue group and then moved on to the next assignment.

If it was Monday, she must be in Fool's Gold, she thought humorously as she stepped into her small, temporary office. Fool's Gold, California. Population 125,482 per the sign she'd seen on her way in. Nestled in the foothills of the Sierra Nevada mountains, the town attracted tourists by the thousands. They came in winter to ski, in summer to hike and camp and all year long to attend the dozens of festivals that had put the community on the map.

None of which concerned her. What was of more interest were the literally hundreds of thousands of acres right outside the city borders. Uncharted wilderness with plenty of slopes, gullies, streams and caves. Places where people got lost. And when someone was lost, who you gonna call?

Destiny chuckled as the *Ghostbusters* theme music played in her head. She didn't know about anyone else, but for her, life was a soundtrack. Music was everywhere. Notes formed melodies, and melodies were little more than memories to be recalled. Hear a song from your high school prom and you were back in your boyfriend's arms.

She settled in her chair and plugged her laptop into the docking station. She only had a week or so to get up and running before the real work began. For the next three months she would be mapping the terrain, feeding the information into the incredibly intelligent software her company used and training the local search and rescue team. She was the point of contact, the human connection. And in three months she would move on to another part of the country and do it all again.

She liked the moving around. She liked always being somewhere new. She made friends easily and then just as easily left them behind when it was time to go. There would be more friends at the next new place. Sure, there was a lack of continuity, but on the upside, she was spared the emotional drama that went with long-term friendships. Whether it was her getting close to them or them getting close to her, relationships could be exhausting.

She'd grown up in a family that made any of the "real housewives" shows look as interesting as reading the phone book.

Reality TV had nothing on her parents. As an adult, she got to choose whether or not she wanted that drama, and she'd decided she didn't. Destiny had deliberately picked a job and a lifestyle that allowed her to forever be moving on.

But for the next few months she would enjoy the small-town quirkiness of Fool's Gold. She'd already read up on the place and was looking forward to sampling plenty of local flavor.

Right on time, the door to her small office opened. Destiny recognized the tall, blond, good-looking guy standing in the doorway. Not that they'd met before—she'd been hired by the mayor, not by him—but she'd seen him on plenty of magazine covers, television interviews and internet articles.

She stood and smiled. "Hi, I'm Destiny Mills."

"Kipling Gilmore."

His eyes were a darker blue than she'd expected, and he had that easy grace that most likely came from a lifetime of being an athlete. Because he wasn't just Kipling Gilmore. He was *the* Kipling Gilmore. Famous athlete. Superstar skier. Olympic gold medalist. The press had called him G-Force, because on skis, at least, he went for speed. Rules of physics be damned. He could do things that had never been done. At least until the crash.

They shook hands. He handed her a small, pink bakery box. "To help you settle in."

She lifted the lid and saw a half-dozen doughnuts. The scent of glaze and cinnamon drifted to her. It was intoxicating and made her instantly want fifteen minutes alone with her sugar fix.

"Thank you," she said. "Way better than flowers."

"I'm glad you think so. When did you get to town?"

"Yesterday. I got to Sacramento the night before and made the short drive in the morning."

"You're settling in okay?"

"I am, and I'm excited to get to work."

"Then let's get to it."

They both sat. She angled her laptop toward him and tapped on several keys.

"There are two major parts to getting the search and rescue software functional," she began. "Mapping the physical geography of the area and then getting you and your team trained on how to use it."

"Sounds easy enough."

"It always does, and then reality sets in."

One eyebrow rose. "Is that a challenge?"

"No. I'm simply saying the process takes time. STORMS can adapt to nearly any situation. The success or failure of a search is usually a combination of information and luck. My goal is to take luck out of the equation."

STORMS—Search Team Rescue Management Software—worked with the rescue team. Data was fed into the system, and the program then projected the most likely areas to search first. The more information known about the person missing, terrain, time of year and weather conditions, the faster the search went. Each searcher had GPS tracking information on his or her person. That information was sent back to the software so the search could be updated in real time.

As more areas were eliminated, the search was narrowed until the missing person was found.

"I'll start mapping the area in the next day or so," she continued.

"How does that happen?"

"First by air. We use a helicopter and various kinds of equipment to supplement the satellite data we already have. The heavily wooded areas and steep mountainsides will have to be mapped on foot."

"You do that?"

While the question was polite enough, the tone suggested he wasn't a believer. *Silly man,* she thought with a smile.

"Yes, Kipling. I can hike when necessary. If the areas are too remote, I take in local guides."

"I thought you were a city girl. Didn't someone tell me you live in Austin?"

"That's home base for me, yes. But I grew up near the Smoky Mountains. I can hold my own in the great outdoors."

What she didn't mention was that when she'd been younger, she'd spent several years living with her maternal grandmother in those same mountains. In addition to knowing her way around rugged terrain, she could fish and knew three ways to cook squirrel, but she wasn't going to share that. Tell someone you grilled a mean steak and you were applauded. Mention squirrel stew with root vegetables and they looked at you like you were in league with cannibals. People were funny, but she'd known that for a long time.

"Then I'll trust you to take care of business," he told her. "When does your helicopter arrive?"

She checked her calendar. "By the end of the week. It's going to be a busy summer. Once we get the geography into the data-base, we'll start testing the system. That means looking for people who aren't really lost."

Humor pulled at the corner of his mouth. "I read the material."

"Good to know. Does that mean you also open instruction manuals?"

He hesitated just long enough for her to start laughing.

"I didn't think so," she said. "What is it with men and in-structions? Or asking for directions?"

"We don't like to admit when we don't know something."

"Ridiculous. No one knows everything."

"We can try."

No surprise there, she thought. Bravado seemed to go hand in hand with being male. Another reason she'd had so much trouble finding the right one. She wanted an absence of bravado and minimal ego. When emotions got riled, the opposite sex could be counted on to act crazy, and there was no place for crazy in her life.

"Are you going to have a problem taking instructions from me?" she asked. "Because if you are, we need to get that taken care of right this minute. I can arm wrestle you into submission, if necessary."

Kipling laughed. "I doubt that."

"Be careful with your assumptions. My grandma taught me a lot of dirty tricks. I know places to dig in a knuckle and make a grown man scream like a little girl. And not in a happy way."

"There's a happy way to scream like a little girl?"

She wrinkled her nose. "I've had to use that threat before, and some men think I'm talking about sex. I'm not."

His gaze settled on her face. "Interesting."

"So, am I going to have a problem with you?"

"No."

"Then this will be a good summer. I've never had a job in California before. I'm looking forward to getting to know the area."

"The town is a little strange."

"In what way?"

He sat easily in his chair. There was no squirming, no sense that he wanted to be somewhere else. He had patience, she thought. He would have to. Waiting out bad weather, waiting out the seasons. Needing conditions to be right.

Kipling Gilmore had won big at the Sochi Olympics, then disaster had struck a few months later. She wasn't one to follow sports, so she didn't know many of the details. Obviously, he'd recovered enough to take the job of heading the Fool's Gold search and rescue team. She wondered if he'd had trouble adjusting to regular life.

She knew it could be difficult for those cursed with fame to try to live like ordinary mortals.

"Everybody here knows everybody's business," he said.

Right. She'd asked him about the town. "That's not uncommon for small towns."

"Yeah, but it's different here. People here are more involved. We'll talk in a couple of weeks and see what you think. The festivals are interesting, and you don't have to lock your doors at night. If you live near the center of town, you don't need a car very often."

"Sounds nice." Despite having her home base in Austin, she wasn't really a big-city girl. She preferred the eccentricities of a small town.

"Have you met Mayor Marsha yet?" Kipling asked.

Destiny shook her head. "No. She hired me, but it was all done through my boss. I have a meeting with her later today."

Amusement returned to his eyes. "I'll be there, too. I think you're going to like her. She's California's longest-serving mayor. She looks like a sweet old lady, but she's actually pretty tough and keeps firm control over her town. She gets things done, and sometimes I've left wondering what just happened."

Qualities she could totally get behind. "I like her already."

"I thought you might." He stood. "Welcome to Fool's Gold, Destiny."

She rose, as well. "Thank you."

As he left her office, she let her gaze drift over his body. He was in great shape, she thought, admitting he was just charming enough to make her wonder if there was any potential there.

She shook her head, because she already knew the answer, and it was no. No way, no how. She wanted ordinary. Regular. The kind of man who understood that life was best lived quietly. Kipling, aka G-Force, had roared down a mountain at who knew what speed. He was a thrill seeker at heart, which meant not for her.

She would simply keep looking. Because the man of her very own calm, rational dreams was out there, and one day she would find him.

Kipling crossed the street. As he waited for one of the few traffic lights in Fool's Gold to change to green, he glanced up at the mountains. Now that it was late spring, he could look at them and not feel anything. The only remaining snow was up at elevations that didn't allow for skiing. So there was no sense of loss, no reminder that he would never again be able to fight the mountain and win. That the sense of flying on snow was lost forever.

He knew what his friends would say, what the doctors would tell him. That he was damned lucky to have made as much of a recovery as he had. That he could walk and that was its own miracle. Anything else was gravy.

Kipling heard the words. On his good days he even believed them. But the rest of the time, he avoided thinking about what had been lost. When it got bad, he simply stopped looking at the mountains.

The light changed, and he crossed the street. As he walked he considered the fact that it might have been easier to simply find a job somewhere there weren't mountains. There were flat places. Maybe in the Midwest or Florida. Only he couldn't imagine what that must be like. To look up and see nothing but sky. He might have an uneasy relationship with the mountains; he might equally love and hate them, but there was no way he could be away from them. They were a part of him. It would be easier to cut off an arm than live without them.

"Hey, Kipling."

He waved automatically at the woman pushing a stroller who had greeted him. Fool's Gold was a friendly kind of place. Where neighbors knew each other and tourists were welcomed as much for their presence as the money they brought with them.

He was used to people he'd never met knowing who he was. That came with the celebrity he had been. Only being in Fool's Gold was different. More intense, maybe. This town wasn't just a place. It was a living, breathing essence.

He shook his head, wondering where all that had come from. He didn't usually think too much about things. He was a doer, preferring to move than sit still. Which had made his recovery a particular brand of hell. But that was behind him now. Except for the scars, the limp and the dull aches that would be with him always, he was healed. And walking.

He headed into his offices at the corner of Eighth Street and Frank Lane, right by one of the fire stations and the police station. No one was going to break in, he thought with a grin. Or party too hard in this neighborhood.

As he unlocked the front door and stepped inside, he reminded himself that years ago he would have chafed at being so close to any kind of authority. That he'd believed that with the ability to fly down a mountain came the right to party as hard as he wanted, and damn the consequences. As long as he beat the clock by even a thousandth of a second, he was a god. At least until the next race.

But time had a way of maturing people. He'd been dragged kicking and screaming into adulthood, and here he was, running the town's search and rescue program. Who would have guessed?

And while his younger self would have mocked authority, even as a kid he'd respected the mountains and those who saved those unfortunate or stupid enough to get themselves lost. He'd been caught in an avalanche once. The local ski patrol had saved his ass.

He'd always been lucky, he thought. Until last summer when he'd had his crash. He'd known one day his luck would run out, and he accepted that it had. Now he was onto another chapter in his life. He had a problem, and he'd fixed it. That was what he liked to do. And in this job, there was going to be plenty of fixing. Or finding.

He walked to his desk and turned on his computer. The office was new enough that he could still smell the fresh paint, and the plants that had been delivered as a sort of welcome were still alive. Kipling considered himself more of a people person than a plant person. Eventually, there would be staff, and he could rope one of them into watering and feeding the plants.

He turned his chair so he could study the huge map that dominated the main wall. It showed the fifty or so square miles around Fool's Gold. There were vineyards to the west, and the road to Sacramento went south. So his main area of concern was east and north. The rugged mountains of the Sierra Nevada rose up quickly. There were a thousand ways to get lost out there, and he was confident tourists and locals alike would find every one of them.

He rose and walked closer to the map. The terrain grew rough within just a few miles of town. There were dozens of popular hiking trails and camping spots. Just last year, there'd been a flash flood through a campground. The rushing waters had endangered a group of girls and their leaders. He wanted to make sure that didn't happen again. That if someone got lost, he or she would be found quickly and safely.

With the new software program, searching would be easy. He knew there would be a learning curve, but in the end, the effort would be worth it.

As soon as Mayor Marsha had told him about the new program, he'd started reading up on it. The results were impressive, and he was looking forward to learning the ins and outs of the system.

And maybe of Destiny Mills, as well, he thought with a grin. She was beautiful. Tall, curvy. A redhead—his personal weakness. There was something about the combination of red hair and pale skin that got his attention. And if she had freckles, all the better. A man could go looking for freckles and not resurface for days.

She was his type in other ways. Single, according to scuttlebutt, and in town for a limited amount of time. He was a man who enjoyed serial monogamy. Having a predetermined expiration date on a relationship was his idea of perfection. If the lady was interested, he was more than willing. At least in the short-term.

Every now and then he wondered if he should want more. That forever thing other people seemed to seek. He'd seen love. He even believed in it. But he'd never felt it. Not the romantic kind. Lust, sure. Liking, absolutely. He loved his sister and his country. He would do anything for a friend. But fall crazy, let's-get-married in love? That hadn't happened.

At this point, he figured it wasn't going to. And he could live with that.

Mayor Marsha was in her late sixties, with white hair swept up in a loose bun and piercing blue eyes. Her suit was tailored, her pearls luminous, and she had a kind smile that made Destiny feel immediately at home.

"Welcome to Fool's Gold," the mayor said, her voice warm. "It's lovely to finally meet you."

"Likewise."

Destiny shook hands the way Grandma Nell had taught her—firmly, while looking the other person in the eye. *You're a human being, not a fish. You should act like it.* Because Grandma Nell had advice for every situation. Not all of it was appropriate, or even helpful, but it was nearly always memorable.

"I'm happy to be here," Destiny told the mayor. "We're going to have a good summer getting STORMS in place."

"Your boss, David, said I would enjoy working with you, and I can see he was right. I like your attitude," the mayor told her.

The other woman looked past her and nodded. "Here comes the rest of our meeting."

Destiny turned and saw Kipling strolling into the mayor's office. There was no other way to describe the easy way he moved. A neat trick, she thought, taking in the slight limp that no doubt came from the horrific crash he'd survived the previous year. What must he have been like back before the accident?

If she were someone else, looking for something different, Kipling would be a temptation, she thought. But he wasn't or she wasn't. Regardless, he was wrong for her, and she knew better than to start down the wrong path. She'd seen way too many emotional disasters in her life to take the chance. *Sometimes you take on the bear and sometimes the bear takes you on. If it's the latter, then you'd better run like hell.*

Destiny held in a chuckle. Yup, Grandma Nell had always had a practical streak in her. She would take one look at Kipling, push Destiny aside and ask for a little privacy. Then she would have her way with him and toss him aside. Because the relationship drama she'd grown up with hadn't started with her parents, although they'd been the worst offenders. No, bad marriages and broken hearts went back generations on both sides.

Kipling hugged the mayor, then kissed her cheek before nodding at Destiny.

"Good to see you again," he said.

"You, too."

Mayor Marsha led them to a seating area in the corner of her office. Once they'd claimed their places, she began the meeting.

"Destiny, the town is thrilled to have you here, helping us launch our HERO program."

Destiny nodded even as she glanced at Kipling. She saw him wince, and couldn't resist pretending she didn't know what the mayor was talking about.

"HERO program?"

"Help Emergency Rescue Operations," Mayor Marsha told

her. "What we're calling Fool's Gold's search and rescue organization. We held a contest, people submitted names. The city council narrowed it down to ten, and then we voted. HERO won."

"It's still a stupid name," Kipling grumbled.

Destiny held in a grin. "You don't like being a hero?"

"Let's just say I take a lot of crap about the name."

"Challenges build character," she murmured, thinking he'd probably liked G-Force a whole lot better.

"Yet another place I'm not lacking."

He winked as he spoke, which made her want to laugh. But this was supposed to be a professional setting, so instead she turned her attention back to Mayor Marsha.

"STORMS will work well for what you have in mind."

"I'm counting on it," the mayor told her. "We were very lucky to get the money we needed. Between our federal and state grants and a very sizable anonymous local donation, we're fully funded for the next five years. Including your part in this."

Impressive, Destiny thought. STORMS didn't come cheap. With the software itself, the equipment required, the expense of mapping and training a team, the price was over a million dollars. And that didn't include the cost of running a search and rescue operation.

"We've had excellent success with our software," she said. "Your terrain is perfectly suited for what we do best."

"Excellent. You and Kipling have a plan?"

Kipling sat as relaxed as he had before. "We're getting one together. Destiny has to map the area and feed the information into her software. Then we'll do some beta testing on the program. We'll make the August first deadline."

"Good." Mayor Marsha nodded at Kipling, then turned back to Destiny. "Do you agree that we'll meet our deadline?"

"We're on schedule to have the program up and running

by mid-July. The extra two weeks are a buffer I'm hoping we don't need."

Destiny didn't like unexpected problems. Part of her job was anticipating issues before they happened. She prided herself on a smooth rollout.

"And how is Starr settling in to life in Fool's Gold?"

The mayor's shift in topic caught Destiny by surprise. Worse, it took her a second to remember who Starr was and why, for the first time in over a decade, she suddenly had someone other than herself to worry about.

"She's, ah, doing okay. I guess. We just got into town yesterday."

The mayor nodded knowingly. "Yes, it must be difficult for both of you. She's your half sister, isn't she? You have the same father but different mothers?"

Destiny felt her mouth start to drop open. She consciously kept her lips together as she nodded. "Yes, that's right," she said cautiously, not comfortable discussing her family. Because it was so much better when people didn't know.

She glanced at Kipling, who looked only mildly interested in their conversation. Did he know who she was? He hadn't hinted that he did.

"Fifteen is a difficult age." Mayor Marsha shook her head. "That's about when the trouble started with my own daughter. She was a headstrong girl. And that was a very long time ago. As for you and Starr, I hope you'll consider Fool's Gold your home as long as you're here. If you need anything, just let me know. Oh, I have something for you."

She walked back to her desk where she picked up a folder. She returned to the sofa and handed it to Destiny.

"We have a summer camp here. End Zone for Kids. It's up in the mountains. There are a lot of interesting programs for young people. I think Starr would enjoy the drama classes, along with music, of course. You're going to be busy, and a fifteen-year-old shouldn't be left home alone all day."

"I, ah, thank you."

Destiny didn't know what else to say. How had the mayor known Starr's age? Or that she was home alone? Although maybe the latter wasn't hard to figure out. After all, Destiny wasn't home with her, and they'd been in town less than two days.

Guilt followed that realization. Because Starr was by herself. At fifteen she should be fine, but that wasn't the point.

"There are charming festivals all summer," the mayor continued. "I hope you'll take advantage of them while you're here. Fool's Gold is a wonderful place to live."

Somehow Destiny found herself outside the office. She didn't remember walking there or saying goodbye. It was the strangest sensation.

Kipling stood next to her. He flashed her a grin. "Kind of wondering what just happened?"

"Yeah."

"You'll get used to it. Nice idea about the camp for your sister."

Destiny nodded. There was no way she was going to explain that until ten days ago, she'd never even met Starr. That between them, her parents had been married twelve or fourteen times, and there were dozens of step-whatevers and a few half siblings floating around the country. No one could keep up with it all, and Destiny had stopped trying years ago.

She held the folder tightly. "Speaking of my sister, I should probably get home and check on her."

"Sure. I'll catch you later."

Right. Work. She forced herself to focus. "We need to talk about the training schedule."

"Give me your phone."

She handed over her cell. He punched in some numbers, then handed it back to her.

"Now you can get in touch with me anytime you want."

He waved and headed for the stairs. For a second Destiny stared after him. Kipling was a good distraction. But when he disappeared from view, she was left with the reality of a new job, a new town and a sister she barely knew.

One problem at a time, she told herself firmly. And right now that meant dealing with her family.

CHAPTER TWO

Destiny traveled constantly for work. While on assignment, she worked 24/7 until the job was done then had a few weeks off until she had to report to the next location. Except for a beautiful summer in northern Canada, she'd only been sent to clients in the US.

She was used to not knowing the best places to eat or where to find a good doctor if she needed one. She'd learned to ask questions and shop local. She preferred corporate housing to hotels.

On her time off, she retreated to her condo in Austin, where she caught up on whatever she'd missed while she'd been gone. Being alone was a natural state for her. One she liked. Sure, her mother visited every three or four months, and there were phone calls from friends or the few of her siblings she'd grown up with, but for the most part, Destiny took care of herself. She didn't have to worry about someone else's preferences.

When people asked if she was ever lonely, she only smiled and shook her head. Grandma Nell had taught her the pleasure of solitude. How with a good book or a guitar, she was never truly by herself. Books and music were constant companions. Better than people, they never argued or demanded. And they were always familiar. Unlike the fifteen-year-old waiting at home.

Destiny stood in front of the small house she'd rented for the summer. It was older in a charming, lived-in kind of way, with two bedrooms and baths. There was an attached garage and a fenced backyard. The house was comfortable. Huge by her normal corporate housing standards. She would never have rented it for herself, she thought as she walked up the front steps. But this summer was different. This summer she had her half sister with her.

She opened the front door and walked inside. Starr sat curled up in a corner of the sofa, reading on her tablet. She looked up at Destiny, her green eyes similar to the ones Destiny saw in the mirror every morning, although the wariness was unfamiliar. They'd inherited their eyes and their red hair from their father. But everything else was different.

Destiny was tall. She'd always felt she was all arms and legs. Starr was shorter and more delicate. Destiny was right-handed, Starr left. Destiny was an early riser, and Starr seemed to be a night owl. But they were sisters, and Destiny knew that trumped any differences.

Two weeks ago, Destiny had been getting ready for her trip to Fool's Gold when she'd received a call from her father's lawyer. The man had been on retainer for as long as Destiny could remember and was responsible for picking up the pieces after each of Jimmy Don's mishaps. Her father was a legend, and cleaning up after him was a full-time job.

He'd told Destiny that one of Jimmy Don's daughters was coming home from boarding school and had nowhere to go. Jimmy Don was out of the country, and the girl's mother had overdosed the year before. There was no one to take Starr Mills for the summer.

While keeping up with her father's women took more time than she had to spare, Destiny remembered the torrid affair and the illegitimate child that resulted. From all she'd heard, Starr was truly alone in the world. Saying no to the implied request hadn't been an option.

But although she and Starr were biologically half siblings, in truth they'd never met until ten days ago when Destiny had picked up the teen at the Austin airport. So far all their conversations had been of the superficial "Hi, how are you" variety. Starr was quieter than Destiny had expected. There weren't a lot of cell calls to friends or frantic texting sessions.

"Hi," she said as she closed the front door behind her. "How's it going?"

"Fine." Starr put down her iPad. "I was reading."

"Have you been out today?"

Starr shook her head.

Destiny might not have a family yet, but she knew that a fifteen-year-old cooped up in a strange house for days at a time wasn't good. It wouldn't be good even if the house wasn't strange. Kids needed to be going and doing. Making friends.

Destiny let her small backpack fall to the floor, then sat on the chair kitty-corner to the sofa and held out the material Mayor Marsha had given her.

"I had an interesting meeting this afternoon," she said, determined not to mention the fact that the mayor had known way more than she should about Destiny's personal life and her nonexistent relationship with her half sister.

"It turns out there's a summer camp in town. Or maybe up in the mountains. I haven't read all the information yet. But it's close, and I thought it might be fun for you."

The wariness never left Starr's eyes. "Why?"

"There are kids your age there. And different classes. Drama, singing, music. You'd be outdoors. That's better than being stuck in here."

Given the choice, Destiny always preferred to be outside. She wasn't sure if she'd been that way before she'd gone to live with

Grandma Nell, but she certainly was after. The sky seemed to beckon her. Trees were tall friends who provided protection and shade on a hot, sunny day. There were a thousand discoveries to be made and the magic of the music Mother Nature created with rustling leaves or the call of birds.

Starr took the offered brochure and opened it. "I'd like to study drama," she admitted. "And music." She looked up. "Get better on the guitar."

There was no accusation in the statement. Just fact. Which didn't prevent Destiny from squirming. The day she'd picked her half sister up at the airport, Starr had asked if Destiny could help her learn to play her guitar better. She'd admitted to being self-taught and frustrated by a lack of instruction. Destiny had lied and said that she didn't play much and couldn't help.

Two weeks later, the lie still sat heavy on her shoulders. Music had been as much a part of her upbringing as breathing. Given who her parents were, it was inevitable, she supposed. She'd been playing a child-size guitar before she could read, and by the time she was six, she'd added piano to her skill set.

Nearly twelve years ago she'd made the decision to put that part of her life behind her. To focus on what she saw as the normal world. She rarely played anymore and did her best to ignore the lyrics that bubbled up inside her head. Sometimes she gave in and spent a long afternoon playing and writing. Usually, that was enough to get it out of her system until the next time the feeling overwhelmed her.

She told herself that she had the right to make that decision. That she didn't owe Starr that piece of herself. And while that might be technically true, she knew she shouldn't have lied about it.

"I looked," Destiny said with a smile. "There are guitar classes. Piano, too, if you're interested."

"Do you play piano?"

"I used to."

"You don't have one in the house."

No, she had a portable keyboard with a great set of head-phones instead. It was tucked under her bed.

"I move around too much to have a piano," she said with a shrug. "It would be tough to bring a piano on a plane as my carry-on."

Starr's full mouth pulled up slightly. Not a complete smile, but closer than she'd gotten before, Destiny thought.

"I think the camp would be fun for you. I know it's tough being away from your school friends. There have to be a couple of cool kids in town, right?"

"I don't hang out with the cool kids," Starr told her. "But I'd like to make some friends."

"Great. Then look that over and tell me what you think."

Starr nodded. She didn't ask about the cost. Jimmy Don's lawyer had explained there'd been a life insurance policy on Starr's mother, and the money from that had been put into a trust. Their dad had kicked in some, as well. No doubt the teen assumed her expenses would be paid from that.

While Destiny knew that legally she could take money from the trust, she didn't want to. She would cover the cost of the camp herself, just like she planned to pay for Starr's living ex-penses. They were family. Sort of. At the very least, they were related, and that counted.

"Come on," she said as she stood. "You can read about the camp while I start dinner."

They went into the kitchen. Starr settled at the small kitchen table while Destiny pulled out the ingredients for fried chicken. As she opened the refrigerator, she saw a few unfamiliar cas-serole dishes.

"Did you cook?" she asked.

"No. A couple of ladies came by with them. There's instruc-tions on heating them. They both look good."

Destiny glanced at the labels. One simply said *lasagna*, with

suggestions on warming in both the oven and the microwave.
The other label said it was *Denise's Many Layered Tamale Pie.*
Destiny was pretty sure she hadn't met anyone named Denise,
but that didn't matter. Small-town folks took care of each other.
Anything noteworthy brought out the casserole brigade.

"We can have these for lunch," she said. "If that's okay with
you."

"Sure."

She dumped flour, salt, pepper and paprika into a large plastic
bag. After washing off the chicken, she patted it dry and then
soaked it in buttermilk for a few seconds before putting the
pieces in with the flour. A couple of shakes later, the chicken
was coated. She set the pieces on a plate. The trick to really
good fried chicken was hot oil and letting the flour mixture
get a little gooey.

As she waited, she glanced at Starr. The teen read the camp
information intently.

There was a stillness about her. Or maybe it was just sadness.
Starr's young life hadn't been easy. She rarely saw her father;
her mother had been in and out of rehab and had eventually
died of an overdose. Now Starr lived at a boarding school. She
had no grandparents, and all her siblings were either half or step
and total strangers.

Destiny's guilt returned, but this time for a different reason.
She needed to make time for Starr, she thought. They had this
summer together. They could get to know each other.

She supposed that in a lot of families, half sisters would already be friends. But not in hers, and that was because her father couldn't resist a beautiful woman, Destiny thought grimly.
Jimmy Don loved the ladies, and they loved him back. Over and
over. He'd married young and often, divorcing and remarrying
again and again. Not that her mother was any different. Lacey
Mills was on her seventh husband. Or maybe her eighth. It was
difficult to keep track.

Destiny was Jimmy Don and Lacey's firstborn. She'd been witness to the early years of their relationship. She'd grown up with the screaming, the plate throwing, the drama. She'd learned early to get out of the way when tempers flared and that the good times were always temporary. She'd vowed to be different. She wanted a calm, quiet, practical marriage. No great highs or lows for her. She was looking for a man she could respect and have children with. Not one that got her heart beating faster.

Her determination was the reason she avoided the Kipling Gilmores of the world. Sure, he was a handsome devil with an easy smile and a charming way about him. She was sure that he knew things that could make her beg. But she didn't want to beg. She didn't want to yearn, lust, dream or even long. She wanted certainty. A solid, dependable, comfortable kind of love.

Sex was the root of all evil. She'd learned that early, too. She'd never let herself be swept away, which was a point of pride for her. No hormone was more powerful than her determination, and nothing about that was ever going to change.

The Man Cave had been an old hardware store, back in the day. When Kipling had first gotten the idea of opening a bar where guys could be comfortable, he'd immediately thought of the store for sale on Katie Lane. As the seller also happened to be one of his business partners in the bar, he'd gotten a good deal on the place.

Renovations had gone quickly. It helped that several of his new business partners knew the local trades, and things got done. Now they were only a few weeks from opening.

Kipling stood by the double front doors and glanced around. There was a long bar along the east wall that housed a self-serve beer fridge. Tables filled the front area. There were pool tables and dartboards, a poker room in back and plenty of TVs, including a couple in the bathrooms so no one had to miss a play.

The second floor overlooked the main bar and had plenty

of seating. Sports memorabilia covered the walls. Not just the usual *Sports Illustrated* swimsuit covers, but actual trophies and other items. Josh Golden, a partner and the guy who had owned the building, had brought in one of his yellow jerseys from the Tour de France. There were footballs and helmets donated by the former pro players at Score, a local PR firm, and dozens of trophies from them and former quarterback Raoul Moreno. Kipling's contribution was one of his gold medals from the 2010 Vancouver Olympics.

But what he liked the best was the big stage and state-of-the-art karaoke machine he'd ordered. Sure they could have bands come in and perform, but for him karaoke was the real draw.

Back when he'd been competing and traveling year round, karaoke was what had always pulled the teams together. No matter where they were in the world, they found a place with a machine and spent many a night making fools of themselves. Kipling could carry a tune. Barely. But singing well wasn't the point. It was about having fun.

The idea for the bar had been with him for a while. When he'd come to Fool's Gold, he'd realized this was where he could make it happen. Jo's Bar in town did a good business, but catered mostly to women. The pastel color scheme and TV stations tuned to fashion and shopping kind of freaked him out. Where did guys go to just hang? A few conversations later, he had partners and a long-term lease from Josh.

He flipped on lights and surveyed the room. They were still waiting on some tables and chairs. The liquor license had been approved the previous week. Now they were getting suppliers lined up.

The front door opened, and Nick and Aidan Mitchell walked inside.

The two men were locals, born and raised in Fool's Gold. From what Kipling had heard, there were five Mitchell brothers. The youngest two were twins. The twins and the oldest brother, Del, had moved away.

At his partners' suggestion, Kipling had hired Nick to manage the bar. Aidan, a year or two older, ran the family business—Mitchell Adventure Tours. The company catered to tourists and offered everything from easy day hikes to white-water rafting.

"Looking good," Aidan said as they approached. "You're going to be opening soon."

"Three weeks max," Nick said easily. "I'm already hiring servers."

Both men were tall, with dark hair and eyes. Aidan glared at his brother. "Seriously? Hiring servers."

Nick's relaxed expression tightened. "Don't start on me."

"You're not worth the trouble."

There was both frustration and affection in Aidan's tone. From what Kipling had been able to piece together, the family was close, but not without its troubles. The father was Ceallach Mitchell, the famous glass artist. He was known both for his brilliance and his temper. Nick had apparently inherited his ability but not his interest. From what Kipling could tell, Nick had been tending bar for years, rather than working with glass.

Aidan was on his brother a lot—complaining that the younger Mitchell could do so much more than simply run a bar. As Kipling had a complicated relationship with his own sister, he did his best to stay out of these family dynamics.

"You given any thought to what we talked about?" Kipling asked Aidan.

The older brother raised one shoulder. "You know I don't have time."

Kipling knew when to keep quiet. It was a trick he'd learned from his coach. Let 'em talk it out, and they'll almost always come round to your way of thinking.

"Yeah," Aidan continued. "I know it's a volunteer assignment, but we get busy in the summer."

"You're busy all year round," Nick said cheerfully. "What if it's one of your customers who's lost?"

Aidan swore at his brother. "No one asked you."

"I'm a giver. I don't need to be asked."

Kipling held in a chuckle.

Aidan glared. "Don't pressure me."

"Wouldn't dream of it," Kipling told him. "Did I mention it was Mayor Marsha who suggested I ask you?"

Aidan swore again. "Fine," he grumbled. "I'll be one of your damned volunteers."

"Good to know. I'll get you the paperwork within a day."

"There's paperwork?" Aidan shook his head. "No good deed."

Nick slapped him on the back. "You know it."

"Don't think you won't be right there beside me," Aidan told him.

"Never planned for it to be otherwise."

Two for the price of one, Kipling thought with satisfaction. The search and rescue team, which he refused to think of as HERO, would be staffed mostly by volunteers. He would be in charge, and he was hiring a second-in-command, not to mention a couple of support staff. But everyone else would work on a volunteer basis. It was the easiest way to keep costs down.

Given the willingness of the community to get involved, Kipling didn't think he would have a problem getting everyone trained. He'd already spoken to both the police and fire chiefs, and they'd assured him he would have plenty of their folks showing up.

Aidan was the one he wanted, though. With his business, he knew the area better than almost anyone. When someone was lost, Kipling wanted Aidan on the ground, looking.

"When does training begin?" Nick asked.

"Not for about a month. The facilitator from STORMS arrived a couple of days ago. She has to get the terrain mapped and the software up and running first."

Aidan nodded. "The tall redhead, right? I've seen her around town. What's her name?"

"Destiny Mills."

Kipling wanted to say more. Like the fact that her green eyes reminded him of spring leaves against the last snow of the season. Only he wasn't a guy who talked like that. No one did. At least no one he knew.

"You could use a woman," Nick said, nudging his brother.

"She's not my type."

"How do you know? You haven't met her."

Aidan's expression tightened. "She isn't. Let it go." He turned and walked out.

Nick waited until his brother was gone to shake his head. "He won't date anyone longer than fifteen minutes. One day that lifestyle's going to bite him in the ass. What about you? What are your thoughts on Ms. Destiny Mills?"

Kipling wasn't sharing them with anyone but the woman in question. "I'm working with her, not dating her. Why all the interest?"

"I'm the bartender. I need to know things."

Kipling thought briefly about warning Nick off. He had his own plans for Destiny. Then he realized there was no point. If Destiny was interested in the same thing he was, he would know soon enough. If she wasn't, then Nick was welcome. Kipling had never had much trouble getting or keeping women. His problem was more along the lines of never feeling he wanted more than a temporary arrangement. But until it was time to walk away, he was interested in wherever Destiny wanted to go.

Destiny woke up earlier than usual. By the time she'd showered and dressed it was still a few minutes before six. She grabbed her wallet and stuffed it in the front pocket of her jeans then walked quietly to the front door and let herself out.

It was still cool, although the weather guy had promised a

nice warm day. The sky was clear, and the neighborhood quiet. She zipped up her hoodie and turned toward town.

One of the advantages of constantly moving around was discovering local businesses. So far her Fool's Gold finds were a street truck that served incredible sandwiches by Pyrite Park and Ambrosia Bakery. The former solved her lunch problem and the latter was going to require her to add a little exercise to her routine.

She crossed empty streets. As she got closer to the bakery, she saw a few people and a couple of cars. A jogger nodded as he passed her.

Destiny liked discovering the rhythm of each town she worked in. They were all similar, with just enough differences to keep things interesting. In a way, like the rhythm of a song. Stanzas told a story, and the chorus was the exploration of a theme. The backbone that held it all together.

She turned on Second Street and saw the bakery ahead on her left. The doors stood open, which meant it was now after six. She walked in and inhaled the sweet combination of sugar, cinnamon and freshly baked bread. Talk about heaven.

A petite blonde stood behind the counter. She had blue eyes and a pretty face. There was something familiar about her, although Destiny knew they hadn't met. Her name tag said Shelby.

"Morning," Shelby said with a smile. "You're up early."

"Not as early as you." Destiny motioned to the display case full of pastries. "Unless these were baked last night."

Shelby laughed. "No such luck. I was here at three."

Destiny winced. "Okay, I like to get up early, but that would challenge even me."

"I know. When I have a day off, I sleep late. Which means four-thirty. It's an odd schedule, that's for sure. What can I get you?"

Destiny chose a half-dozen Danish. She would leave most of them for Starr and maybe take one to work.

Shelby put the pastries in a silver-and-white-striped box. "Are you new in town or visiting?"

"I'm new. Here for the summer to set up software for the search and rescue program."

Shelby nodded. "HERO." She laughed again. "My brother is Kipling Gilmore. I don't know if you've met him yet. He's running the program. And totally hates the name, by the way. If you want to torture him or something, just keep saying it out loud."

"I have met him, and I appreciate the advice."

Destiny studied the other woman, realizing now why she looked familiar.

Shelby handed over the box. "You know, you don't have to come here for Danish. Not that I don't appreciate the company. But most people want coffee, too, and we don't do that. You can get our baked goods over at Brew-haha."

"I'm not much for coffee. Just sugar." Destiny thought about her conversation with Kipling and what Mayor Marsha had said about the program. "Have you lived in town long? I got the impression that Kipling was a relatively new addition to the population."

"Nearly a year." Shelby's smile faded. "I moved here last summer. My mom died and, well, it's complicated. Kipling was in rehab until January. Physical, not the other kind. Oh, do you know who he is? The skiing and all that?"

Destiny nodded. "I figured it out. The accident was pretty bad. I'm glad he's okay now." She hesitated, not sure what to say about Shelby's mother. "I'm sorry about your mom."

"Thanks. It never goes away, but I'm dealing with it. Having Kipling around helps. I mean he's totally annoying, but I love him. He's the only family I have left. I'd be lost without him."

"It's nice to have family around," Destiny murmured, thinking of Starr. The girl was only fifteen and pretty much alone in the world. It was good they were going to have the summer to get to know each other.

A couple of guys walked into the bakery. They were tall and broad-shouldered and wearing shorts and T-shirts. They looked familiar, too, although she couldn't place them. Was everyone in this town related?

"Loser buys," the dark-haired guy said. "That means you."

"Nice, Sam. I am so kicking your ass on the court today."

"See you tomorrow," Destiny told Shelby and headed for the door.

She passed by the two men. They were both wearing wedding rings. Not that she'd been attracted to either of them. She was strong and powerful and never sucked in by something as temporal as sex. She had goals and rules and a plan. And if all that failed, she had Danish.

She started back for the house. There were more people out on the street now, and the sun was rising in the sky. She smiled and greeted those who waved at her. She liked the friendliness of the town.

At the corner, she checked before crossing. As she glanced to her left, she saw a man jogging away from her. His stride was slightly uneven, and his pace slower than most. As the information registered in her brain, she recognized Kipling.

There were scars on his legs and a hitch to his gait. She thought about all that he would have gone through after his accident and wondered about the courage it took to recover from something like that. No, not recover. Thrive. It spoke highly of his character.

She crossed the street and made her way to her rental house. Once inside, she left the Danish on the table and hurried into her bedroom. After closing the door, she got her guitar out of the closet and sat on the edge of the bed.

Words tumbled around a half-formed melody. Aware of Starr sleeping on the other side of the hall, she strummed quietly, pausing every now and then to write down lyrics or notes.

Too many ways and too many days. Testing and hurting, I see you alone. Too many nights of wanting it right and I'm walking...

She pressed her palm against the strings as she struggled with the line.

The song beckoned. The need to get lost in finding the right combination of notes and syllables grew. Of meaning and phrases. She glanced at her small bedside clock. She had to be at work, and she didn't want Starr to hear her. Better to start her morning.

She drew in a breath, then compromised by setting her phone timer for forty-five minutes. When the beeper sounded, she forced herself to put away her guitar and shoved the worn notebook into her nightstand.

She had a real job, she reminded herself. A regular life. The rest of it—the songs and the music—were just play. She made deliberate choices for a reason. Staying in control was all that kept her safe. Vigilance, she reminded herself. Determination. She was stronger than her biology. She always would be.

CHAPTER THREE

Kipling set up the new computers on the desks that had been delivered the previous week. He sorted the packing material into recycle and trash piles, then carried it all out back. When he returned, Destiny was walking into the HERO office.

"Right on time," he said, taking in the jeans, boots and short-sleeved T-shirt she wore. She'd pulled her long hair back into a ponytail.

From what he could tell, she wasn't wearing makeup. She used a small backpack for a handbag and certainly didn't dress to impress anyone. She wasn't the kind of woman who kept a man waiting "just five more minutes" while she primped. All pluses in his book.

"I see the computers arrived," she said by way of greeting. "I'll let my tech guys know. They'll be here in a couple of days to load and test the software. While they're doing that, I'll be mapping the terrain. Then we'll get started on training you and your volunteers on STORMS."

"Good morning," he said. "How was your evening?"

She raised her eyebrows. "I didn't take you for someone who

lived for social niceties, but sure. I can do that. Good morning, Kipling. Did you have a nice jog this morning?"

"How did you know I was out jogging?"

She shifted her weight from foot to foot. "I went out to get some breakfast and saw you. Going the other way. I would have called out, but you were too far away. I wasn't spying or anything."

"I never thought you were."

She'd been watching him. A year ago, he would have read that as a good sign. One of interest. Today he was less sure. She could have been put off by the scars or his limp. Although she didn't strike him as overly concerned about that sort of thing.

"It's the small-town thing," she continued. "You can't really escape anyone. Not that you were trying to. Or anything."

She dropped her backpack on the desk and crossed her arms over her chest.

"Feeling awkward?" he asked.

"Very."

"Want to move on to another topic?"

"More than you know."

He grinned. "Then let's get down to business."

Unlike the mayor's office, there was no comfortable sofa-and-chair arrangement. In the command center, conversations took place around a metal table with folding chairs. He and Destiny settled at one corner. She pulled a laptop out of her backpack and booted it. While it did its thing, she handed over a couple sheets of paper.

"This is the preliminary schedule," she told him. "Mapping and testing will take about a month. We'll have multiple practice rescues that will all go badly. For those, we want as small a group participating as possible. So no one gets discouraged."

"You're assuming the worst."

"I've done this before," she told him. "Man and machine don't work well together without training. Once we get the kinks worked out, we'll broaden the practice areas and bring in more people."

She was sitting close enough that they could both see her laptop screen, which also meant he could inhale the scent of her shampoo. Something floral, he thought. A bit of a surprise considering how she didn't seem all that interested in being girly with her clothes or accessories.

Unexpected nuances. Everyone had them. They were some of his favorite things to discover. What else was she hiding? Was there a passionate woman behind the "all business" exterior? Was she quiet in bed, or a screamer? He was open to either.

She turned to get something out of her backpack. As she moved, her ponytail swung toward him. Dark red hair curled slightly at the ends, begging to be touched. He knew the strands would be soft. For a second he allowed himself the fantasy of her pulling out the band holding her hair in place and shaking her head. Like in one of those cheesy perfume commercials. Maybe she would crook her finger at him.

Unlikely, he thought, holding in a grin at the image. Destiny didn't strike him as the sultry type. He would guess she was more practical than seductive. Again, not a problem for him.

She set more papers on the desk and scanned the top sheet. "You're going to be hiring a second-in-command?"

He forced his attention back to the job at hand. "Yes. I have interviews lined up for the next few weeks. There will also be a couple of paid staffers." She made a couple of notes as he spoke. "The volunteer force is impressive. Mostly firefighters and cops, along with a few locals who—"

She turned to him. "Sam Ridge."

"You know him?"

"What? No. I saw him today. At the bakery. He and another guy came in as I left. The one said Sam. I've been trying to figure out who he is." She leaned toward him. "He's a former NFL kicker. There are a lot of former pro athletes in this town. You, the football guys and some cyclist, too… There was an article about him on the Fool's Gold website. You're in good company. Is that why you wanted to move here?"

"Not exactly."

Her mouth curved up in a smile. "Let me guess. It has something to do with Mayor Marsha."

"As a matter of fact, it does. She came to see me in New Zealand after my crash and offered me the job."

He hadn't cared about the job, he thought grimly, remembering the helplessness he'd felt trapped in a hospital bed, not sure if he would ever walk again. He'd cared about his sister and what she was going through. People said love was a big deal. He'd never thought that. Love didn't get the job done. When Shelby had been dodging their father's fists, Kipling's love hadn't been able to do a damn thing to save her.

Then Mayor Marsha had shown up and offered a miracle. He didn't know how the old lady had known what was happening, but she had. As promised, she'd protected Shelby and in return, he'd moved to Fool's Gold.

He knew he'd gotten the best end of the deal. Shelby was safe, and he had a place to start over. A place where he was simply Kipling Gilmore. Not world famous G-Force. Which probably sounded good enough to most people. He was healed, and he could settle down. What few realized was after years of being a god, sometimes it was hard to settle.

"That's a long way to go to hire someone," Destiny said.

"I'm worth it."

Destiny laughed. "Okay, I'll pretend to agree with you. Was she on vacation?"

"I don't know," he admitted. "I never much thought about it. I was pretty banged up and out of it. There were things to deal with."

He still remembered Mayor Marsha standing beside his hospital bed and telling him she could take care of his sister. He hadn't believed her, but she'd come through. His old man had been thrown in jail, Shelby had been safe and when he'd healed enough, he'd shown up to take the offered job.

"And?" Destiny prompted.

"She made an irresistible offer," he said, not wanting to share the truth with anyone. More to protect Shelby than himself. "And here I am."

"You're uniquely qualified for the job. You know your way around mountains."

"Less on foot than on skis."

"Does that bother you?"

He thought about what it had been like to fly down the snow. To go faster than anyone. He thought about the feel of the wind, the sounds, the fact that for those few seconds, it was only him and the impossible odds against winning.

"Sometimes," he admitted.

"Giving up the dream?" she asked.

He nodded. "It was going to happen eventually, but I wanted it on my terms."

"But what you did was dangerous. You could have hurt yourself."

He looked into her green eyes. "I did hurt myself."

"I mean it could have been worse. Was it worth it?"

He didn't have to consider his answer. He knew what it was like to defy gravity. He'd been the best. "Absolutely."

"I'll never understand that. Why would you deliberately take that kind of risk?"

"For the reward."

Her nose wrinkled. "A trophy and some arm candy?"

"The thrill of winning. Doing what hadn't been done before."

"So you break a record. Someone else will break yours. The glory is fleeting."

"The mountain is forever and when I skied, I was part of it."

★ ★ ★

As Kipling spoke, he seemed to be looking past her, to something she couldn't see. Destiny couldn't understand what he was talking about. Not the meaning behind the words, anyway. Why would someone willingly put themselves in harm's way? Of course she'd often asked her parents why they were willing to risk their marriage and family for a few nights of passion, and they hadn't been able to explain that, either.

She supposed her inability to understand was more about her than them. She wasn't looking for the thrill in any form, while it seemed that nearly everyone else sought it no matter the cost. But although she could usually dismiss her parents' choices with a shrug, she found herself wanting to know more about Kipling's. To understand what had driven him to take the risks.

"So you're part of the mountain?" she asked. "A part of something larger than yourself?"

He gave her one of his easy smiles. "Something like that."

"That one I get," she told him. "When I'm alone in nature, there's a peace. A connection. But you can feel that sitting still."

"*You* can," he corrected. "I do it with speed."

Her gaze locked with his. In that moment, the world seemed to shrink just a little bit. Or maybe go out of focus was more accurate. She could hear the beating of her heart and knew that she was breathing, but all that seemed separate from the act of looking into his dark blue eyes.

They were sitting closer than she'd realized. Close enough that she was both uncomfortable and a little bit jumpy. Leaning forward seemed the most logical thing to do, although she couldn't for the life of her say why. Lean forward and then what?

Rather than give in, she drew back slightly and searched for a neutral topic. "I met your sister this morning."

"You went with the breakfast of champions, then?"

"I bought Danish for my sister."

One brow rose. "Now you're lying."

"Fine. I bought them for myself, but I left most of them with her." She shuffled the papers in front of her. "It's nice that Shelby could move to Fool's Gold, too. Have you always been close?"

"Mostly. I traveled a lot, and that made it harder, but we've stayed in touch. You know how it goes."

"Not really," she said before she could stop herself. "My parents had me nine months after they got married. They split up when I was five. While they were apart, my dad married someone else and had a baby with her. My mom got pregnant by some other guy, then my parents got back together. It was confusing."

There was so much more. Other marriages, separations and divorces. Lacey and Jimmy Don believed in living large. Destiny had been passed around to relatives and friends. She'd spent time on the road with her parents. Finally, Grandma Nell had stepped in, taking her away from all the craziness. From the first moment Destiny had set foot in the small house in the mountains, she knew she was where she belonged.

"I don't really know Starr," she admitted. "We have the same father, but until two weeks ago, I'd never met her."

"That's tough. How are things going?"

"Okay, I guess. I hope they are. She doesn't talk much, and I've never been responsible for a teenager before. She seems excited about the summer camp Mayor Marsha told me about. I think it would help if she got out and could make some friends." She hesitated. "I don't know what she wants. From me or her life. When I was her age… Let's just say it was different."

"Different how?"

Before she could figure out how to answer, a familiar low rumble sounded overhead. It grew louder, then quieter.

"I can't believe it," she said with a grin. "What is it about your gender? Can't you just walk into a room? Do you always have to make an entrance?"

"I have no idea what you're talking about."

She pointed to the ceiling. "That noise you just heard? It's

Miles, buzzing the town on his way to the airport. Because he thinks it's cool. My helicopter pilot is one of the best, but he has the emotional maturity of a toddler. Come on. You'll want to meet him, and I have to warn him that he's not to make trouble while he's here."

"Does he usually?"

She thought about the string of broken hearts and shattered dreams Miles left in his wake. Sort of the reverse of bread crumbs. Because once Miles walked away, he never came back.

"Always. He says it's part of his charm."

"What do you say?" Kipling asked.

"That he needs a good smack upside the head."

They took his Jeep out to the small airport. Sure enough, a helicopter sat on the tarmac. As Kipling came to a stop, a guy climbed out and waved. Destiny scrambled out of the Jeep and raced toward him.

Kipling saw the other man, Miles, was about his height with dark hair. He wore an LA Stallions baseball cap. Destiny launched herself at him, and the man caught her in a tight embrace.

For a second Kipling wondered if he was going to have some competition for his planned short-term affair with the sexy redhead. Or if he'd misread the fact that she was single. But as he watched, the hug, while friendly, never progressed past affectionate. There was no trace of sexual tension between them. No lingering chemistry.

Miles released her, and she stepped back. They were talking animatedly. The man shook his head stubbornly, and Destiny slugged him in the arm.

Okay then, Kipling thought with a grin. More like brother and sister, not lovers. Excellent news. He'd been looking forward to seducing Destiny but wouldn't go there if she belonged to someone else.

They approached. Destiny rolled her eyes. "Kipling Gilmore, meet Miles Thomas. He's a good pilot and a complete dog when it comes to women. Please tell him to go easy here in town."

The two men shook hands.

"It's a family place with a lot of women in power," Kipling warned him. "Our police chief has sons in high school and college. She's not one to be reasoned with."

Miles winked at Destiny. "Then I won't ask her out. Sweet Destiny, you're going to make this nice man think I'm a total bastard."

"Yes, I know. Like I said. Brilliant in the sky. A jerk in his love life. I can't tell you how many sobbing phone calls I've had to deal with over the past couple of years."

"I've never made a phone cry," Miles told her.

"Very funny. Don't make me hit you again."

Miles rubbed his arm. "You do pack a punch. More of Grandma Nell's work, I presume."

"Yes, and had she met you, she would have castrated you, just like she did the hogs."

Miles's good humor faded as he took a big step back. "Thanks for sharing. She'd dead, right?"

"You're talking about my favorite grandmother," Destiny told him. "Show a little respect."

"Yes, ma'am."

Kipling leaned against the Jeep and took in the show. "How long are you in town?" he asked Miles.

"As long as the job lasts." He looked up at the mountains. "Six weeks maybe, give or take." He sighed heavily. "Not that her work fills my days. Know anyone who wants to hire a helicopter pilot for odd jobs?"

"No, but I'll ask around. There's a company in town that offers different wilderness tours. I'll give you the owner's number. Aidan might want to offer helicopter tours. There may be others. Let me think on it."

"Sure. That would be great." Miles fished a business card out of his shirt pocket and handed it over. "I'd appreciate anything that would break up the boredom of going over terrain, inch by fricking inch."

"We pay you very well for your time," Destiny said.

"That you do, my love, but the money doesn't make the work interesting."

"He's a diva," she told Kipling. "You're the one who should have attitude, and you don't. Miles has no reason to think he's all that, yet he acts like he is."

"I can hear you," Miles said.

She started for the Jeep. "We have to give him a ride back to town so he can rent a car. I hope that's okay."

Miles shook his head. "She's always like this. Acting as if I'm her…"

"Annoying younger brother?" Kipling asked.

"Yeah. Why is that?"

"No idea."

All he knew was Miles wasn't going to get in his way. Which meant it was time to get on with his plan.

"I don't get it," Starr admitted as they stepped off a curb on their walk to town and the festival in progress. "Who is Rosie the Riveter?"

"She worked in a factory during World War II," Destiny said. "She symbolized women helping out during the war. Before that, not many women had been in factory work, but when the men went off to war, factory positions had to be filled."

Starr's eyes widened. "How do you know that?"

"I read a brochure. Someone dropped off a whole folder filled with brochures on the various town festivals. Some of them look fun." More important to her summer with Starr, there were a couple every month—giving them things to do on the weekend.

Today was the start of Rosie the Riveter Days, a festival that celebrated all of the women of Fool's Gold who moved to San Francisco during World War II to work in the factories there.

While the schools in Fool's Gold were still in session for a few more weeks, Starr's boarding school had already ended for the summer. The teen was certainly old enough to be left alone, but Destiny didn't think day after day by herself was good for her half sister.

"Maybe we could get a book about Rosie the Riveter from the library," she offered.

Starr rolled her eyes. "No, thanks. If I want to read about her, I'll go online."

"Sure."

They crossed the street and headed for the park. The day was sunny and warm, the sidewalks filled with people. There were booths set up, selling everything from olive oil to jewelry, and posters promised live music all afternoon and evening.

Destiny paused in front of one of the posters. At least here was something she and Starr had in common. Something they could talk about.

"We can stay and listen to the bands," she said. "Which ones look interesting to you?"

"Hello, girls."

Destiny turned and saw a gray-haired lady in a track suit walking toward them.

"Don't tell me," the older woman said. "Let me guess." She paused, then pointed. "Destiny and Starr. Do I have that right?"

Destiny nodded. "Yes. Hello."

"I'm Eddie Carberry. You two are new in town. Welcome. We like new people, as long as you don't make trouble." Her expression turned stern as she raised her hand and pointed her finger at Destiny. "No texting and driving, young lady. Do you hear me? It's dangerous."

"Yes, ma'am."

"I don't drive yet," Starr added quickly, taking a step to the side, so she was half-hidden behind Destiny. "And I would never do that."

"See that you don't." Eddie's face relaxed as she smiled. "Have fun at the festival."

"Yes, ma'am," they said together.

Eddie walked away.

"How does she know who we are?" Starr asked. "Why was she mean?"

"All good questions," Destiny told her. "It's a small-town thing."

"The smallest town I lived in was Nashville. From there we moved to Atlanta and then to Miami." Starr paused for a second. "Dad took me on tour once. I was eight. We went to small towns, but that was different. I don't know if I like it here."

"You have to give it time. It can be more intense, but it's also easier to get to know people because you'll see them again and again."

"Which is great unless you don't get along."

Destiny laughed. "So you're not an optimist?"

"I guess not." Starr's green eyes brightened. "Isn't moodiness a sign of, like, having talent?"

"I think it's more about being a teenager."

"Were you moody?"

"Grandma Nell didn't believe in moods. She always said the chickens didn't care how I felt about feeding them, as long as I got the job done."

"She sounds, ah, really great."

Destiny grinned. "She was, but she wasn't easy. Still, I loved being with her." She turned back to the poster. "All right. Let's choose our bands. You first."

They looked at the offerings and had a heated discussion of rock versus bluegrass. Ten minutes later, their day was scheduled, musically, at least. It was early for lunch and with the music not starting for a couple of hours, the afternoon loomed long.

Destiny wasn't sure what they should talk about. School? Was that a safe topic?

"Are you keeping in touch with your school friends?" she asked.

Starr shrugged. "Some."

"If you want to invite anyone to come stay for a few days, that would be okay. A weekend would be better so I wasn't working," she added.

"Thanks, but no. They all have plans with their families. Becky's going to Europe, and Chelsea's going to a language school." Starr sighed heavily. "Her dad works for, like, the government or something, and she has to learn a bunch of languages."

"That would be kind of hard."

"I know, right? But she's good at it. Becky's good at math. I'm not really good at anything. I thought maybe music but..." Her voice trailed off, and she shrugged.

For a second Destiny felt a flood of guilt. She'd only heard her sister sing a couple of times, but she had a pretty voice. She knew she could teach Starr how to play the guitar better. Maybe they could start on the keyboard. Only Destiny didn't want to go there. Didn't want to get involved or have anyone she knew in that business. It was seductive and dangerous. From the outside, the music world was glamorous, but from the inside, it was anything but.

A tall woman with a baby strapped to her chest approached them. She smiled engagingly.

"Hello. You must be Destiny and Starr Mills. Nice to meet you both. I'm Felicia Boylan. I run the festivals here in town." The woman paused. "Interesting that we're all natural redheads. Only about two percent of the population has red hair. The gene itself is recessive. I believe the color is caused by a mutation of the MC1R. That's a gene that—"

Felicia paused then shrugged. "Sorry. Pretend I never said all

of that. Most people don't find my bursts of knowledge particularly interesting, but they are, I assure you, harmless."

"Is that true?" Starr asked. "What you said about a mutation?"

"Yes. But not in a way that gives you super powers, like in the
X-Men movies. Although, curiously enough, red hair doesn't
go gray. It simply fades over time." Felicia smiled again. "Not
that you'll care about that now, but in forty years, it will be
comforting."

Starr looked more confused than reassured.

"Cute baby," Destiny said. "How old?"

"Eight months." Felicia beamed. "This is my daughter, Gabrielle-Emilie. She's named after Gabrielle-Emilie Le Tonnelier
de Breteuil, a French courtier who collaborated with her lover
Voltaire on many physics projects. However, if you ever meet
my brother-in-law Gabriel, please don't tell him that the baby
isn't named after him. He made an erroneous assumption, and
we've decided not to disabuse him of it."

Starr looked even more confused, but nodded and touched
the baby's hand. "Hi, Gabrielle."

"We call her Ellie for short. Humans bond through the use
of nicknames, and my son, Carter, requested this one in honor
of his mother."

Destiny was having trouble keeping up. "You're not Carter's
mother?"

"No. It's complicated." Felicia turned to Starr. "Mayor Marsha told me you were thinking of coming to the summer camp.
I wanted to stop by and let you know that according to my son,
it's really great and you'll enjoy yourself. He's fifteen, too."

Destiny was willing to accept that locals might know her
and Starr's names and maybe even why they were in town. But
knowing ages and about the camp was a little strange.

"Thanks for the information," Starr said shyly.

"You're welcome. One of the things they do at the camp is
assign you a buddy. That's someone who's been there before.

She'll show you around and introduce you to people. It can be difficult when you're new. Or odd. I was always odd when I was growing up. I'm better now. My husband says falling in love mellowed me, but I think it's more that our intensely personal interactions have allowed me to develop my social skills."

Felicia touched Starr's shoulder. "As a teenager, your natural emotional state is to feel alienated. It's part of the separation process as you mature into adulthood. And while the concept is helpful for you to learn to be a functioning member of society, you can easily find yourself feeling out of step and alone. Which is less comfortable. I think the camp would be helpful in nurturing feelings of connection with peers."

"Okay," Starr said slowly. "If you say so."

"Good. I'll tell Carter to look out for you." Felicia smiled at Destiny. "Several of the women in town will be having lunch today at Jo's Bar. You and your sister are invited. I can't go because I'll be working, but I encourage you to attend. Making friends really helps a place seem like home."

"Thank you," Destiny said. "That's very nice."

"You're welcome. Look for Shelby Gilmore. She said she knows you. She'll be there. Now if you'll excuse me, I heard there was a problem with the seating by the smaller stage. Someone didn't pay attention to my plan. I must now go explain why he's wrong."

"Good luck with that," Destiny murmured.

Felicia waved and walked away.

Starr stared after her. "She scared me."

"Me, too. At the same time, I kind of want to be more like her. Talk about smart."

"You're smart. Look at the job you have."

"I'm intelligent enough," Destiny said with a laugh. "But not compared with Felicia." She put her arm around her sister. "On the bright side, apparently we don't have to worry about going gray."

"I already wasn't." Starr snuggled close for a second then stepped away. "I'm hungry."

"Me, too. Looks like we have plans for lunch now, but that's hours away. Want to go by the bakery and get a doughnut?"

"Sure."

They circled the park then headed up Second Street, maneuvering around families with strollers. Tourists or locals? Destiny wondered, thinking about her plan to sensibly marry and then have a quiet, calm marriage of her own one day.

In college, when she'd come up with the plan, she'd assumed she would have found a husband by now. But it turned out that calm, sensible men were more difficult to find than she would have thought.

Two men stepped out of the bakery. She recognized Miles and Kipling, each holding a silver-and-white-striped box.

She stumbled to a stop as her chest suddenly tightened. How strange. What on earth was—

Everything went still. She focused on her breathing then cautiously let her attention drift to the rest of her body. There was the aforementioned tension in her chest, plus a distinct quiver in her stomach and something almost like tingling in her thighs. If she hadn't felt totally fine a second before, she would swear she was getting the flu. So if it wasn't that, then what?

She looked at Miles. He saw her and grinned. He appeared self-satisfied, which meant he'd been successfully flirting with someone. As she studied him, she felt only pity for whatever woman had endured his attentions. Not that most of them seemed to mind. Many conquests had lamented losing Miles, but few of them regretted the short-term thrill of being with him.

Something she'd never been tempted to experience herself, so Miles wasn't the cause of her reaction.

She turned to Kipling and instantly got lost in his dark blue gaze. He looked less happy than his new friend. Irritation tugged at the corner of his mouth and when he glared at Miles, she had a clear view of his chiseled profile.

Your words were like a beacon, I was looking for a home.

Destiny sucked in air. No, she told herself firmly. She would not create song lyrics around Kipling. She knew where that led, and it was to a dark, bad place. It led to attraction, which led to sex, which led to jealousy and late-night fits of anger. Love was only a few shades less bad. No way, no how. She was not, under any circumstances, attracted to Kipling Gilmore. Ski gods did not make for sensible relationships.

"What part of 'my sister' don't you understand?" Kipling demanded as he and Miles reached her. "Hey, Destiny."

"Hi. What's going on?"

Miles shrugged. "I don't know. I saw a beautiful woman and complimented her. This one nearly took my head off."

Destiny winced. "Not Shelby. I like her. Stay away from her."

"Thank you," Kipling said, then smiled at Starr. "Hi. I'm Kipling."

"Starr."

"The sister. I see pretty runs in the family."

Starr blushed and ducked her head.

"Hello," Miles said. "We were talking about me. Shelby's an adult. She can date who she wants."

Kipling took a step toward the other man. "No, she can't. You hurt her, and I will break every bone in your body. Is that clear?"

Miles opened the bakery box and pulled out a cookie. He took a bite. "Attitude, man," he said as he chewed. "You have to work on your attitude." He looked into Kipling's unyielding expression and sighed. "Fine. She's off-limits." He offered a cookie to Starr. "So what am I going to do for fun in this town? No Shelby." He winked at Starr. "You're too young for me." He looked at Destiny. "You're not interested in me."

"You're right. I'm not."

Miles groaned. "You don't have to be so blunt. You could

pretend you think I'm hot." He turned to Kipling. "We've had this problem from the start. It's the princess thing."

Destiny had been enjoying the exchange right up until that second. Now she stiffened, hoping she was wrong. That he wasn't going there.

It always happened, she thought frantically, searching for a distraction. Someone found out, then word spread and then everything changed.

"Princess?" Starr asked. "Destiny?"

"You, too, your highness."

"What?" Starr studied her cookie. "I'm not anybody special."

Kipling turned to Starr. "Sure you are."

A kindness, considering he had no idea what Miles was talking about.

Miles wiggled his eyebrows. "He doesn't know, does he?"

"No, and he doesn't have to."

"Sure he does." Miles grinned at Kipling. "Destiny is the oldest daughter of Jimmy Don and Lacey Mills. You know who they are, right?"

Kipling looked at Destiny. Confusion darkened his eyes, then it cleared. "No way."

"Way," Miles told him. "I've met Lacey a couple of times. She usually comes to visit Destiny on her jobs. Wow, is she still hot. And that voice. I heard her live once. They really are country music royalty. All those hits, all that passion."

And drama, Destiny thought grimly. The pictures in the tabloids, the arrests, the divorces, the broken promises. Yeah, it had all been so incredibly wonderful. Who wouldn't want to be her?

She made a point of glancing at her watch. "Look at the time. We need to be going."

She turned away, hoping Starr would follow. The teen fell into step with her.

"Why didn't you want Kipling to know about your parents?" Starr asked when they were out of earshot.

"It changes things. People act differently when they know."

"They respect you more?"

If only, Destiny thought. "Not exactly. They think they know me, because of them. And they don't."

"Is that bad?"

"Sometimes."

CHAPTER FOUR

Destiny and Starr arrived at Jo's Bar for lunch. Destiny wasn't sure what to expect. As a rule, she avoided bars. She didn't drink all that much and certainly wasn't looking to be picked up by a man. But Felicia's lunch invitation offered a chance to get to know some of the women in town and fill part of the day—at least until it was time for the bands to start playing. A twofer in the win department.

She was surprised to find the place was the antithesis of a traditional bar. There was lots of light, a high ceiling and soft, pastel-colored walls. The place was clean, the TVs tuned to what looked like shopping shows, and the background music was barely audible.

A few tables were already taken, mostly with groups of women. Destiny saw Shelby sitting with several other women and walked toward her. Shelby looked up and waved vigorously.

"You made it," Shelby called out as Destiny and Starr approached the table. "Great. Come meet everyone." She motioned to the blonde at the end of the rectangular table. "This is Madeline. She works at Paper Moon."

"I'm on the wedding gown side," Madeline said with a grin. "So if you're thinking of getting married, come see me."

"Thanks," Destiny murmured, thinking that while marriage was appealing, finding the right guy was especially difficult. At least for her.

"Bailey, you probably met at Mayor Marsha's office," Shelby continued.

"No, she didn't," the pretty redhead said. "I was out that day. Chloe was home sick." Bailey smiled. "My daughter. She got what's been going around. Isn't that always the way?"

Destiny nodded and tried to pay attention to the rest of the names. There was a Larissa, a Consuelo and maybe a woman named Patience, but she wasn't sure.

"I'm Destiny," she said when everyone else had been introduced. "This is my half sister, Starr. We're new, but then you probably already know that."

Bailey pulled out the chair next to her. "Starr, honey, come sit by me. I think our hair's the same color, and that almost never happens to me."

Starr hesitated only a second before taking the offered seat. Destiny settled across from her, by Madeline.

"How long have you been in town?" Madeline asked.

"A week."

"I can't imagine what that must be like," Madeline admitted. "I've been here forever. Patience, too."

Patience nodded. "Born and raised. I never left. Madeline, didn't you spend a year or so in San Francisco?"

"I did. I tried a lot of different jobs before finding the one I love. Helping a bride find the right dress is so satisfying."

Shelby leaned forward. "Patience owns Brew-haha."

"The coffee shop," Starr said then shrugged. "I've been reading about the town. It's an interesting place."

"We have a history of powerful women."

The last speaker was Consuelo, Destiny thought. She was petite but looked strong. With her dark hair and eyes, she was the most striking of the group. Destiny momentarily wished she looked more exotic. Or maybe she was simply hoping not to look so much like her parents. So far no one had said anything. Maybe Kipling hadn't gone out and told everyone she was Jimmy Don and Lacey Mills's daughter. And wouldn't that be nice?

She supposed she shouldn't spend so much time hiding who she was, but honestly, she just didn't want to answer all the questions. What was it like growing up with famous parents? Could she sing? Was Lacey really that sexy in person? That was one of the worst. No child wanted to hear about how sexy people found their parents. With her dad, it was worse. She'd had groupies give her their phone number, their email address and one particularly pushy older lady in Dallas had offered a naked picture of herself for Jimmy Don. Destiny had refused to take it, let alone deliver the photograph.

"Centuries ago, a group of Mayan women migrated north to this part of the country," Patience said with a grin. "They set up a matriarchal society. I'm not saying it's mystical or anything, but I think their power, or whatever you want to call it, lingers."

"I'm sure it does," Larissa said. "Haven't you ever walked into a place and just known it had a happy vibe? Or an evil one?"

Several of them nodded. A waitress walked up to the table, a notepad in her hands. "Hi, everyone," she said, then looked at Destiny and Starr. "You two are new. Sisters?"

"Half," Destiny said and introduced them.

"I'm Jo. Welcome. First drink is on me. What would you like?"

Consuelo sighed. "It's been a long week. I vote for margaritas." She glanced at Starr. "Make one of those virgin."

Everyone nodded eagerly.

"My only appointment of the day was this morning," Madeline said. "I'm in."

"I'm not working, either," Patience said. "Bring 'em by the pitcher, Jo."

Destiny was both shocked and amused. Grandma Nell would have loved this group, she thought, even as she wondered at the wisdom of day drinking. Still, it was Saturday, and it wasn't like she had to drive.

"Will do," Jo told them. "Nachos to go with that?"

"You know it," Larissa said.

Jo nodded and left. When she was gone, Patience leaned in and lowered her voice. "Has anyone seen the inside of The Man Cave yet?"

"You have got to let that go," Consuelo told her. "Businesses are allowed to open."

"But this one is different."

Madeline nodded. "There's going to be trouble."

"What are you talking about?" Destiny asked.

Madeline glanced over her shoulder, then returned her attention to the group. "There's a new bar opening in town."

Destiny waited for the rest of the announcement, but there didn't seem to be anything else.

"Okay," she said slowly. "And that's bad why?"

"Because Jo's Bar is *the* bar in town. Now there will be two. That's not how things work here."

"But that's not true. I've seen more than one restaurant. More than one dry cleaners."

"Sure," Bailey said. "And several of the hotels have bars. But this is more like direct competition. I don't know what's going to happen. Mayor Marsha hasn't said anything yet, but I'm sure she will."

Patience pointed at Madeline. "Have you heard? Nick's the manager."

Madeline shook her head and sagged back in her chair. "Don't go there, I beg you."

"Nick, huh?" Larissa teased. "You have a thing?"

Consuelo rolled her eyes. "Do you even know who he is?"

"He's the manager of The Man Cave."

Consuelo groaned. "Have you ever *met* him?"

Larissa laughed. "No, and why does that matter? What if they have a romantic thing going on? Don't you want to hear their story? How they met, and how they fell in love?"

Destiny waited for a snappy comeback. Consuelo surprised her by sighing. "You know what? I would like to hear it. Which is horrifying. I used to be so tough."

"You still scare me," Bailey told her.

"Really? You're not just saying that?"

"I promise."

"Can we get back to Madeline and Nick, please?" Patience asked. "So how long have you two been going out?"

Madeline stretched out her arms on the table and rested her head on them. "I give," she mumbled. "Someone shoot me. Or her. I don't care which."

"You do care," Larissa told her. "So what's Nick like?"

Everyone laughed. Madeline straightened.

"Nick is one of the Mitchell brothers," she said. "Their father is a glass-blowing artist."

"Ceallach Mitchell," Bailey told everyone. "He's world famous. His pieces are exhibited everywhere." She turned to Starr. "I work for the mayor. I have to know these things."

"Does he live here?" the teen asked.

"He does. With his wife. Two of his sons are still in town." Bailey frowned. "Is that right?"

"Yes," Patience said firmly. "Del left years ago. He was in college, and there was this girl, Maya. They were totally in love and then she left and he left, but not together. I'm between them in age, so it was all very exciting. She wasn't from around here. Then there's Aidan. He's in Fool's Gold. He runs the family tour business. Nick is in the middle. He's the one with the artistic talent, like his dad, only he doesn't work with glass anymore. I have no idea why. Then the twins."

Destiny's head was spinning, and she hadn't had any of her margarita yet. "How do you keep this all straight?"

"I live here. It's not hard." Patience grinned at Madeline. "Are you the reason Nick lost his ability to create? Did you wound him?"

"We had one summer," Madeline protested. "Years ago. We were seniors in high school, and it was hot and heavy and then it ended. Nick created this big glass piece, and I remember being terrified because I thought maybe it was going to be about us or sex or him taking my virginity, but it wasn't. It was trees. So I was fine."

Madeline pressed her lips together then cleared her throat. She turned to Starr. "Sorry. I probably shouldn't talk about that in front of you. We were in love, but still. Not married. Bad me."

Starr smiled. "I know people have sex and that it's supposed to be romantic, but it still sounds kind of gross to me."

"It is," Madeline said quickly. "Very gross. Not something you want to be doing."

Jo appeared with the margaritas. As they were passed around, Destiny thought that the group of women was very welcoming. A little out there, but when it came to friendship, that was okay.

She was grateful Starr didn't seem to be in a hurry to fall in love. Or have sex. That was a complication neither of them needed.

Honestly, she'd never understood the appeal of getting so lost in another person that you totally went crazy. What was the point? Take Kipling. Sure he was a nice guy and good-looking. While she didn't get the whole ski-at-the-speed-of-sound thing, she respected that he'd had a dream and had worked to achieve it. Hard work made sense to her.

But throwing herself in front of him and begging to be taken? Why? Yes, she liked thinking about him, and being around him was nice, too. And she wouldn't go so far as to think touching him would be gross. But thinking about kissing wasn't the same as sex at all. She was very clear on that. She could enjoy Kipling's company and admire his body and not have sex with him. She wasn't some wild animal.

"So you're saying no sparks with Nick," Larissa said.

"Not anymore."

Shelby smiled at Destiny. "I'm totally lost. You?"

"Pretty much, but in a good way. Sounds like life here is interesting."

"It is," Shelby assured her. "I've enjoyed it."

"You have a hot brother," Patience announced. "Not that I'm the least bit interested. I'm married to the best guy in the world, and he's fabulous. I'm simply noting that Kipling is hot from an intellectual place. I am allowed to observe things."

Consuelo groaned. "Even you can't be drunk that fast. You've had two sips."

"I know, but I haven't eaten today."

"Lightweight," Consuelo grumbled, but her tone was affectionate.

Destiny was more interested in her conversation with Shelby. If Kipling had told anyone about who she was, it would have been his sister. But Shelby didn't give the slightest hint that she was the least bit intrigued by Destiny's parents.

"Kipling might be hot," Shelby said. "But sometimes he's annoying—he has this burning need to fix things. Not every situation needs fixing. But aside from that, he's basically a good guy." She brightened. "And single. Anyone want to date him?"

Everyone looked at Destiny and Madeline, which made Destiny realize they were the only single adult women at the table.

Madeline held up both hands. "I'm not interested. He and I have met, and there's no chemistry."

Destiny thought about her sensible plan and knew she didn't want to get into that with anyone else. She'd discovered that most people simply didn't understand her reasoning. Of course most people hadn't grown up with her parents.

"I'm only in town for a couple of months."

Patience raised her eyebrows. "You notice Destiny didn't say anything about a lack of chemistry."

Shelby laughed. "You can say he's hot. It's okay. I won't read anything into it."

"Thank you. He's hot."

Patience sipped her margarita. "There are a lot of hot guys in town. It's interesting. And nice for us."

"My husband is totally dreamy," Larissa said with a sigh. "That body." She paused as everyone looked at her. "TMI?"

Patience pointed to Starr and raised her eyebrows.

Larissa nodded. "So, um, Starr, who's hot in your world? You're what? Seventeen?"

Starr blushed. "Fifteen."

"Really? You look so sophisticated. It's the hair." Larissa sighed. "Everyone thinks the blond thing is so cool, but there are a million of us. Redheads are special."

Starr smiled impishly. "Destiny and I just found out we won't be going gray. Redheads don't."

"Okay, now I'm bitter," Patience said cheerfully. "So who do you like? Not Justin Bieber, please. I worry about him."

"One Direction?" Bailey asked. "I like their music. And I can't help it. I love Taylor Swift."

"No one here is surprised," Consuelo told her.

"I like Cody Simpson," Starr said. "For pop music. I'm more into country, though."

Destiny froze in the act of swallowing. Was Starr going to out them? But her sister didn't say anything else.

Destiny waited to see if anyone would pick up on the country part, but Shelby only said, "I know he's kind of old but I have a thing for Matt Damon. He's just so sexy and nice."

Madeline laughed. "And married. I like to crush on the single guys. You want to talk about hot? What about Jonny Blaze? OMG, he's incredible. That body, those dark green eyes. The way he moves." She used her hand to fan herself.

Starr giggled. "He's pretty cute."

"I love him in all his movies," Larissa said. "He's an action star with a brain. And the muscles don't hurt."

Consuelo made a fist with her thumb up. "He gets the fights right. The hand-to-hand stuff. Most movies don't even try, but he's into the details."

Madeline leaned close to Destiny and lowered her voice. "Consuelo used to be in Special Forces or something. She teaches the most amazing classes at the bodyguard school here in town. She started with self-defense, but now she does these killer exercise classes. I've been taking them since the first of the year, and I now have muscles in places I didn't know you could have muscles. But every now and then she scares me. I swear, she could kill someone with a paper towel."

"I'm impressed and intimidated," Destiny admitted.

"Tell me about it. Let me know if you ever want to go to class with me. It's hard, but it's fun."

"Thanks. I will."

Jo arrived with two big platters of nachos. Starr laughed at something Larissa said. Conversations at the other tables in the bar flowed just as freely.

Destiny had to admit that she was more than a little surprised by Fool's Gold. She generally had a good time on her assignments, but she'd been worried about this one. Mostly because of Starr. But from everything she'd seen so far, Fool's Gold was welcoming and an easy place to live. She already felt as if she'd been here for months instead of only a week. There was a sense of connection she wasn't used to. Belonging. She liked the women she'd met and was grateful they were being so nice to her and Starr. Not that she was looking for permanent, but it would be nice while it lasted.

★ ★ ★

Family Man Air Charters was housed in a hangar by the air-port. Finn Andersson, a tall man in his midthirties, leaned back in his chair while Kipling explained about Miles and the heli-copter. Aidan Mitchell sat in the other visitor's chair and listened.

"Helicopter time isn't cheap," Kipling explained. "But it of-fers a unique perspective."

Aidan and Finn glanced at each other.

"Interesting," Aidan said. "Finn and I have been bouncing around the idea of getting something permanent going for the tour company. A helicopter would offer some interesting ad-vantages."

Finn nodded. "Right. We could take people up into the mountains, and they could hike down. Or into the backwoods that are too remote to reach any other way. How long is Miles around?"

"Two months," Kipling told him. "The mapping should be done by mid to late July."

"Enough time to see if there's interest," Aidan said. "Because if we move forward with a helicopter, that's a big investment."

"I could get my helicopter license." Finn sounded excited by the prospect. "It would have to make business sense, but that would be a fun challenge."

Aidan chuckled. "Any excuse to fly." His expression turned thoughtful. "You know, we could talk to Mayor Marsha about the city going in on the helicopter with us. You and I could buy it, and then the city could contract with us when there was an emergency."

"I can talk to Destiny about how a helicopter fits in with the STORMS project," Kipling offered.

"This is good," Aidan said.

"I agree," Finn added. "We should have thought of this our-selves. We'll be in touch with Miles and see if he wants some extra work while he's in town."

"Happy to help," Kipling told them. "I hope it works out." Because he enjoyed solving a problem when he encountered one.

When the meeting finished, he walked toward his Jeep. The mountains seemed closer today, which wasn't possible. But he felt them all the same. Looming. Insistent. Taunting.

He hurt. The places where the bones had shattered were the worst. Most of his joints knew when it was going to rain two days before the local weather guy. He reminded himself he'd survived. That he was walking, and the odds had been against him ever getting out of a wheelchair. He should be grateful.

When he reached the Jeep, he glanced up at the mountains and imagined them covered in snow. If there was snow, he could take them, he thought grimly. Or he had been able to. Once. Just not anymore.

"They're intense," Kipling said.

Destiny watched the two tech guys work on the computers. They wore headphones and typed intently. She would guess they had no idea there were other people in the room.

"They're the best," she told him. "They'll get everything up and running, work out the bugs and disappear into the night. When we're near the end of the training, they'll come back and put in all the customization we've figured out you're going to need for your program. Then we test it, and you're good to go."

They headed outside. The day was warm and sunny. To the side of the office was a small garden with a few tables and benches. A good place for volunteers to collect, Destiny thought. And for them to get updates and rest before heading back out on a call.

Other arrangements would have to be made for the winter, she thought. Maybe they could meet at the nearby fire station. Not that it was her problem to solve, she reminded herself. When she was finished with her job, she would move on. No matter how much she enjoyed a particular location, she never came back.

They sat across from each other at one of the tables.

"I talked to Miles this morning," Destiny said. "He told me you've found him some part-time work."

Kipling shrugged. "He said he got bored. I knew a couple of guys who might want to expand their business using a helicopter. It seemed like a win-win."

"Shelby said you liked to fix things. I can see what she meant."

"Is that a bad thing?"

"No. It's just an interesting trait. Is there a psychological reason, or were you born that way?"

He chuckled. "Which do you think?"

"I don't know. I think how we're raised has a big impact on how we act later in life." She'd learned a lot of lessons watching her parents. Of course those lessons had mostly been about things she needed to avoid. But there had been positive lessons, too.

"I agree with you on that," he said, then hesitated. "What Miles said about your parents. You weren't happy."

She resisted the urge to duck her head and bolt. "No. I don't tell a lot of people. They ask questions that I don't want to answer."

"Or assume things that aren't true."

"How did you know?"

"Let's just say I'm not a famous country singer, but I've been in the limelight before. It's not all positive attention."

"Of course. You're that hot skier guy."

One eyebrow rose. "You think I'm hot?"

Heat instantly burned on her cheeks. She cleared her throat. "I was speaking in generalities, not specifics."

"So you don't think I'm hot."

He was teasing her. Flirting maybe. She almost never got to that point with any guy, so she wasn't sure what to do. Destiny suddenly realized that her plan to find someone sensible and ignore everyone else had a giant flaw. She was twenty-eight years old, and she didn't really know how to deal with a man outside of a work setting.

Miles was easy. She thought of him as a brother. The tech guys and her boss were colleagues. People she met as she went from town to town were kept at a careful distance. No one got close, which kept her safe, but what happened when she found the one? How was she supposed to get close to him?

"It wasn't supposed to be that hard a question," Kipling told her, his eyes twinkling with amusement.

"You know you're very good-looking. You don't need more compliments from me."

"More implies there have been some. So far, you're a disappointment in the compliment department. I was hoping for more."

"Handsome is as handsome does."

He frowned. "What does that mean?"

"I don't know. It's something my Grandma Nell used to say. But it sounds wise."

"Or confusing. Is the flip side of that 'ugly is as ugly does'?"

"I have no idea."

"So who's Grandma Nell?"

Destiny felt herself relaxing as she remembered the other woman. "My maternal grandmother. She lived in the Smoky Mountains all her life. She was wonderful. Loving and smart and an emotional rock for me, if a bit flirty when it came to men. No matter what happened, I could count on her."

Destiny smiled as memories flooded her. "My parents were young when they had me. My mom was still eighteen, and my dad was only a few months older. Apparently, four weeks after I was born, they went off on tour and left me with her. I spent the first couple of years of my life with her. I don't really remember. Then I was with my parents for a while and other family members. My early years weren't exactly stable."

"Was that hard?"

"Sometimes. I would go on tour and have a nanny. The guys in the band always looked out for me."

Kipling studied her. "Didn't you have a hit record when you were maybe seven or eight? I would swear I remember that."

Destiny felt the second blush of the day on her cheeks. "Yes," she said with a groan. "'Under the Willow Tree.' I was eight, and the song did very well."

She'd been nominated for a Grammy, which should have been a terrific experience, only that very morning her father had told her that he and her mother were divorcing for the second time. She'd been devastated, and it had taken all she had not to sob when walking the red carpet.

The reporters had wanted to talk to her. To ask about what it was like to be so young and so talented. She'd wanted to explain to them that she would give up all of it simply to have her parents stay together.

"Right after that, my parents split up again. There was a huge custody battle over me. I'm not sure either wanted me as much as they said. I think it was more about hurting each other." She shrugged. "I went back and forth between them for a couple of years. They both married again and again. When I was ten, Grandma Nell showed up and said I was going to live with her."

"Was that better?" he asked.

"Much. She had a small house. There was running water, but not much else. Electricity was spotty. We had a wood-burning stove, and we grew a lot of our own food. There were times I was lonely, but mostly I was so grateful to her for taking me in."

As she spoke she was aware of Kipling watching her intently. She had no idea what he was thinking, but didn't feel it was bad. From what she could tell, he was a nice man. He fixed things, which was an admirable trait. If her parents had been more interested in holding the family together…

But they hadn't been. Which left her with a half sister she didn't know and left Starr with no one else to take care of her.

"Tell me more about Grandma Nell," he prompted.

She smiled. "She knew about plants and how to can and sew. She was a big reader. We would drive into town every Wednesday afternoon and go to the movies, then stop at the library and get lots of books. I was homeschooled until I was sixteen. She sent away for lesson plans, and she made me stick to a schedule."

"What happened when you turned sixteen?"

"She said I had to go join the real world. That I couldn't hide forever. I didn't want to go, but she was right, as usual. I stayed with my father while I took college entrance exams and applied to different universities."

She remembered how she'd been so scared that she wasn't going to know enough. She should have trusted Grandma Nell. "I got accepted everywhere I applied. My scores were really high, and I ended up being able to test out of half my general education courses."

Neither of which had made up for missing the woman who had taken her in and loved her like a mother.

"She visited me at college every semester, and everyone adored her," she continued.

"I'd like to meet her," Kipling said.

"She's gone." Destiny felt her smile fade. "Three years ago, she came to stay with me for a couple of weeks. When she was leaving, she said it was her time. I didn't understand. She died three days later."

"I'm sorry."

"Thanks. Me, too. I miss her every day. Even more so now that I have Starr. Grandma Nell would have known what to do."

"You do, too."

"I'm less sure of that." She shook her head. "Sorry. I'm not sure where that all came from. I'm usually more private."

"I asked."

"Still." She stood. "I should go check on my tech guys. Every now and then they remember they have to eat. I can do a lunch run for them."

Kipling rose and walked around the table. He gazed into her eyes. "Grandma Nell sounds like she really loved you."

"She did."

"You'll always have that."

They walked toward the front door of the building.

"The Man Cave is opening soon," he said. "It's this bar I own with a few business partners."

"I've heard some people talking about it," she admitted. "You must be excited."

"I am. Come to the opening with me. We're going to have a killer karaoke setup. You could sing."

"I don't sing," she told him firmly.

"Ever?"

"Not in public."

"But it has to be in your blood."

"There are a lot of things in my blood. I deny most of them. It makes life easier."

"Who said easy was the right path?" he asked. "I'd like to hear you sing."

"It's never going to happen." She narrowed her gaze. "I don't need fixing."

"I didn't say you did."

"Shelby warned me, and she was right. Let me repeat myself. No fixing required. I'm perfectly fine. I have everything under control. I prefer life without surprises."

Kipling studied her for a second then leaned in. She had no idea what he was going to do so wasn't the least bit prepared for the feel of his mouth brushing against hers.

The contact was brief, soft and rocked her down to her tiniest toes. She went hot then cold. Her chest got tight, and somewhere deep inside, a dark, lonely place she rarely acknowledged, warmed up at least three degrees.

"Why did you do that?" she demanded when he'd straightened.

One corner of his mouth turned up. "Two reasons. First, because I wanted to. And second, everyone needs a good surprise now and then."

She struggled to speak, but there were no words. She could only stare as he gave her a wink then turned and walked away.

CHAPTER FIVE

Destiny gently strummed her guitar. The music was elusive to-night. Taunting her with melodies attached to half phrases. But when she tried to capture the notes or even the words, they faded away.

You could be my best regret. I could be your peace of mind.

She made a few more notes then put down her guitar and flopped back on her bed. She immediately sat up and began playing the hillbilly music Grandma Nell had loved. Mostly the songs didn't appeal to her, but they were a connection. Many a winter's night, she and Grandma Nell had played and sung by firelight as the snow fell outside. There had been an old piano in the front room. A man came by every spring and tuned it. The rest of the year, they made do.

Now she sang about the mountain and God and life until she started to relax. Unfortunately, the second she did, she remem-bered Kipling's kiss and tensed up all over again.

Stupid man, she thought as she put down her guitar again. Stupid, stupid kiss. Why had he done that? And then to walk away. Who did that?

She told herself it didn't matter. So he'd kissed her. It wasn't as if she'd asked. And while she got a little thrill every time she thought about his mouth on hers, it wasn't as if she was letting her hormones run away with her. She was perfectly in control, as always.

In fact, it was probably good Kipling had kissed her. As she'd recently realized, if she wanted to find the man of her somewhat quiet dreams, she was going to need a little more experience. While she doubted he would be the type who wanted to be seduced, she should at least be able to hold her own. So more kissing was a good thing. As long as she didn't let herself get carried away.

It was all so ridiculous, she thought as she stretched out on the bed. The whole boy-girl-sex thing. Why did people give in so easily? Why did they let themselves get swept away? People let their bodies take over, and then they made bad decisions. Which would be fine if those decisions didn't have consequences for other people. But they usually did. Like when Dad and Mom broke up and forgot about their children. Like Jimmy Don with Starr.

Destiny glanced at the small clock on her nightstand. It was nearly ten. She stood and walked into the hallway, then knocked on Starr's closed door.

"Hey, I just wanted to say good-night."

There was an odd sound, then Starr said, "You can come in."

Destiny opened the door. Her sister sat at the small desk in her room. Her tablet was on a stand.

"Emailing friends?" Destiny asked.

"Watching a movie." Starr half turned toward her, her long hair hanging over her face. "I heard you playing."

Destiny winced. She'd been so upset, she'd forgotten to go into the garage. Or wait until Starr was asleep.

Destiny walked over to the bed and sat down. "Yes, you did."

"So you *can* play. You lied."

"I know. I apologize."

"Why would you do that?"

"I don't like playing. Sometimes I can't help doing it, but mostly I ignore it. Music isn't my thing."

"What if it's *my* thing?" Starr brushed her hair back and glared.

Destiny saw what looked like tears on her sister's cheeks. "Are you okay?"

Starr brushed at her face. "I'm fine. You didn't answer the question."

Destiny thought about life with her parents. How every moment had been dominated by music. It had always been playing in the background. There had been jam sessions in the living room. Even putting the dishes away had turned into a music extravaganza with flatware as percussion and water-filled glasses playing the melody. She thought of the laughter and later the tears. The sense of being abandoned over and over again. Of being a pawn.

"It's complicated," she began.

"No, it's not. I want to play better, and you won't teach me. We're sisters. You're supposed to care about me."

"I do."

"No, you don't. Music is the most important part of my life, and you're keeping me from it."

"I'm sorry. Sorry that I lied and sorry you're hurt now." She paused, knowing what she had to say and not wanting to say it. No. It wasn't the words she regretted, it was the actions that would follow.

"I can teach you to play," she said softly. "Guitar and piano. I have a keyboard in my room."

Starr turned away. "Never mind. I don't want to learn anything from you."

Destiny flinched as if she'd been hit. She'd screwed up. "Please, Starr. Don't punish me by punishing yourself. That never goes well. Let's spend some time playing this weekend. I can show you a few things that—"

"I said no." Starr turned back to her computer. "It's late. I'm tired."

In other words, get out of my room, Destiny thought.

"Okay." She stood. "Good night."

She walked out and closed the door.

She told herself she would do better next time. The subject wasn't over. She would give Starr a couple of days then bring it up again. Teaching her a few chords wouldn't be so bad. Maybe it would give them something to talk about. A way to get to know each other.

Because while Destiny might not know everything Grandma Nell would do, she was sure the older woman would make Starr feel welcome and loved. It was a lesson Destiny knew she had to learn.

Angelo's Italian Cuisina was across from the park. The white-washed building had a large patio with plenty of outdoor dining. Kipling tasted the red wine that had just been delivered to the table.

"Very nice," he said.

Their server nodded and poured. When he'd left, Shelby leaned toward him.

"Do you ever send the wine back just because?" she asked with a grin.

"No. Not my style."

"I know. I'm just messing with you. I'm sure in your life, you get enough attention in other ways."

Not lately, he thought, thinking it had been a long time between women in his life. Between recovering from the crash and then moving to Fool's Gold, he'd avoided romantic entanglements. But if all went according to plan, he was going to be tangled up very soon. Which wasn't a subject he would be discussing with his baby sister.

"How's work?" he asked. They were having dinner at five in the evening. A ridiculous time, but Shelby's job at the bakery required an early start.

"Good. I'm learning a lot. Amber is trusting me with more and more responsibility. The tourist season is bringing in a lot of business. I had no idea how many people come back year after year. They remember what they ordered last time, and we sure had better have it now."

He nodded to show he was listening. He admired Shelby's enthusiasm. A year ago she'd been dealing with a mother dying of cancer and a father who thought nothing of putting his fist into his only daughter's face.

"I suggested we have a food cart at the last festival. Amber wasn't sure it would work, but we sold out of everything before noon. It was a huge moneymaker."

"Congratulations on impressing the boss."

"Thanks. I have a lot of ideas." Shelby glanced down at the table then back up. "Amber and I have been talking."

Kipling recognized the tone and the strategy. He braced himself for something he knew he didn't want to hear. "And?"

"When her dad retires, she's going to take over the bookstore. There's no way she can run two businesses at the same time. So she's looking for a partner in the bakery. I was thinking I want to buy into the bakery with her."

Kipling deliberately inhaled, giving himself time to think before speaking.

"That's a great opportunity," he said slowly. "Are you sure you're ready for it?"

"I know what I'm doing. I love the work, and I want to stay in Fool's Gold permanently."

"You're more than capable of making a decision about this on your own. I'm just asking that you think it through. You haven't been here that long. You're coming off a very difficult emotional loss. Buying into a business is a big responsibility.

What if you and Amber want different things for the business? It won't be just a job anymore. You can't quit and walk away."

"I don't walk away," she snapped. "I don't leave. I stay where I am."

He told himself not to take her comments personally. That she wasn't talking about *his* leaving. Because he had left. When he'd gotten the opportunity to work with his ski coach, he'd jumped at it. He'd been all of fourteen. Shelby had been a half dozen years younger. He'd told himself she would be safe. Mostly because their father hadn't started hitting her yet.

"I worry because you lead with your heart," he told her gently. "I worry because I want you to be sure you're doing what you want and not simply acting to help Amber. Helping a friend is a good thing, but in this case it could tie you to something permanently."

She sagged back in her seat, as if the fight had gone out of her. "I know you care. I love you, too. But, Kipling, you have to stop taking care of me. I'm not one of your projects. I don't need fixing."

"Fair enough. I won't try. Besides, there's no point in fixing what isn't broken."

She reached across the table and patted his hand. "Thank you. You're a good brother."

"One of the best."

She laughed. "Now you're annoying me on purpose. Do you think that's safe?"

"I trust you, kid."

"You've known me all my life."

"And most of mine. In fact, I can't remember when you weren't around."

She leaned toward him. "I had lunch with Destiny and her sister a couple of days ago. There was a group of us. She's nice and everything, but I get the impression she and her sister aren't close."

Kipling picked up his glass of wine as a way to buy time. He wasn't sure what to say. A case could be made that he owed Destiny nothing. Only that wasn't true. He liked her, and he'd kissed her. He was hoping for a lot more, in the "let's get physical" department. But more than that, he figured the secret was hers to tell or not.

"I don't know exactly how she and Starr ended up together," he said casually. "But she mentioned something about them not knowing each other. They're half sisters, through their father. Starr's mom died a while ago."

Shelby blinked. "Seriously? That's just like us. Half siblings through our father, and I lost my mom last year."

"Except we grew up together."

"Yeah, that would change things. I can't imagine having a sister I didn't know."

He couldn't, either. Although he did understand family estrangement. His father was currently sitting in prison for various crimes, beyond beating his daughter. He would be there a long time, and Kipling had no plans to go see him.

As a teenager, he'd worried about how much of his father he carried with him. Was his father's darkness like a hibernating monster that would wake with no warning? Because there was no other way to describe a man who beat his daughter.

He'd been afraid he would one day wake up and feel the dark violence growing inside him. Finally, he'd talked to his coach about what he'd seen at home and what he feared.

As always, the advice had been honest and practical.

"Have you ever wanted to hit a woman?"

Kipling remembered being both shocked and humiliated by the question. "Hell, no."

"If you do, go get help. Immediately. Find a shrink. Get on medication. Whatever it takes. You can't choose where you come from, but you can decide how you're going to deal with it."

Kipling had vowed he wouldn't let himself turn into his father, no matter what it cost him. The promise had turned out to be easy to keep. He'd been angry to the point of rage and had never once felt the need to raise his hand to anyone. If there was a genetic component to violence, he'd managed to dodge that bullet. If it was the result of nurture, he would guess the skiing had saved him. Either way, he was grateful.

He thought maybe part of the reason was his connection to the mountains. Flying over snow took a discipline that forced him to control himself. Every action had an immediate consequence, and when he screwed up, the results, or disasters, were unforgiving.

He wondered what Destiny had gone through, growing up as she had. Which demons had she escaped, and which did she carry with her?

Later, after he and Shelby had finished their dinner, he walked back to the town house he'd rented. It was still light, and there were plenty of people out enjoying the evening. He nodded and called out greetings, but kept moving. He wasn't in the mood to talk to anyone right now.

Restlessness pulled at him. He recognized it and knew the cause. Before the accident, the solution would have been easy—hop on a plane and go find a mountain. Get to the top and ski down. That was all. The simple act of movement against snow would take care of the problem.

He stepped off the curb and felt the pull in his back and down his leg. Remnants of what had happened. Of the accident.

It had happened so fast—as they always did. He didn't remember much. Just waking up in a world of hurt. He could have been paralyzed. He could have died. So he couldn't ski. Big deal.

Only some days, it was. Some days he thought about how the best part of him had been lost and would never be found again.

He passed a family out for a walk, a little girl flanked by her parents. Dad pushed a stroller.

There were a lot of families in town. Couples. People in love.

He'd always thought he would get there someday, only he'd never been able to get past the truth. That saying you loved someone didn't mean a thing. Not when love couldn't change anything. Heal anything. Fix anything.

His father had claimed to love his daughter. And then he'd beat her. Shelby's love for her dying mother had put her right in front of the old man's fist. What good had love done any of them?

It wasn't that he didn't believe in love. He did. He knew it existed. He loved his sister. He would die for Shelby. But if she was in trouble, he would get off his ass and do something about it. Not just sit back and love her. Or claim to, as their father had.

He saw other couples all around him. Happy people who made it look easy. Who didn't seem to be working so hard. But he'd never been able to simply believe. To know it was right. That any particular woman was "the one." He couldn't figure out what was different for him. So he stayed with what worked.

He liked serial monogamy. Maybe he should just go with it. And for the most part, he was happy. But every now and then, he wondered if maybe, just maybe, there was more.

If sex was the root of all evil, then men were holding the watering can and making the root go deeper.

Destiny groaned. That didn't even make sense to her, which sort of proved her point. Look at her. A sensible woman with a responsible job spending twenty-five minutes wondering what to wear to a meeting. Talk about a waste of time. She knew what to wear. She would put on work clothes, which meant jeans or cargo pants and a shirt. It wasn't like she had much choice. No way she was going to prance into her business meeting in some frilly dress and high heels.

This was all Kipling's fault. He'd kissed her. And while she'd been kissed before, something had happened this time. A part of her brain had come loose, or she'd had an influx of unusually powerful hormones. Or she needed to be on anti-Kipling medication, but she doubted that had been invented.

She closed her eyes and took a calming breath. Or tried to. Because when she opened her eyes, she still wanted to look pretty for the meeting.

No, she told herself, determined to be honest. Not for the meeting. For the man.

If only she had someone to talk to, she thought as she pulled out her skinny jeans and shimmied into them. A sensible person who could tell her how to shake off the grubby remnants of lingering sexual attraction. But there was no one. She didn't really stay in touch with people she'd met on previous jobs. Asking her mother for advice was like calling a pyromaniac for tips on how to avoid fire. And for once, recalling the many words of wisdom from Grandma Nell wasn't the least bit helpful. Because her thoughts on the subject were incredibly clear.

If he's single and rings your bell, then go get a good ringing.

"I don't want anything to do with bells," she muttered as she chose a tight T-shirt and pulled that on.

She'd already washed her hair and, damn it, used a blow-dryer and round brush to add fullness and a slight wave. Worse, she'd put on mascara. She was pathetic. Kipling was not for her. While he had many excellent qualities, he wasn't sensible. And apparently, she wasn't sensible around him.

The fact that a single kiss could throw her so far off her game only proved her point. No sex. Not until she was ready to have children. It was the slick, steep road to trouble.

She grabbed her backpack, made sure she had her notes for the meeting then left her bedroom. She found Starr in the living room. The teen looked up from her book.

"I'm heading out," Destiny said. "Are you going to be okay tonight?"

"I'm fine."

The words were right, but there was something in Starr's

eyes. Sadness, maybe. Or maybe Starr was still mad at her about lying. Destiny wasn't sure. Once camp started, Starr would be happier, but that was still a few days away.

"We can talk when I get home," she offered. "I could show you some chords."

Starr shrugged and returned her attention to her book.

Destiny wished her sister had come with instructions. Not even a manual. A pamphlet would have helped. But there was nothing.

"I won't be late," she said.

Starr didn't say anything, and Destiny left. She promised she would figure out what to do with Starr when she got back. But between now and then, she had a meeting to get through.

It was after six in the evening, but still warm and sunny. She walked quickly, heading for City Hall. Apparently, there was a small auditorium they would be using for the volunteer meeting.

While the HERO program would have a few key permanent staff, the majority of the search crew would be made up of volunteers. A percentage of those would need to be trained to use the equipment. The purpose of tonight's event was to discuss the program with the community and, ideally, to get people to sign up. Or at least show some interest.

Given the personality of the town as she'd seen it, Destiny didn't think there would be a problem getting people to show up. The plan was to pull the majority of the volunteers from local police and firefighters, who already had the necessary training. She was curious as to how many other people would be interested in signing up for the HERO program.

She got to City Hall and took the stairs up to the main door. There were signs in the entrance hall pointing her toward the auditorium. She walked in only to find that she was the first one there...except for Kipling.

He stood by the stage, studying his notes. Overhead lights seemed to cast some kind of glow about him. Destiny knew all the tricks lighting could play and told herself not to be impressed. Which she wasn't. It was just that she couldn't seem to catch her breath.

Damn him, she thought, nearly stomping her foot. And the kiss. And the hormones. And her body for betraying her. She knew better. She'd seen it, lived it, had felt the pain of watching her parents being swept away by yet another "one true love." She'd been cast aside, ignored and forgotten. Even now she was dealing with the consequences of her father's fling sixteen years ago in the form of a teenage daughter he seemed to have forgotten he had. She wasn't going to give in. She was going to stand strong.

She squared her shoulders, sucked in a breath and stalked up to Kipling.

"Let me be clear," she said by way of greeting. "I will not be your plaything."

He looked up at her and grinned. "Why not? I'm happy to be yours."

Destiny felt her mouth drop open. He had *not* just said that. Who talked like that? But before she could start expressing her opinion in a volume designed to get his attention, two old ladies walked into the auditorium. She recognized one of them as Eddie Carberry.

Destiny lowered her voice. "This isn't over," she promised.

His smile never wavered. "I was hoping you'd say that."

"I meant this conversation. Not the whole..." She clenched her teeth together. "Never mind. I'll deal with you later."

"Looking forward to it."

That man, she thought, turning away from him. He was so annoying. He hadn't been annoying before.

She told herself to ignore him and the strange sensations rushing through her body. This was business. She was here to do a job. Kipling was simply an obstruction she had to get over. Or through. Or something.

More people arrived and found seats. Miles showed up, and Destiny moved to sit next to him. Despite his good looks, she didn't have to worry about being attracted to him.

"What has your panties in a twist?" he asked as she settled beside him.

"I have no idea what you're talking about."

"You look angry. It's kind of sexy."

She rolled her eyes. "You'd find drywall sexy."

"Only if it was girl drywall." He pointed to the stage. "Shouldn't you be up there?"

As the time for the meeting approached, she saw Kipling was walking toward the stairs on the side and knew she should join him. After all, she was going to be speaking to the group.

The room was nearly full, she thought as she reluctantly got up and followed him to the small podium on the stage. There were a couple of chairs behind it. He turned to her. A smile tugged at his mouth. She felt everyone in the room watching them.

"Don't even think about it," she said in a low voice.

He chuckled. "I was going to ask if you wanted to speak first, or if you wanted me to go first."

Like she believed that. The man was trouble. Grandma Nell would have adored him.

"You tell them about the program," she said. "I'll talk about the technical stuff, then we can take questions together."

Kipling nodded and approached the podium. He flipped on the microphone.

"Thanks for coming tonight, everyone. I appreciate the show of support from the community. For those of you who don't know me, I'm Kipling Gilmore, and I'm in charge of the town's search and rescue program."

"You mean you're our head HERO," Eddie yelled from her seat in the audience. The older lady next to her clapped.

Kipling nodded. "That would be me. Help Emergency Rescue Operations is going to save lives. But we're a small organization, just getting started, and we'll need help. Volunteers. Tonight's meeting is to explain how the program is going to work and how you can get involved."

Destiny only half listened as Kipling went through the details of the program. She knew the particulars better than most. When it was her turn, she would explain how the software would make finding those who were lost just a little easier.

She liked her job. She liked knowing that when she moved on, she'd left things better than when she arrived. She liked the people she met and the sense of belonging, however temporary. She'd met a lot of nice people and more than one attractive man. But no one had rattled her as much as Kipling. She was going to have to figure out why he got to her, then find a way for it to stop.

When Kipling was done, Destiny took the podium and talked about the STORMS software and how it would help with HERO, then together they took questions. She tried not to notice how close they stood to each other as they shifted to use the microphone in turn.

Eddie Carberry raised her hand. "Gladys and I want to volunteer. Are you going to tell us we're too old?"

Destiny smiled at Kipling. "I'll let you take that one."

Several people in the audience laughed.

"Thanks," he said, moving forward and clearing his throat. "We appreciate everyone who wants to volunteer. There are going to be opportunities for every level of fitness."

Eddie scrunched up her face. "You're going to stick us in the office, aren't you? We want to be out in the field."

Kipling's expression turned pained. "We can talk about that, if you'd like—"

"And then you'll say no." She stood, as did Gladys. "We want an adventure this summer, before we're too old. If you're not going to give it to us, we'll find someone who will. That'll show you what we're capable of."

The two older women walked out of the meeting. When they'd left, a tall woman stood. She wore a dark blue T-shirt with FGFD emblazoned across the front, and she was clearly pregnant.

"Don't let them get you down," she said. "They love to make trouble. I'm Charlie Stryker, by the way. Fool's Gold Fire Department. I'm interested in volunteering. Most of us on the department are. We're going to sign releases so the HR department can link our work shift information to your database. That way you'll know who's available when. People tend to get lost when it's least convenient to everyone else."

A couple of police officers made the same offer. Kipling took down the names of the two departments' human resources contact and promised to be in touch. By the end of the meeting, they had dozens of volunteers.

"You're not going to have any trouble filling positions," Destiny said when she and Kipling walked off the stage.

"Good to know." He nodded at her. "I'm going to go talk to Charlie before she leaves. I'll see you around."

"Sure."

Destiny's brain was pleased by his all-business attitude. She'd made her feelings very clear and appreciated how he'd obviously listened. The rest of her was just a little crabby that he seemed to have gotten over her so quickly. And that there wasn't going to be any more kissing. Which only proved her point about how things like sexual attraction messed with the mind and left a perfectly rational woman teetering on the mental edge.

CHAPTER SIX

"Try putting your fingers here," Destiny said, shifting Starr's fingers on the fretboard. "Press firmly enough to hold the strings, but not so tight that you exhaust yourself. You don't need a death grip."

Starr moved her hand slightly then relaxed her fingers. "Like this?"

"That's it. How are your fingers?"

They'd been playing for nearly an hour already. Starr had ignored her offer to help her learn to play guitar for a week. But at six-thirty that morning, her sister had approached her. Destiny had been surprised, but pleased.

"Sore," Starr admitted.

"It's going to get worse before it gets better." She glanced at the clock. "We have to get going or you'll be late for camp. We'll practice more tonight. Eventually, you'll build up calluses but until then you can use ice or soak them in apple cider vinegar."

Starr laughed. "I'll start with ice. I don't want my hands to smell."

"Fair enough. You ready?"

Starr put down the guitar and nodded. She was already dressed in jeans and a jacket. It would warm up later, but it would be cool first thing in the morning, especially up in the mountains.

"You have sunscreen and insect repellent?" Destiny asked. "They're giving you lunch."

"I have everything, and if I don't, I'll text you."

"Good. I'll have my cell phone with me."

Destiny grabbed her backpack, and they headed for the car.

Later in the week a bus would take the local kids up the mountain, but for the first couple of days, parents were expected to drive. She had directions, but guessed that she would simply be following a line of cars heading to End Zone for Kids.

"You excited?" she asked as they turned onto Forest Highway.

"A little. I'll be assigned a buddy to help me find my way around."

"Plus, everyone is new on the first day."

"Did you ever go to camp?"

"A couple of times," Destiny told her. "They were the kind where you stayed in a cabin."

"Like boarding school."

"Exactly. Between touring and getting married or divorced, neither Mom nor Dad could take care of me in the summer."

"Is that when you went to live with your Grandma Nell?"

"Uh-huh. I was ten. Scared about living in the mountains, but happy to be with her. No matter what, she was always there for me."

"Did you like living with her?"

Destiny thought about the beauty of the Smoky Mountains. Sure, they'd been isolated, but that hadn't been a bad thing.

"Very much. There's a rhythm to the seasons. Things to do. Putting up fruits and vegetables in the summer. Getting ready for winter in the fall. The first snowfall was always so beautiful."

She turned onto Mountain Pass and as she'd expected, found herself in a long line of cars heading up the mountain.

"Was it hard to leave to go to college?" Starr asked.

"It was. I worried I wouldn't be as smart or educated as everyone else. And I was nervous about being back in the ordinary world. I'd been out of touch for so long. What if I didn't talk right or know what to wear?" She thought about her first couple of days at college. "And I missed Grandma Nell so much."

"Where did you go to college?"

"Vanderbilt for two years, then I transferred to the University of Texas."

"Why?"

"It was hard being in Nashville. There was too much of the industry around." She knew she didn't have to say which industry. In her family, there was only the one.

"You got your degree in music?" Starr asked.

"Computer science."

"What?" Starr stared at her. "Why? That's like math, only harder."

"Computers rule, young lady. We have to respect them."

"Sure, but we don't have to, like, study them. Oh, wait." Starr nodded slowly. "You wanted to get away from your parents and what they did for a living. You wanted to be different."

Or safe, although Destiny didn't say that. "It seemed like a good plan. Once I figured out my major, transferring made the most sense. I ended up getting an internship at the company where I work now, so everything turned out."

"What did Grandma Nell think of your major?"

An interesting question. The older woman had in fact reminded Destiny that running *from* something wasn't the same as running *to* something.

"She always supported me," Destiny said, bending the truth. "I could count on her, no matter what."

"That's nice. I wish I had someone like her in my family. Where is she now?"

"She passed a few years ago."

"I'm sorry."

"Thanks. Me, too."

Destiny pushed away the inevitable sadness and pointed to the sign up ahead. "We're here." She followed the other cars into a large parking lot.

Registration was quick. Starr was given a color-coded wristband, and then it was time for Destiny to leave.

Starr drew in a breath. "Okay, I'll see you later. You remember that lady, Felicia, is driving me home, right?"

"I do." Destiny touched her sister's arm. "You're going to do great."

"I hope so. It sucks being the new girl. I know how to do it, but I never like it. I can't imagine doing what you do. Not just, like, working with computers and stuff, but always going from place to place. Don't you ever want to settle somewhere?"

"Eventually, sure."

Starr looked like she was going to say something else but changed her mind. She shifted her backpack to her other shoulder. "See you later."

"Have fun."

Destiny thought about giving her a hug, but before she could reach out, Starr had turned and walked away.

She let her go and returned to her car. Progress had been made, she thought. She would enjoy that and continue to take baby steps.

She drove back to town and parked at home before walking to Brew-haha. She was meeting Kipling for an update before heading out in the helicopter to oversee more tracking. Miles was making good progress. It wasn't that he needed her along, but she preferred to make random flights to confirm it was all going well.

She crossed the street and walked toward Brew-haha. When she realized she was moving faster and faster, she deliberately slowed. She was *not* excited about seeing Kipling again. She wasn't anything. She was going to have a meeting with a colleague. Nothing more.

As she forced herself to keep to a slower pace, she thought about all the women who gave in so easily to sex. She supposed a case could be made that their way was better. If you simply reacted to attraction, then maybe, over time, it had no power. Maybe it was like an itch that once scratched, didn't return.

Only that hadn't been her experience with her parents. They went from itch to itch, creating havoc in their respective wakes. Maybe the actual problem was she hadn't been looking hard enough for her sensible, reliable mate. There were plenty of single men right here in town. Why not check them out?

There were the Mitchell brothers. Aidan and Nick were both attractive. Although from what she'd heard, Nick was an artist at heart. If he really was denying his gift, then there was a disaster looming, and she didn't want that. Aidan ran an adventure tour company. Not exactly the job description of her ideal calm, staid mate.

There had been talk at the volunteer meeting about a rancher named Zane. He had sounded age appropriate, and a man who made his living off the land was certainly going to understand about being responsible and patient. She should find a way to meet him.

But all plans of casually running into rancher Zane fled the second she walked into Brew-haha and saw Kipling was already at one of the tables. He'd ordered two lattes and had a plate of pastries in front of him.

She hesitated for a second. Her body seemed to go into some kind of cellular happy dance. Her breathing hitched, her heart raced and somewhere deep in her belly she felt a distinct kind of twisting. Probably the beginning of stomach flu, she told herself uneasily.

She refused to show weakness and walked toward him.

"Hey," he said when she took the seat opposite his. "I got you a latte. Hope that's all right."

"It is. Thank you." She clutched the coffee mug in both hands.

"You get Starr off okay? Didn't she start summer camp today?"

"Uh-huh. I hope she likes it."

"Yeah, it's never easy being the new kid."

"That's what she said. Did you move around a lot as a kid? Because of the skiing?"

"Sure, but I had my coach and my team. I wasn't on my own like she is. But she'll make friends and that will help. Too bad you're leaving at the end of summer. If you were staying, she'd have friends when school starts."

"Starr goes to a boarding school. She'll be going back there."

Kipling frowned. "She doesn't live with you full-time?"

"No. Just for the summer. I'm her legal guardian now, but that's more for handling logistics."

"Oh. And she's okay with that? With not having a real home?"

Destiny didn't like the questions. "She has a home."

"Where?"

Destiny didn't have an answer to that. Starr had only spent a few days at Destiny's place in Austin before they'd left for Fool's Gold. The apartment wasn't really big enough for the two of them.

"I guess I haven't thought that part through," she said slowly.

"You should talk to her and find out what she thinks is going to happen in the fall. She might not be as excited about going back to boarding school as you think."

"Why would you say that? You don't know her."

"I know kids. I jumped at the chance to join the ski team and loved every second of it, but there were kids who would rather have been home. No one likes being sent away."

She'd been a kid, too, she thought with faint irritation. For her, being sent away had been the best thing to ever happen to her. But she'd been going to live with a loving grandmother while Starr was going away to school. Those were different destinations.

"She has friends at school," she said, aware she sounded defensive. Partly because if Starr wasn't going back, then Destiny didn't know what that would mean. She loved traveling for her career, but with a fifteen-year-old, moving from place to place every three months wasn't possible.

She shook her head. "You're fixing things again. You need to let that go."

"I can't help it," he said with an easy smile. "It's part of my charm."

"If you say so."

He laughed. "Not impressed? I could get you references, if that would help."

"I can't begin to imagine what they would say."

"It's all good," he promised. "I'm a fun date. Speaking of which, come with me to The Man Cave opening. It's going to be a hell of a party."

"I'm really not the bar type."

"This isn't a regular bar. Come on. It's the opening of my business. How can you not want to be there to see all the magic?"

She tried to figure out why he was so appealing. Other men were as good-looking. Maybe more so. He was plenty smart, but not brilliant. He had characteristics she found mildly annoying, but they didn't seem to diminish her attraction.

A date. She couldn't remember the last time she'd been on one. Did she even remember how?

"I won't sleep with you," she told him.

Kipling didn't bother reacting to the blunt statement. "I don't remember asking, but thanks for the update. Are you saying that night or ever?"

Ever. She should say ever. Because he wasn't what she was looking for. She was clear on her goals. Clear and determined.

"Ever," she said firmly.

He leaned back in his chair. Amusement twinkled in his blue eyes. "Yeah, you are so lying. You want me. Admit it."

Destiny told herself he was teasing. That all she had to do was laugh with him and everything would be fine. Only she couldn't. Not really. Because she *was* attracted to him. More than she wanted to be.

She opened her mouth, then closed it. She felt herself blushing and wished to be miraculously transported somewhere else. Preferably to another hemisphere. When that didn't happen, she grabbed her backpack, stood and mumbled, "I have to go."

Kipling was on his feet in a second. "Destiny, no. Don't. I was teasing."

She shook her head and bolted.

For whatever reason, Kipling didn't follow her. Gratitude and fear propelled her to her office. A ridiculous place to try to hide, she thought, even as she closed the door behind her and leaned against it. Like he didn't know where she worked?

But there was nowhere else to go. She could only hope for a few minutes of solitude. An hour or so to figure out what on earth was wrong with her and how she was going to fix it. Fast.

By five that afternoon, Destiny had managed to put the Kipling issue out of her mind. The reprieve was probably temporary, but she was willing to go with that. Mostly out of guilt. Starr guilt.

While she wanted to try to forget the man, she couldn't seem to let go of his words about her sister. That Starr didn't technically have a home to retreat to. That there was no place she called her own.

Destiny didn't know how to fix that problem, but she knew how to offer a distraction. In the time-honored tradition handed down by generations, she cooked.

First up was a pie. Grandma Nell had taught her the secrets to a perfect crust. She'd used first-of-the-season blueberries. Now the pie was cooling on a rack on the kitchen table.

She'd bought chicken for frying and ingredients for salad. Because there weren't many problems that couldn't be fixed with fried chicken for dinner.

"I'm back," Starr called.

Destiny walked into the living room. The teen looked happy as she dropped her bag onto the sofa and collapsed next to it. Destiny sat across from her.

"How was it?" she asked, then mentally crossed her fingers. Please let the report be good.

Starr grinned. "Great. I'm really tired, but in a good way, you know? The camp is huge. There are all these classrooms and different areas. I'm with the drama and music kids. There's some tech classes and lots of sports stuff, too. It's busy and loud and fun. We had lunch in shifts, which was good because with that many kids, it would be totally impossible."

She paused to breathe. "There are kids that come in for a couple of weeks. They stay up there. They're from, like, Los Angeles. The inner city, one of the counselors said. I talked to this girl who had never been to the mountains before. She'd never seen a forest! She said there were, like, eight trees in this tiny park by her house. She'd counted them."

Starr shook her head. "I've never met anyone like that. She was so fun and had an incredible voice. But everything is different for her. Her family doesn't have any money. I didn't know it was really like that for some people."

"I'm glad she's able to go to camp."

"Me, too. I met a lot of kids who live in town. Some of them are my age." She ducked her head for a second. "Felicia's son is nice. Carter. He has friends he wants to introduce me to. He said we could hang out."

Destiny had been nodding along with the conversation, but right then she got stuck.

"A boy?" she asked, wondering if the fear and outrage showed in her voice.

Starr stared at her. "Duh, most sons are boys, so yeah. We're friends. It's cool. He's nice. I like him."

"Like him how?"

Starr rolled her eyes. "What are you worried about? I'm fifteen. It's okay for me to like a boy. It's what teenagers do."

Destiny told herself to stay calm. That this could be managed. "I get that," she said slowly. "But you have to be careful. We both do."

"Careful? What are you talking about?"

"It's in our genes. Like having red hair. And an interest in music. You get that from your dad, right?"

"Okay," Starr said cautiously. "What does that have to do with Carter?"

"Other traits can be inherited. Things like falling in and out of love. You saw what happened with your parents. Do you want that for yourself? These are decisions you need to think about. Because if you don't think, you might act. Sex is dangerous."

Starr turned away. "Don't say that to me. I don't want to talk about it. I'm *fifteen*. I know some kids are doing…that, but I'm not. Who do you think I am?"

"I think you're Jimmy Don's daughter. Believe me, I've wrestled with the same thing. You have to be careful around boys."

"Is that why you're not married? You're being careful?"

"I know what I'm looking for. I simply haven't found it yet."

Starr frowned. "You mean you have a list or something?"

"Yes. I do. I want to make a sensible decision about the man I spend my life with."

"Love isn't sensible," Starr told her. "Even I know that."

"You're right. Love is words and chemistry. It has little value. Better to make a decision based on reasonable, understandable criteria. That's lasting."

She wasn't sure if Starr would see her point or call her an idiot. What she didn't expect was for the teen's eyes to fill with tears.

"Is that what you really think?" Starr demanded, coming to her feet. "There's really no love? That my mom didn't love me?"

Destiny wanted to slap herself. She stood. "No! Of course she loved you. I don't mean the love between parents and a child. I was talking about romantic love. Your mom treasured you."

"You don't know anything," Starr yelled. "She only cared about my dad and her drugs. She didn't love me. She abandoned me over and over again, and then she died. I know my dad doesn't care. Obviously. He barely knows who I am, and he sure doesn't want me. I'm only here because you got stuck with me. I get it, okay? I get it."

Her voice rose with the last three words.

"I know I don't have anywhere to go. I know that no one wants me. I get it!"

She took off at a run and bolted into her bedroom, slamming the door behind her. The harsh sound reverberated through the house.

Destiny sank back onto the chair and covered her face with her hands. The distance between what she'd wanted to say and what had come out of her mouth was so great, it couldn't be measured. She'd only been trying to protect Starr. Instead she'd hurt her.

She stood and walked to the closed bedroom door. After knocking, she spoke.

"Starr, honey. I'm sorry."

"Go away."

"We need to talk."

"No, we don't. If you don't believe in love, then knowing I hate you won't matter at all. I hate you, Destiny. Leave me alone."

There was a sharp click as the lock was engaged, followed by a few seconds of silence, then sobs that tore through Destiny's heart. She sank onto the floor outside her sister's bedroom door and tried to breathe. Honest to God, she had absolutely no idea what to do.

Before moving to Fool's Gold, Kipling had never had anything to do with city government, or government of any kind. He'd assumed the day-to-day running of a location simply happened. Like most people, he'd groused about laws that seemed an unnecessary interference. He hadn't known there were so many complex steps that ended with a seamless stream of services that affected people's lives.

But since the move, he'd attended monthly city council sessions. At first he'd worried about being bored, but now he looked forward to the details of what went on behind the scenes. Mayor Marsha ruled her town well, and she had a lot to contend with. Thanks to the constant flow of tourists, the growth of the town, a major university and dozens of successful businesses, all with different interests and needs, there was always a crisis, a problem and something incredibly funny going on.

At today's meeting, the comic relief was supplied by Eddie and Gladys, who wanted to host a cable access show—the same two old ladies who had wanted to sign up to be volunteers at his recent HERO meeting. Mayor Marsha was doing her best to discourage them, and while Kipling would normally put his money on the mayor, she didn't seem to be making much headway against a very determined Eddie and Gladys. The ongoing conversation made him wish he'd brought popcorn. Talk about entertainment.

"You can't stop us," Eddie said, leaning in as she spoke. "This is a free country. I know my rights. The community access channel is just that. For the community. Gladys and I will include everyone on our show."

"Especially the men." Gladys cackled.

"That's what has me concerned." Mayor Marsha studied them both. "There are strict laws about nudity."

Eddie's eyebrows rose nearly to her hairline. "Are you implying I'd have naked people on my show?"

"We should be so lucky," Gladys muttered.

"Yes," the mayor said firmly. "Or pictures. I've been in touch with my friends at the FCC, and they're going to be watching you two."

Patience Garrett, the owner of Brew-haha, sat next to him. Now she leaned close. "It's always dangerous when Mayor Marsha starts talking about her friends anywhere. If I were Eddie and Gladys, I'd be shaking in my shoes."

"They wouldn't really have nudity, would they?"

"In a heartbeat. A couple of years ago there was a calendar done as a fund-raiser. A bunch of male models flew in and did a photo shoot. Naked. Eddie and Gladys were front and center, watching the show."

"They look so innocent."

Patience grinned. "Don't confuse old with innocent. They could so take you."

"Those two?"

"Sure. You're a nice guy. You'd never fight back."

"Point taken."

He returned his attention to the ongoing discussion, then allowed it to slide to his left. Destiny sat a few rows in front of him. She'd come in late and had found a seat off to the side.

At first he'd wondered if she was avoiding him. While he'd found their last conversation intriguing, he thought maybe she'd been embarrassed. Maybe she didn't want him to know she was attracted to him. She was a little tightly wound. But as he watched her now, he wondered if something else was going on. She seemed tense in a way that had nothing to do with him. She'd barely glanced in his direction.

If he had to guess, he would say she was upset about something. Not work related. He received an email update every morning, and they were right on track. So it had to be something else. Family, maybe?

He looked back at Mayor Marsha and did his best to pay attention to what she was talking about, all the while keeping tabs on Destiny. He wanted to speak to her before she left. If there was a problem, maybe he could help.

The meeting wrapped up after about an hour. Kipling had thought Destiny might bolt, but she stayed to speak to a few people. He made his way over to her. Everyone else left the meeting, and by the time he was standing in front of her, they were alone.

"How's it going?" he asked.

Destiny shook her head. "Badly. Starr and I had a huge fight last night. It's my fault. I totally screwed up. She talked about a boy she liked, and I overreacted."

"She's dating?" Wasn't Starr too young?

"I hope not. I told her that love was just chemicals and words, and she misunderstood. I was talking about romantic love. She thought I was saying no one loved her." She turned away. "I want to say she's wrong, but I don't know. Our father hasn't seen her in months. Her mother's dead, I'm her temporary guardian and I barely know her. She's lost, and I'm the last person to know what to do."

He put his arm around her and pulled her close. "That's not true."

"We have the same father. Believe me when I say I don't come from an emotionally stable family situation."

"You had Grandma Nell. She was stable. She loved you and made you feel safe. So do the same for Starr."

She felt good tucked against him. Feminine and warm. He wanted to step between her and whatever was going wrong so he could make it right.

She relaxed against him for a second before stepping away.

"You're right. I need to think like Grandma Nell would. This morning Starr wouldn't even speak to me. She's too young to be dealing with all this. I have to find a way to help her."

"What about your dad?"

Destiny sighed. "I talked to him after I heard from his lawyer about Starr. Jimmy Don is touring in Europe this summer. He has no plans to come back before October. As for Starr, he's sure she'll be fine."

Kipling felt a familiar anger stirring. Not all abuse came from a fist. "In other words, he doesn't give a shit."

"Not exactly how I would have phrased it, but yes. Famous people don't have to clean up their own messes. There's always someone ready to step in and do it for them. Not that I'm calling my sister a mess. You know what I mean."

"I do. What are you going to say to her?"

She looked up at him, her green eyes wide with emotion. "I have no idea. The truth, I guess. That I made a mistake. That I care about her and want her to know that."

"She needs to know she'll always have a place with you."

Destiny nodded slowly. "I know. But I haven't figured out how to make that work yet. My job requires me to travel all the time. I can make sure I have an assignment that covers most of the summer months, but then I'll be moving on."

"Which makes boarding school practical," he said. "Does she like it?"

"She hasn't really said. You're right. We need to talk more so she can feel safe. The whole conversation about Carter really threw me."

"I'm sure they're just friends."

"That's what she said. Six weeks ago I barely knew who she was. Now this. It's too much."

Instinctively, he pulled her close. She went easily into his arms and hung on to him.

They fit well together. He breathed in the scent of her hair and enjoyed the warmth of her body. When she stepped back, he let her go.

He knew not to read too much into her willingness to get close. She was hurting, and he was an available shoulder. But he found he liked being Destiny's shoulder to lean on, at least for the moment. Because like her, he was always moving on. Emotionally if not physically.

"Making friends with people her own age is the best thing for her right now," he said. "So she can feel like she belongs."

Destiny nodded. "She did seem really happy yesterday when she came home from camp."

"One of my partners has a daughter about her age. Why don't I call Ethan and see if we can set something up for Starr and Abby the night of The Man Cave opening? The girls can go to a movie and hang out. You can come with me. You'll both have fun, and being away from the situation at home will give you both perspective."

She gave him a smile. "Always with the fixing."

"But you'll admit it's a good idea?"

She paused for a second, then nodded. "It's a very good idea."

CHAPTER SEVEN

Destiny sat in the living room and waited for Starr to get home from camp. She'd been doing a lot of thinking about what had gone wrong between them. Talking to Kipling had really helped. She appreciated how nice he'd been about the whole thing. She tried to remember the last time she'd had someone to lean on, however briefly, and couldn't think of when it had happened. Because she didn't have friends, she realized. Her friendships were of the brief, temporary kind.

There were probably a lot of good reasons. She was always leaving for the next assignment. So why get too involved? And while that was a great idea in theory, in practice it meant she was always starting over, and she had no real continuity in her life. Not emotionally. Not only was that not particularly healthy, it was also kind of lonely. Something she hadn't seemed to notice until the blowup with Starr.

She hadn't had anyone to call. No one to talk things over with. She could have phoned her mother, but wasn't sure Lacey was the best person to give advice under the circumstances. Lacey loved her daughter and stayed in touch, but Destiny didn't think her mother would want to be pulled into a situation involving her ex-husband and one of his mistresses' children. As for her other half and step siblings—she barely knew some and hadn't met the others.

Kipling had been an unexpected rock.

The front door opened, and Starr walked in. Unlike the previous night, she didn't look the least bit enthused or happy. She glanced at Destiny then away. But instead of heading directly for her room, she sat on the sofa and stared at her hands.

"How was your day?" Destiny asked.

"Fine."

"Still liking camp?"

Starr nodded.

Destiny wished for wisdom, but there wasn't any. And despite Kipling's great advice, she couldn't imagine what Grandma Nell would say, mostly because she was too smart to ever get in this situation.

"I'm sorry about yesterday," Destiny told her sister. "About what I said. I blew the whole thing with Carter out of proportion. I have my own worries and fears, and I shouldn't project them on you."

Starr raised her head. "You're afraid of men?"

"No. Just of making a mistake. Of being swept away. And that doesn't matter. I want to talk about you right now. Us. Starr, you're my sister."

"Your *half* sister. That's how you always introduce me."

Destiny felt her eyes widen. She wanted to protest, only she had a feeling that Starr was right.

"I'm sorry for that," she said. "I won't ever do it again. Because we're sisters. Not half or three-quarters. Just sisters."

The teen stared at her for a long time. "Okay."

"This is a difficult situation for a lot of reasons, but mostly because we don't know each other. I want that to change. I want you to be happy here. With me, I mean. We'll be leaving Fool's Gold when my assignment is finished."

"Where will you go after that?"

"I don't know."

"You move around every couple of months?"

Destiny nodded. "I can try to be in one place for the summer, but other than that, my job means I'm always somewhere new."

"That means boarding school for me." Starr studied her hands again. "I guess that's how it's going to be."

Which didn't sound like a ringing endorsement for going back to boarding school, Destiny thought grimly. But what was the alternative?

"We'll have holidays and the summer," she said. "If you'd like that."

"Because you're stuck with me." Starr sounded more scared than defiant.

"I don't think of it as stuck," Destiny said. "It's actually kind of nice. You're right, I am always the new girl, and it does get lonely. Having family around helps. I'm not sorry you're here, Starr. In case you were thinking that."

Her sister looked at her. "Really?"

"I promise." She smiled. "I have all the ingredients to make fried chicken. I was going to prepare it last night, but with everything that happened, I never got around to it. We've had it once already, and now I want to teach you the old family recipe. Are you in?"

Starr smiled. "Sure. Let me put my stuff away."

Destiny watched her walk to her room. Tonight, after dinner, they could play guitar together. She would teach Starr more chords and how to play a couple of her dad's songs. If they both kept at it, they could find their way into being a family in deed and not just in name.

The caveman statue by the door turned out to be a bigger hit than Kipling had expected. Nearly everyone coming through the door stopped to take a picture or have their picture taken with their mascot. There were also some hilarious selfies.

In honor of opening night, the pictures were then texted to the bar and loaded up onto the TVs. The resulting slide show had the crowd clapping and cheering.

Kipling circulated through the throngs of people. He wasn't keeping count, but he had a feeling they were nearing capacity. He had no idea how seriously the local fire department took that sort of thing. Not that having a line outside the building was a bad thing.

He greeted his guests, kept an eye on the servers and watched for Destiny's arrival. Given how early he'd had to show up for the opening, they'd agreed to meet at the bar. He wanted to make sure he saw her the second she showed up.

Anticipation, he thought with a grin. It made for a very good day. She was a complex woman, but he liked that. Easy was for sissies. Working hard to get what he wanted only made the reward sweeter. And he would have his reward. Destiny might be a little tightly wound, but he knew she would loosen up eventually. All she needed was to feel safe.

He walked by the bar, stopping to talk to people as he went. He'd been in town less than six months and knew just about everyone he saw.

Nick waved him over. He excused himself and went to talk to the bar's manager.

"What's up?" he asked.

Nick grinned. "It's official. Jo's closed every night through the weekend."

"Jo as in Jo's Bar?"

"That's the one."

"Why is that a big deal?"

Nick's expression turned pitying. "You still don't get it. The women in this town are powerful, my friend. Jo's is their place.

If we cut into her profits, Jo won't be happy, and then the ladies won't be happy."

Kipling dismissed the information. "We serve a different clientele. Most of our customers won't have gone to Jo's. We're not taking anything from her. Plus, we're going to get about half our business from tourists."

He knew. He'd been to every one of the meetings where he and his partners had discussed their business plan. They figured they would be most successful in summer with the tourists. Guys watching sports would sustain them in the winter. Jo could keep her lady clients.

"We're meeting a need," Kipling told Nick. "When I moved here, all I heard was guys complaining about Jo's place. How they were stuck in the back room, and the TVs weren't big enough."

"That's one way to look at it."

"You're worrying about nothing." Kipling had seen a problem and put together a group of investors to fix it. That made today a very good day.

Nick shrugged. "Just spreading the news," he said, then pointed. "You have company."

Kipling turned and saw Destiny standing by the door. From his perspective, the noise in the bar faded and the lights shifted to a spotlight that focused entirely on her. He was pretty sure he was seeing things the way his dick wanted, rather than how they were, but he was willing to go with it. Especially when it meant staring at a beautiful woman.

She'd curled her hair and put on makeup. He couldn't remember seeing her all done up before, and the results were impressive. Her green eyes looked huge, her hair was all curly waves and her mouth was a glorious, kissable pout of shiny pink.

He walked toward her, not bothering to talk to anyone as he went. She was all that mattered. All he needed. As he got closer, he saw she'd pulled on a short jacket over some kind of white lacy fitted shirt. She had on tight jeans and boots. The perfect combination of comfortable and sexy, he thought as he approached. It was the kind of thing only women could do, and speaking on behalf of all men everywhere, he appreciated the effort.

"Hey," he said as he got closer.

She looked up and smiled. "Hey, yourself. Congratulations. There's a crowd milling outside, and the rest of the town is oddly empty. You're a success."

"At least for tonight." He took her hand in his and drew her against him. He inhaled the sweet scent of her shampoo and maybe a little perfume, then lightly kissed her cheek. "Thanks for coming."

"It's going to be fun."

He stared at her for a second. "You're better. You make up with Starr?"

"How did you know?"

"You're more relaxed."

"I don't like how you can read me. Most people have trouble knowing what I'm thinking."

"Think of it as a gift."

"I'm not sure I'm willing to commit on that one," she told him.

"Then let's get you liquored up and see where that leads."

She laughed. "At least you're honest with your intentions."

He leaned close. "My intentions are bad."

She looked away. "I suspected as much. I'm afraid tonight is going to be a bit of a disappointment, then."

He dropped his hand and put his arm around her. "Not if you're going to tell me no. Because I'm interested in working for it. Don't you worry."

"Because you like the conquest?"

"I like all of it."

They made their way to the bar. People were standing three and four deep, but Kipling went to the end where he knew he would be spotted. One of the advantages of being a partner, he thought. No waiting for service.

"What would you like?" he asked Destiny.

She looked up at him. "Okay, don't laugh, but I would love an Old Fashioned."

"You're a Southern girl at heart. I would expect no less." He ordered her drink and a beer for himself. With everyone jammed into the space, there wasn't much room, which forced her to press up against him. Something he wasn't going to complain about.

When they got their drinks, he led her toward the back room. It was quieter there. They also had the rear door open to let in more air.

He greeted people as they walked. When he saw the Hendrix brothers together at a table, he stopped to say hello to them.

"Destiny, meet Ethan, Kent and Ford Hendrix," he said. "This is Destiny Mills. She's here putting together the search and rescue software program."

Ethan raised his beer. "Nice to meet you." He paused, then grinned. "Starr's sister, right? You met my wife, Liz, earlier."

"I did." Destiny turned to Kipling. "I took your advice. Starr is hanging out with Abby and her friends tonight."

"I'm glad." He wondered if the hanging out included a sleepover. That would be convenient. Although he doubted Destiny was one to put out on the first date and with her, he was happy to wait.

Ethan nodded at Kipling. "Good job. This place is great."

"Thanks. Where are the ladies?"

"They said it wasn't their thing," Ford said. "They're hanging out with our mom, baking."

Kipling nodded. "How's the bet going?"

Ford and Kent eyed each other.

"Fine," Kent said. "I'm winning."

Ford shoved his brother. "You don't know that."

Kent shoved back. "I have every faith in my wife."

Ethan, on the other side of the table, shook his head. "You're both idiots. You know that, right?"

Kipling smiled at Destiny. "Apparently, the Hendrix brothers have a bet going. Who can get his wife pregnant first."

"You're betting on it?"

Kent shrugged. "Yeah, but it's not that serious a thing."

"Which is why I'm going to win," Ford said smugly. "Just wait and see."

"What do your wives say about the bet?" Destiny asked.

"They, ah, don't exactly know," Kent murmured. "We'd be obliged if you didn't say anything."

"Because if Isabel finds out, the most that will happen is she'll be mad," Ford pointed out. "If your wife finds out, she's perfectly capable of killing you."

"True," Kent said cheerfully. "But she never would."

"You wish."

Ethan sipped his beer. "My brothers are idiots. I'm not proud of that fact, but I can't avoid the truth forever. Total and complete idiots."

Kipling laughed. "Can't wait to hear how it all turns out."

He put his arm around Destiny again and led her through the back room and out onto the patio. There weren't many people here, and they could breathe in the cool night air. With a little luck, she might get chilly and snuggle close.

She sat at one of the tables. He took a seat across from her. She shook her head.

"I'm not sure betting on who gets who pregnant is a good idea."

"They're brothers," he pointed out. "They can't help being competitive. I'm glad things are better with Starr."

"Me, too." She sipped her drink without meeting his gaze. "Kipling, what do you want from me?" she asked suddenly.

"Tonight or in general?"

"Both."

"Tonight I'd like you to have a good time. After that, I'd like to see where things lead."

He could have been more specific, but something told him Destiny wasn't going to deal with that well. For someone who was so confident at work, she was surprisingly restrained when it came to her romantic life. At least that was how he was reading her.

"You know I'm leaving," she said.

"Yes, I do. I'm not looking for always. I'm a serial monogamy kind of guy."

"No interest in anything more?"

Sure he had interest. But he couldn't seem to get to the "wow, I'm in love" place. Mostly because he couldn't wrap his mind around love having much in the way of value. Doing the right thing was so much more productive than thinking it.

"Sure. I'd like to get married, have a family," he said, going with the dream rather than reality. "One day. What about you?"

"The same. One day."

"There you are!" Shelby walked over to the table. She sat next to him and hugged him. "You did it, big brother. This place is a success. Congratulations."

Shelby's arrival gave Destiny a chance to excuse herself on the pretext of wanting to say hi to some friends. While she hadn't seen anyone she knew all that well, she needed a moment to catch her breath. Sipping bourbon and staring into Kipling's eyes was having an unsettling effect on her equilibrium. Or maybe it was the talk about marriage and kids.

Not that he'd been offering, she reminded herself. He hadn't. And he wasn't sensible enough for her. But a girl could dream and if she was, then he certainly fell into the "dream-worthy" category.

She wandered back to the bar area and was immediately hit

by a wall of noise. If possible there were even more people than before.

Overhead fixtures provided plenty of light, and the music was at a good level. You didn't have to shout to have a conversation. Liquor flowed freely, and pictures taken at the door flashed on the various TVs. Several people were playing pool. While the poker room was currently serving as additional seating, there was a sign saying when the games would start, along with a sign-up sheet.

If she closed her eyes, she could be five again. Or eight, or any age she'd traveled with her parents. While they'd been huge stars and didn't perform in bars, they'd enjoyed going to them after the show, and she'd been taken along. There was always a back room where she could be made comfortable on a bed of coats.

She remembered the smells and the sounds. The bursts of laughter, the lingering scent of cigarettes and fried food. Not exactly a nurturing environment, but it had been what she'd known.

It was only after her parents had split up that they'd started having more children. Half siblings she may or may not have met. Would things have been different if Lacey and Jimmy Don had had more kids together? Would additional offspring have forced them to be more like other parents, or was that simply wishful thinking on her part?

"Here you go," a server said, handing Destiny a fresh drink and taking her previous one. "Nick said to tell you he makes a great Old Fashioned, and not enough people drink them these days."

"Thank you."

She raised her glass toward the bar, and Nick waved in response. Just as she took a sip, Madeline rushed up to her.

"OMG, seriously? You're the only child of Lacey and Jimmy Don Mills? *That* Mills family? You're like country music royalty."

Madeline sounded more intrigued by the information than upset Destiny had tried to keep it a secret, which was good. But she was still a little cautious as she asked, "How did you find out?"

"Miles told me. We went out for drinks last night. You never said a word."

Which was just like Miles, she thought. Poking his nose where he shouldn't. She was going to have to have yet another chat with him soon. "I don't talk about it much."

"Obviously not." Her friend had a glass of champagne. She linked arms with Destiny and led her to a small table in the corner. "I guess I can see why. That's all anyone would talk about, right? Your famous parents? But wow. I was stunned."

They sat across from each other. Madeline had on a pretty blue dress that was the same color as her eyes. She'd pulled her blond hair back into a braid.

"So can you sing, too? You must be able to. Why are you working where you do? Don't you like the business?"

Destiny took a big swallow of her drink and wondered where to start. "I never wanted what my parents had," she admitted. "It looks really glamorous from the outside, but from the inside, it's a tough business. There's so much travel and craziness. It's not for me."

"So you're a regular person." Madeline laughed. "That makes me like you so much more."

"Thanks. Do you know if Miles told anyone else?"

"I have no idea." Her friend leaned toward her. "Look, this obviously bothers you. I won't say anything to anyone. I promise. But if Miles told me, he's going to tell other people."

"I know. I've asked him to stop talking about my family before, but he won't listen. He's very chatty when it comes to other people's personal lives." Destiny pressed her lips together. "Wait. Are you two dating? I don't want to say anything I shouldn't."

Madeline shook her head. "No. We went out for drinks, but he's not my type."

"He's good-looking and charming."

"Right? So I should totally fall for him. But I don't know. There wasn't any chemistry. And now that I know you've asked him to be quiet and he wasn't, I could never trust him. I want someone with integrity. Someone who cares about family." Madeline sipped her champagne. "It's pretty funny. I spend my days helping brides find their dream wedding gowns, and I can't find my one true love."

"Have you been looking?"

"Good question. Not for a while now. I grew up here so I know most of the guys my age. Either I dated them or a friend did. My parents have been married forever. I was a change-of-life baby. They'd been trying to get pregnant for years and finally gave up. Then I came along. They're sweet and still in love after forty-five years."

"That's nice." Destiny did her best not to sound wistful. She knew that romantic love could work out for a limited few, but hadn't seen it herself. Not up close.

"It does set a pretty high bar," Madeline admitted. "I don't want to make a mistake. My mom always told me she knew right away with my dad. That it was like a lightning bolt. He felt the same way about her. I'm still waiting. I swear, when I feel that lightning bolt, I'm going after the guy. I don't care who he is." She paused. "Unless he's, you know, married. If that's the case, I'll have to become a nun or something."

"Are you Catholic?"

Madeline grinned. "No, but that seems like a problem I can overcome, right?"

They laughed together. Shelby joined them and invited them both to lunch the following day. Destiny liked being included. This was different from the casual relationships she usually made on the job. Better.

She was also pleased that Madeline didn't mention anything about Lacey and Jimmy Don. More drinks were delivered. She felt her tensions ease and knew she was feeling the false courage brought on by too much bourbon, but as she rarely indulged, she figured she was due.

Somewhere around ten, someone turned on the karaoke machine and people started singing. Kipling found his way back to her. They sat together in a booth, his arm around her.

She liked the feel of him next to her. A few couples were dancing to the songs. She wondered what he'd been like before the accident. Not physically. Obviously, he would have moved more easily. But emotionally. Had confronting first death and then later the fact that he might never walk again changed him? Or had he always been one of the good guys?

She heard the familiar opening of Garth Brooks's "Friends in Low Places" and turned to the stage. Sure enough Miles was up there preparing to launch into the only song he ever sang. Not that she minded hearing his version, it was what was going to happen when he was done.

"I should go," she said, sliding out of the booth as she spoke.

Kipling followed her, grabbing her hand before she could make her escape. "Not so fast. It's still early. Stay."

It wasn't him, she thought frantically. She was enjoying herself with Kipling. He was easy to be around. Even the personal questions didn't bother her when he was the one doing the asking.

"It's not you," she said, aware of the song progressing and time running out. "It's something else. I really have to go."

"But we haven't danced yet. Destiny, you can't run out on me."

"I'm not. There are things that—"

The song ended, and the applause began. Miles held the microphone. She didn't have to see him to know he was grinning in anticipation.

"I know," Miles said over the crowd. "Pretty damned good,

huh? But if you think that was impressive, wait until you hear our next singer. Destiny, darlin', where are you?"

She froze. Kipling looked confused.

"You sing in public?" he asked. "I thought you didn't want people to know."

"I don't," she whispered as the spotlights circled the room before finally landing on her. "Miles has done this to me before."

"There you are," Miles called. "Come on up, Destiny. Let's have a song."

She shook her head.

"Oh, she's shy. Come on, everyone. Let's give her some encouragement."

Destiny felt people moving away from her. Making a path so she could get to the stage. Kipling stayed where he was, but she didn't seem able to reach out to him. It was like a force greater than herself had sucked her in, and when she was spit out, she was onstage. She had no memory of walking there, yet the proof was irrefutable. Once again, she'd given in, and now she would have to sing.

Her mother would tell her that the need to perform was in her blood. That she could resist, but eventually she would find herself exactly where she was meant to be.

Miles handed her the microphone.

The second she took it, everyone cheered. Miles stepped up to the machine and scrolled through the songs. He paused on one, and she nodded. Might as well just go for it, she thought, as the familiar notes played.

The crowd went silent. The words scrolled onto the screen, but she didn't need them. She still remembered sitting quietly while her mother wrote the song that was eventually to become her biggest hit.

"Accidentally Yours" had won Lacey a Grammy, along with a CMA Award for Single of the Year. She'd also scored as Female Vocalist of the Year.

The music surrounded Destiny as memories filled her. Her parents together. Her parents fighting. The tears and how scared she'd been.

The words to the song came without her thinking as she got lost in the melody. She sang from the heart—the only way she knew how. As if she were alone. So when she was done and people applauded, the sharp sound brought her back to reality with a bit of a thud.

She stared into the crowd, momentarily lost. She shoved the microphone into Miles's hand and started for the stairs.

"More," someone yelled. "Sing another song."

She kept moving. When she reached the floor, she started for the closest exit. In this case, it happened to be the back door.

"Did you know she could sing like that?"

"Who *is* she?"

"...Lacey Mills and then they got a divorce."

"My mom loves Jimmy Don. I wonder if she could get me an autograph."

She ignored it all. She could nearly taste her escape. Only a few feet more.

By the time she pushed against the door in the rear room, she was shaking. The door gave easily, and she stumbled out into the dark night. Music still played, but it was muffled. Her head spun, probably from both the drinks and the singing.

She shouldn't have done it, she told herself. She shouldn't have given in. But while mostly she could ignore that part of herself, every now and then she was unable to resist. Her mother would tell her that biology was inescapable. That if Destiny simply gave in to the inevitable, her life would be a lot easier.

The door opened, and Kipling joined her.

"You okay?" he asked.

She nodded without speaking. Breathing was still difficult, and words would be impossible.

He looked at her. "You surprised the hell out of a lot of people tonight."

"That's one way to put it." She drew in a deep breath, pleased the words had returned. "I didn't mean to do it. Sing. I should have said no."

"You have a beautiful voice."

"Thank you."

"You're welcome. So much for keeping a secret."

She felt her lips twitch. Then she was smiling. A small giggle escaped. "Word will get out."

"Want to come back in and sing another song?"

"No."

"I didn't think so."

He took a step toward her. His gaze was intense, and she felt a pull nearly as strong as the one that had propelled her onto the stage. Only this time, the message was to stay put rather than to move.

When Kipling put his arms around her, she was glad she'd listened, and when he drew her against him, she went willingly.

Maybe it was the singing or the night, but for some reason, she needed to be in his arms. She needed to know what it felt like to absorb the warmth and strength of him.

"Destiny."

He only said her name. Just once. Softly. Then he pressed his mouth against hers in a kiss that both comforted and challenged.

She melted against him, letting him support her weight even as she moved her lips against his. Usually, she was a pretty passive kisser, but not tonight. Tonight she wanted to know what kissing him felt like. She wanted to explore the man and the unexpected tension and heat building inside her.

She rested her hands on his broad shoulders and felt the pressure of her breasts flattened against his chest. She breathed in the scent of him, and when he touched her lower lip with his tongue, she parted immediately.

He swept inside, taking control from her. But the electricity that followed made it worth the shift. Delicious tingles vibrated through her. She ached, she squirmed, she needed. When his tongue stroked against hers, she returned the attention in kind. When he drew back, she followed.

They kissed over and over again. He shifted his hands to her hips and then down to her rear. He squeezed the curves, and she instinctively arched against him.

Her lower body felt heavy. Her breasts hurt. The deep ache made her want to place his hands there. Because somehow his touching her would make everything better.

The thought should have shocked her, but all she could think was how much she wanted the kissing to never stop and how good it would feel to have his fingers on her tight nipples.

The back door banged open. Destiny was aware of laughter then a quick, "Sorry, man." The door slammed shut.

Kipling stepped back and cleared his throat. "I should, ah, get you home."

Destiny sucked in air. Her head cleared a little and she knew that tonight she'd done more than sing one of her mother's songs. She'd also flirted with her mother's lifestyle, and she knew better.

"Don't worry about it," she said, pleased she could speak in actual sentences. "It's opening night. You should stay here. I'm walking. It's Fool's Gold, and I'll be fine."

He hesitated. She gave him a little push toward the bar. "I promise, it's all good. I'll text you when I get home."

"If I don't hear from you in twenty minutes, I'm coming after you."

A tempting reason to not text, she thought as she waved and started toward the sidewalk.

Seventeen minutes later, she was in her bedroom and sending the text that would allow Kipling to forget about her for the night.

It was late, and Starr was already asleep, but Destiny couldn't relax. Her body still ached for the man who had kissed her, and her mind swirled with words and images. Not knowing what else to do, she pulled out her guitar and the notebook full of half-written songs. She flipped through it until she found one that made sense to her, then started to play.

You spoke to me, in careful tones. Your words were like a beacon, I was looking for a home.

She made a few notes and started the song from the beginning. As she played, she relived Kipling's kiss over and over until it was etched into her brain.

CHAPTER EIGHT

Destiny hesitated outside Jo's Bar. It wasn't the hangover that was slowing her down. Although she'd awakened with a headache and the need to drink about a gallon of water, that had all passed. No, what stopped her at the door was old-fashioned embarrassment.

She fully remembered what had happened the previous night. All of it. And while her date with Kipling had gone way better than she'd expected, and she'd been blown away by the kiss they'd shared, what she couldn't get out of her mind was the rest of it. How she'd stepped onstage and sung her mother's song.

She knew what happened when she opened her mouth. The connection was instantly clear. There was no hiding who she was and where she'd come from.

The comparisons were inevitable—and she was fine with that. Once people knew about her family, they saw the similarities in appearance, heard familiar elements in her voice. What she couldn't get past was that she'd done it to herself. She could say she'd been compelled by a force she didn't understand but the truth was she'd walked onstage with her own two feet. She'd opened her mouth, and she'd chosen to sing. While she planned to have it out with Miles later, in the end, the choice had been hers.

What she didn't know was why she'd done it. Sure, she'd sung in public before. When she'd been little. But as an adult, she avoided the limelight. Miles only knew she could sing because he'd heard her one time when the hotel window had been open, and she hadn't known he was in the room right next door. He'd questioned her until she'd admitted who she was. Since then he'd refused to let the information go. He loved bringing it up at the worst possible time. And encouraging her to perform.

Until last night, she'd always refused. So what had been different?

There was no way she was going to get her question answered, she thought. So she sucked in a breath for courage and walked into Jo's.

Several of her friends were already waiting at a table. Madeline was there, along with Bailey. She recognized Isabel, Madeline's business partner, and Taryn, the tall, dark-haired woman who ran the PR firm, Score. Shelby waved from the other side of the table.

"Hi, everyone," Destiny said as she sat down in the empty chair between Madeline and Dellina. They all greeted her normally with no mention of the previous night. A few of them hadn't been there, so she wondered if word hadn't spread. She hoped that was true, but didn't think she was that lucky.

Bailey, from the mayor's office, leaned forward. "Dellina, you have to help me plan my wedding. I honestly can't decide what to do, and Kenny's getting impatient."

"What's the problem?" Dellina asked.

Madeline leaned toward Destiny. "Dellina's our local party planner. If you need a wedding put together, she's your girl. She can do nearly anything in almost no time."

Dellina laughed. "I heard that, and please don't oversell me. I'm not a miracle worker." She turned back to Bailey. "The first question is what kind of wedding you want. Big or small? Formal or informal?"

"I don't know," Bailey admitted.

"That was my problem, too," Taryn said. "I secretly wanted the big dress, big wedding, but I'd been married before and wasn't sure."

"And I didn't want any hassle," Dellina said cheerfully. "So we eloped. There are lots of options."

They were a marriage- and family-friendly town, Destiny thought, realizing that nearly every woman at the table was married or engaged. In fact, Madeline and Shelby were the only other single people there. Taryn was pregnant, Isabel was part of a get-pregnant bet she might or might not know about and the rest of them had kids.

It was all so normal, she thought wistfully, thinking how when she was a kid, normal sounded like heaven. While other people dreamed of fame and fortune, she'd imagined living on an ordinary street where the rhythm of life was dictated by the changing of the seasons or school calendar and not a record dropping or a tour schedule.

"I guess Kenny and I need to have a talk," Bailey said. "Chloe wants to be a bridesmaid for sure, so eloping isn't an option."

Patience Garrett raced into Jo's and hurried over to their table. She claimed the last empty seat. "Sorry," she said. "I was talking to Zane Nicholson."

Isabel and Madeline sighed while the rest of them just looked confused. Well, not Bailey, who shook her head.

"You are all totally insane," Bailey said. "You get that, right?"

"I don't care," Isabel said dreamily. "Zane is amazing."

"He's just a guy," Bailey corrected. "He puts on his pants one leg at a time."

"Which means sometimes he takes them off," Patience said, then giggled.

Bailey rolled her eyes. "Ignore them," she told the rest of the group. "They're acting like five-year-olds."

"We're acting like sixteen-year-olds," Isabel corrected. "There's a difference. And it's just silliness. Zane Nicholson grew up here. He has a ranch about twenty miles away. He's very hunky. Taciturn. Manly." She waved her hand in front of her face. "Is it hot in here, or is it me?"

"You're married," Destiny said, before she could stop herself, knowing the talk about the mysterious Zane was simply done in good fun, but still finding it strange.

"I know." Isabel didn't sound the least bit repentant. "I love Ford with every fiber of my being. Zane was a high school crush. It's just fun to remember what it was like back then."

"He's no Jonny Blaze," Shelby said with a grin.

Madeline laughed. "You're right. My eternal love for Zane is overshadowed by my movie star crush on Jonny Blaze. I think that makes me kind of slutty."

Jo appeared to take their orders. No one discussed getting margaritas today, and Destiny was grateful. She planned to avoid alcohol for a very long time.

When Jo had left, Taryn rested her elbows on the table and smiled at Destiny.

"We haven't had a chance to get to know each other very well yet. Where are you from, and how did you end up here?"

Everyone at the table froze. Destiny told herself to remain calm. That Taryn meant the question in a general way. She wasn't fishing for information on the Mills family. But in the second before she could summon an answer, she had to admit she felt more than a little trapped.

Taryn straightened. "What?" she demanded. "What did I say? I didn't ask anything outrageous." She slapped her hand on the table. "Something happened last night, didn't it? I knew it! I told Angel we had to go to the opening, but he wanted to stay home because I was tired. Being pregnant means I miss all the fun."

Bailey put her arm around Taryn. "I didn't go, either," she told her friend. "Nothing happened."

"Something did," Taryn insisted. "Tell me."

"I sang," Destiny said quietly.

Taryn frowned. "That's it? You sang? Okay, I don't get it. Either you're really, really good, or really, really bad."

"She's good," Madeline murmured.

Destiny knew there was no point in avoiding the topic. Nearly everyone knew, and maybe if she talked about it, they could move on to something more interesting.

"My parents are country singers," she told Taryn. "Lacey and Jimmy Don Mills."

Taryn brightened. "I've heard of them. You're their daughter?"

"They married when they were eighteen and nineteen, and I came along nine months later."

"But you work with that computer tracking program."

"STORMS," Destiny offered.

"Right. For the search and rescue guys. So why do that if you can sing?"

"I don't like the business. I don't want to be touring and living out my life in public." Destiny did her best not to sound defensive.

"I get that," Shelby said with a sympathetic smile. "It can't be easy."

"Not if it's anything like what I've seen with my business partners." Taryn nodded as she spoke. "I know what they went through. Interesting. Well, I'm sorry I missed your karaoke performance."

"Me, too," Jo said, appearing with their drinks. "I heard it was crazy busy over at The Man Cave. Good thing I closed for the night, or I would have spent the whole time being lonely."

"You could have called me," Taryn said. "I missed the fun, too."

"Fun, huh?" Jo said. "Lunch will be along in a bit."

She left. Destiny hoped there would be an organic change of topic, but Taryn turned back to her.

"Tell me next time you're singing. I want to be there."

"I doubt it will happen again."

"But you have an amazing voice," Madeline said, then slapped her hand across her mouth. "Sorry. It's your decision. I'm not pushing."

Destiny grinned. "Thanks."

"What about Starr?" Shelby asked. "Does she want to be part of the business?"

"More than I'd like." Destiny sipped her iced tea. "She didn't grow up seeing the hard work and long days on the road. She thinks it's glamorous."

"She's a lot younger than you, isn't she?" Bailey asked.

"Fourteen years. She and I have different mothers."

Shelby smiled. "Kipling and I are the same. We have different mothers, too."

Destiny didn't think she'd known that. She would never guess they were only half brother and sister. Although she supposed that was simply the biology of their relationships. In their hearts, they were family. Something she and Starr needed to work on.

"So where is Starr's mother?" Taryn asked.

"She died about a year ago. Starr's been in boarding school. When summer break came around, there wasn't anyone to take her. Jimmy Don is touring in Europe, and Starr doesn't have any other family on her mother's side. None of her other half siblings are old enough to take her, so I said she could come stay with me."

Madeline's eyes widened. "That is the saddest thing. Not you taking her in, of course. That's great. But the other part. I come from a small family, but I always knew my parents adored me. I can't imagine what it must be like to be her age and have nowhere to call home. I'm so glad she's with you now."

Kind words that made Destiny feel guilty. Because she hadn't exactly been excited to have Starr show up in her life.

She waited for someone to trash her dad. God knew the man deserved the censure, but it would leave her in the uncomfortable position of having to defend him. Surprisingly, no one said anything, and conversation shifted to the upcoming X-treme waterski festival.

Destiny let all the words wash over her. She felt as if she'd run miles. But the exhaustion was more emotional than physical. Belonging was hard. Staying on the outside, never getting involved was so much easier. Yet she didn't regret making friends. The connections, however brief, felt good. Real. Or maybe, more important, normal.

Kipling had been looking forward to his meeting with Destiny. He hadn't seen her since The Man Cave opening a couple of days before. And while he'd thought about seeking her out, his gut told him she needed some time.

Not because of the kiss, although he hoped she'd been as intrigued as him by the chemistry that had flared between them. Instead he thought she would need to figure out how to deal with the truth now that her secret was out. Everywhere he went, people were talking about her and her performance. About who she was and how come she wasn't out making million-dollar records instead of working as a software facilitator in Fool's Gold. Or living off what must be a hell of a trust fund.

He didn't know how much of the talk was getting back to her. He thought maybe people were trying to be discreet. But eventually, she would figure out everyone knew, and he had a feeling that would bother her.

She arrived right on time, looking as good as ever. The makeup from the other night was gone, and she was back in cargo pants and a T-shirt. Which, in his opinion, was just as sexy and appealing. He liked her fresh face and sensible fashion. There was less for him to muss, and she would be ready for anything. Although what he had in mind didn't exactly require a special wardrobe. Or any.

"How's it going?" he asked as she walked into his office.

"Good." She glanced past him, and her mouth dropped open. "No way."

"Way." He walked over to the giant maps on the wall. Accurate maps that showed elevation and more detail than anything they currently had. "Mayor Marsha came through."

"I must remember to never doubt her," Destiny said, walking over and tracing a nearby river. "These are fantastic. And expensive. You don't just order them from an online retailer. They're custom."

"She said she got a grant from somewhere and put the money to work for us." He handed her a thumb drive. "Here are the same maps in digital form for you."

She laughed as she took the drive. "Thank you. An unexpected bonus."

She pulled her laptop out of her backpack and set it on one of the desks. Once it had booted up, she shoved in the thumb drive and began to download the information.

"I have software to compare these maps with the flyovers I've been doing with Miles. Once we combine the information, we'll be able to figure out what areas will require mapping on foot. The more detail we have, the better, and with your very fluffy budget, we can afford the time."

She typed on a few keys then stood up. "Okay, it's doing its thing. It'll take a while, so we can move on to other topics while we wait."

They talked about the schedule and the beta testing that would take place later in the summer. The tracking equipment had been shipped. Destiny seemed relaxed as they spoke, which pleased him. It meant she'd been okay with them kissing.

He briefly wondered about doing that now. Kissing. He wanted to. He'd liked the feel of her mouth on his. He knew some guys were interested in moving things along quickly, but he liked to take his time. Sure, the destination was great, but getting there could be a lot of fun.

He enjoyed a second or two of fantasy then reminded himself that they were both working. This wasn't the time or place.

"I didn't know you and Shelby were only half brother and sister," she said suddenly. "She mentioned it yesterday at lunch."

"Same father, different mothers."

"But you grew up together."

"Mostly. She's a few years younger, but we've always been close. When I left to work with my ski coach, I made sure we stayed in touch. I got home when I could, and Shelby came to see me."

He didn't mention anything about their father. That was Shelby's secret to tell, and unlike Miles, he knew how to keep his mouth shut.

"Families are complicated," Destiny said. She sat on one of the empty desks. "I had lunch at Jo's yesterday with a group of women, including Shelby. Do you know that more than half of the women there were married, and most of them had kids?"

"No," he said slowly. "And I'm missing the point. Is that unusual?"

"I guess not. In a town like this, it makes sense that families are a big thing. Most people have a biological or social need to procreate."

He sat across from her and grinned. "Now you're scaring me. A social need to procreate?"

"I don't know what else to call it. You're expected to grow up, get married and have kids. Nearly everyone does." She tilted her head. "Why haven't you?"

"Grown up?"

She chuckled. "You know what I mean. Is it because there are too many women and why pick just one?" Her humor faded. "I'm asking this for real. Not just making conversation."

"Why aren't I married?" He shrugged. "Lots of reasons. You're right. I did play 'the more, the better' game for a while. They were offering, and I wasn't going to say no. But after a while, that got old."

"So you switched to serial monogamy?"

"Something like that."

"And it works for you?"

"Mostly. I do think about wanting more. But I can't figure out how to deal with the love part. Love is just a feeling. It doesn't get the job done." How could he trust love when so many horrendous things were done in the name of love? If you asked his dad, the old man would swear he loved Shelby. But he thought nothing of putting a fist through her face.

Being in love didn't protect anyone or mean everything was going to turn out okay. It was just words. Hard to get excited about that.

She sighed. "Love. Everybody wants to be in love."

"You don't?"

"I'm not sure. Romantic love seems sketchy to me. People fall in and out of love all the time. I think it's better when people truly commit to each be there for the long haul. When it's not about hormones, but about real feelings. Like when normal parents love their kids. Or friendships that last sixty years. That's what I want."

There was a mountain of information in those few sentences, he thought. The fact that she'd define a subset of parents as normal. Because hers weren't?

He agreed with her concerns about romantic love. He'd found that women wanted the words. Words he refused to say, because in the end, talk was cheap. Actions mattered.

"Did you get your heart broken?" he asked gently, knowing plenty of other people simply believed the words and then were shocked when things didn't turn out.

"Not in the way you think. I saw what my parents went

through. How much they claimed to love each other, only to have it explode in their faces. They would get back together and swear it was forever, then one of them would take off or cheat or both."

"Words without the actions to back them up."

"Exactly," she said. "They were ruled by their hormones. It's ridiculous."

"Hormones are powerful."

Her mouth twisted. "I think it's an excuse. We can act rationally. We simply choose not to. It's like sex. People claim to be swept away. Really? Are you saying you can't control yourself, or you simply don't want to? Oh, please. We all know what it is. If you want my opinion, sex is the root of all evil. If people stopped having sex, things would be better."

"For who?" he asked, incredulous.

"You know what I mean."

"I kind of don't."

She raised her shoulders then lowered them. Her gaze was steady, as if she'd thought this all through and had all the answers.

"Like I said, I saw what my parents did. I watched other people in the band, both men and women, act like idiots because of sex and supposed love. I think there's a better way."

He was almost afraid to ask. "Which is?"

"A sensible plan. Finding someone who gets that it's all a game and refuses to play. We'll get married and care deeply about each other without all the drama. Just two committed people who want the same kind of emotionally stable life together."

Like that was going to happen, Kipling thought, not sure if he should laugh or bolt. "Will there be sex in this sensible marriage?"

"For the purposes of procreation. There's really no need to do it otherwise."

He stared at her. "If you believe that, then you've been doing it wrong."

She waved her hand. "Blah, blah, it's transformative. I know. There's no feeling like it."

"You don't sound convinced."

"I'm not. I think my way is better."

"The sensible marriage without sex between two like-minded people. For the greater good."

She brightened. "Exactly."

"Good luck with that."

She looked away. "I knew you wouldn't be interested."

He swore silently. "You considered me as a candidate?"

"I wasn't sure. You seemed to have a lot of really good qualities. But I figured the sex thing would be an issue."

He had no idea what to make of what she'd told him. Or what to think. He supposed there was a compliment buried in there somewhere. "You're completely not interested in sex?" Because when they'd been kissing, he'd felt a lot of interest coming from her side of things.

She studied her boots. "I think that staying in control is important and ultimately healthier. I refuse to give in to my base emotions. Hormones are not stronger than my will."

He turned that information over in his mind until everything got clear. Okay, now he got it. Some dork, or maybe a couple of dorks, had done the deed and moved on without taking her over the edge. If she'd never had an orgasm, she'd been left hanging without knowing what she was missing. He was a little surprised she hadn't taken care of business herself, but with all her rules about sensible relationships and defying her urges, maybe it was to be expected. He might not trust emotion, but he totally trusted a good plan.

It was, he realized, a problem that needed fixing.

"There are a few flaws in your master strategy," he told her.

"I know, and I'm still working out the details."

"Like finding a willing partner."

She smiled. "Yes, that is one of the bigger details."

"And the sex thing."

She groaned. "What is it about men and sex?"

"We like it."

"So I've heard. Over and over again." She stared at him then narrowed her gaze. "You're not going to change my mind on any of this. I don't want you to try."

"Me? Try to change you? Why would you suggest that?"

"There's nothing wrong with me. I don't need to be fixed or healed or anything."

"Uh-huh. What I find interesting is how you think you know what you're talking about, and you don't. I can't wait to see you fall on your ass."

She looked away. "If you had your way, I wouldn't be falling on my ass, now would I?"

Kipling laughed. "And the first point goes to Ms. Mills."

She stood and walked to her computer. "I'll get enough points to win. Just you wait and see."

He knew she was wrong, but it was going to be fun letting her find that out for herself. Because he'd gone from a man who was interested to a man on a mission.

For a second he considered the fact that they were kind of on the same side of the love issue. They'd both seen people who claimed to love each other do awful things, and had decided not to trust the feelings. They both wanted a rational response to a potential intangible. With one big exception. He was a firm believer in the power of passion, while she was convinced passion was the problem. She was wrong about that. Which meant he was going to be the one to show her exactly what it was she'd been missing.

Destiny hurried toward Ambrosia Bakery. She'd planned on making a pie for dessert, but hadn't been able to leave work on time. And while it was true that neither she nor Starr *needed* pie in their life, she'd thought it would be nice to have. She would've had time to make one herself if she hadn't stayed so long talking to Kipling. Which explained her visit to the bakery. This was guilt pie.

He was fun to talk to. Fun to hang out with. Fun to kiss. Just as interesting, she'd told him about what she wanted from life, and he hadn't said no. He hadn't been thrilled, but he'd seen the conversation through. Which made her wonder if he would consider what she was interested in. Because the more time she spent with Kipling, the more she wanted to spend time with him.

That had to be a sign or something. While it was too soon to know enough about his character or her feelings, for the first time she felt a sense of…maybe. Just maybe she could find what she was looking for. A good man who wanted a family and wasn't going to get all weird about the sex thing.

Because he'd already had a bunch. He'd admitted it to her. So maybe that could be enough. It wasn't like anyone needed to keep doing it.

She paused just outside the bakery as a little music video played in her head. The song was one she'd written, and the images were all of her and Kipling. Talking together, walking through the woods, holding hands. At the end, she imagined them kissing. Because that had been really nice. Maybe she wasn't interested in doing the deed, but she wouldn't mind daily kissing. And hugging. A married couple should hug. It established connection.

She shook off the daydream and stepped into the bakery. Shelby smiled.

"Hey, I didn't expect to see you so late in the day. You're one of my morning customers."

"I was hoping you had a pie I could take home for Starr." Destiny walked to the counter. "You're working late. Don't you get in at four in the morning?"

Shelby laughed. "Yeah, it's been a long day. Amber had a bunch of appointments so I said I'd work a double shift. She's hired more part-time help for the summer, but they haven't started yet." She covered a yawn. "I'll be in bed early tonight."

"You'd have to be."

"Until then, pie. So cold or hot? We have a few cream pies left, or double-crusted fruit pies."

"Cream pie," Destiny said, thinking she would have made a fruit pie, so a cream pie would be a nice change.

Shelby pointed out various options, and Destiny went with the double chocolate mousse pie that included a layer of both light and dark chocolate along with plenty of whipped cream.

Shelby rang up the purchase. "I know you probably don't want to talk about this, but I have to tell you, you have an amazing voice."

Destiny did her best to keep smiling. She'd brought the attention on herself, and now she had to deal with it.

"Thanks."

"You really don't like singing in public?"

"No."

"But you looked so comfortable. Totally at ease. I figured you'd sound amazing, but I had no idea what you could do." She handed Destiny change and then placed the pie box in a bag and passed it across the counter. "You and Miles must have known each other awhile."

"We've been working together a couple of years." Destiny shifted the bag to her other hand. "My mom visits me a few times a year, and she happened to come while I was working with Miles. He was completely smitten with her, as most men are."

Shelby pressed her lips together. "You and Miles aren't involved, are you?"

"No. We're friends. He's not..." Destiny remembered her

encounter with Miles and Kipling a couple of weeks ago. "Are you seeing him?"

"We've been out a couple of times." Shelby sounded both pleased and defensive. "He's nice."

"He's also seeing other women. Miles isn't into relationships. He likes the ladies. A lot." Because not everyone was interested in her sensible plan, she thought. They wanted to feel the rush and have sex, and then they got their hearts broken. Something she knew would never happen to her. Because she was thinking with her head and not her hormones.

"You think he's dating someone in town?"

"I know he went out with Madeline a few days ago. Drinks, I think."

Shelby's happy expression faded. "Oh, I didn't know that. She's so fun and pretty."

"You're both adorable," Destiny said firmly. "And neither of you is the problem. Look, I like Miles. He's not a bad person. But when it comes to women, he's also not going to give you more than a quick good time. So if that's what you want, go for it. If you're looking for more, he's not the one."

"Thanks for the advice."

"You're welcome."

Destiny waved and left. As she walked home, she wondered if Shelby would listen. Or if she would think she could change Miles. That somehow with her, things would be different.

Destiny had seen that happen again and again. With her father, especially. Women knew his track record, but they always thought that things would be different with them, that he would change. And he never did.

She, on the other hand, saw things clearly. Rationally. She might be missing a few highs, but if the price of that was avoiding the lows, then she was all-in.

CHAPTER NINE

"I don't know," Starr said as they left the bleachers by the lake. "They were good and all…"

Destiny linked arms with her sister. "Oh, I so understand what you're trying not to say. It was a great performance, but just a little strange."

Starr laughed. "Right. Because they're, like, you know, old."

Destiny would guess that to a fifteen-year-old, a group of women over the age of sixty would be more ancient than just old.

X-treme Waterski Fest had started the previous day and would continue through tomorrow. There were various demonstrations, competitions and even a place on the lake where you could take lessons. She and Starr had just watched the famous Don't-Call-Me-Grannies, a group of synchronized skiing women all over sixty.

"They were in great shape," Destiny said. "We should be so lucky to look that good at their age."

"I guess."

Destiny grinned. "Can't imagine ever being that old?"

"Not really. But I suppose it will happen."

"The alternative isn't a pleasant one," Destiny told her.

Starr grinned. "You're right. It's going to be weird not to look forward to birthdays. Now I want to be sixteen so I can get my driver's license."

"I suppose part of the reason people don't look forward to birthdays as they get older is that there aren't as many milestones."

"You're not excited about being twenty-eight and a half?" Starr asked with a laugh.

"Not as much as you'd think."

They walked into the main part of town. There were booths set up everywhere. Crafts, food and demonstration booths had their own sections. The flow really worked, Destiny thought. Whoever planned all this had done a good job of managing the crowds.

"I should invite my mom to visit during a festival," she said.

"Lacey is coming here?" Starr sounded both excited and nervous. "This summer?"

"She usually visits me at my various assignments. She says those trips help her stay connected to her fans, because they keep her real."

Starr nodded. "That makes sense. She's not on a bus or a plane. She's just living with normal people."

Destiny smiled. "You know it's all a crock, right? My mom will never be like her fans. She's Lacey Mills, superstar."

"What about when it's just you? Isn't she like a regular mom?"

"She is," Destiny admitted, realizing she'd never thought about her time with her mom that way. "When she's out on her own, she always has an entourage. She gets dressed up and waits to be mobbed by her fans. They generally don't disappoint her. But when she visits me, it's just her. And while she'll never be confused with your average suburban mom, when she's with me, she tones it down."

"Only one bodyguard?"

"Yes, and he keeps his distance."

"Can I meet her?" Starr asked.

"Of course." Destiny started to say she was surprised Starr hadn't yet, only to remember the teen and Lacey had no biological connection. "She's great. You'll like her. She loves to talk music, so have your questions ready."

Starr looked at her. "OMG. Really? You mean that?"

"Absolutely. She'll stay up all night talking about music and the business. And she has energy to spare, so she'll be awake way longer than you."

Starr clutched her arm. "I have to start practicing more. I have to get better before she comes here. What if she asks me to play? I can't embarrass myself."

"Deep breath. You won't. Lacey doesn't judge. And to be honest, she prefers to be the best musician in the room."

"But Dad plays."

Destiny sighed. "I know. It was a source of friction between them. They would have friends over and both play and then ask them to say who was better. That rarely ended well." She pointed. "Let's get elephant ears."

"Sure."

They headed to the booth and waited in line.

"It must have been so great, having all that music in the house," Starr said. "Being able to listen to them and their music friends play."

"I learned a lot," Destiny admitted. "But it wasn't one giant jam session. They traveled all the time. I'd go on tour sometimes, but often I was left behind. I missed school a lot. It was hard to make friends because I was gone and then back and then gone again."

She wondered if that was where it had started—her not having friends. Back when she'd been younger than Starr. She remembered having a best friend when she was seven or eight—Mandy, a girl from down the street. Only something had happened, something with her parents. She'd never been sure if Jimmy Don had come on to Mandy's mom or if Lacey had flirted with the husband. Either way, there had been a big fight, and she and Mandy had never been allowed to play together again.

There had been a couple more incidents like that, and then she'd simply stopped trying. It was too hard to get close, to confide in someone, to believe they would always be there, and then have it ripped away.

After she'd gone to live with Grandma Nell, there hadn't been any girls her age close by. By the time she'd gotten to college, she'd forgotten the art of making friends. For the first time in as long as she could remember, she was hanging out with other women and enjoying their company. She would miss them all when she left.

"Ladies."

Destiny turned and saw Kipling walking toward them. As he approached, she felt an odd tightness in her chest, followed by a ridiculous urge to flip her hair and giggle.

"Hi, Kipling," Starr said. "We're getting elephant ears. You want one?"

"Yeah, that sounds great."

No one was in line behind them, so he stepped next to them.

"How's summer camp?" he asked Starr.

"Good. I like the different classes. A couple of us are talking about forming an a capella group. You know, just girls singing, but it could be fun."

Destiny did her best not to stomp her foot as she listened to Starr's easy conversation with Kipling. How did he do it? He asked one or two simple questions, and Starr wouldn't stop talking. An a capella group? She shared all kinds of things she didn't tell Destiny.

While they were making progress toward getting to know each other, there was always something in the way, and Destiny had no idea what it was. For reasons she couldn't explain, her sister held back with her.

"No musical instruments?" Kipling asked. "That's ambitious."

"It's harder than it sounds," Starr admitted. "Just singing without music isn't bad, but when you try to make the other sounds, like percussion, it can get silly pretty fast. But we're going to try it."

A couple of families got in line behind them. Kipling moved closer. Destiny found herself wanting to lean against him, to ask him to help her with her sister, because she was obviously not doing as good a job as she thought.

"Making friends?" Kipling asked.

"Oh, yeah. A lot. Some of my friends are from LA, but a few are from here in town."

"That's nice," he said. "You can see them on the weekends."

"Sure!" Destiny jumped in. "Anytime. Or if you wanted to invite some of them over for dinner or something, I'd be happy to cook or just order pizzas."

Starr glanced from Kipling to her. "Seriously? You wouldn't mind if I had friends over?"

"Of course not. I want you to have fun this summer."

"Cool. Thanks."

They moved up in line. Starr turned her attention to the menu. Destiny looked at Kipling and mouthed "thank you." He grinned and shrugged, as if saying it was nothing. Which, to him, it probably was. He had an easy way with people. One she would like to share.

She told herself to be grateful for the improvement in her relationship with her sister and to take her small victories where she could. Having Starr enjoy the summer was one that would make both of them very happy.

Destiny followed the course laid out on the tablet screen which, she thought as she circled yet another downed tree, was easier said than done. She and Aidan Mitchell were about thirty miles

northeast of Fool's Gold in a rugged area just past the small val-
ley where wind turbines spun in the constant canyon breeze.

They'd left all signs of civilization behind several miles ago,
and the noise of the turbines had long faded. Out here there was
only the hum of nature.

"I was thinking up here," Aidan said, pointing.

She looked up from her screen and studied the relatively flat
ledge where he had indicated. The area looked big enough, and
the location was good.

"I like it," she said, then eyed the steep terrain between where
they were and the ledge. "Can we get there from here?"

"I'm game if you are."

She handed him her tablet and turned so he could tuck it
into her backpack. When the flap was secured, she gave him a
thumbs-up. "Lead on."

Aidan set a brisk pace, but she was able to keep up. These
woods were not all that different from those in the Smoky
Mountains. Trees, underbrush and scurrying animals. She
smiled, thinking Grandma Nell would be appalled to know Destiny had reduced her beloved Smoky Mountains to generalities.

She started up toward the ledge, following Aidan. He climbed
over a downed tree, then turned back to help her scramble over
the huge trunk.

When she put her foot down on the other side, she started
to slip on damp leaves. Aidan immediately grabbed her around
her waist. When she was steady, he released her.

In that moment of contact, Destiny found herself wondering if she would have any reaction. A tingle or a desire to lean
closer. There was nothing. Not the slightest whisper of interest.

They climbed the last twenty or thirty feet up to the ledge.
Once there, Aidan pulled two water bottles from his backpack
and handed her one.

"What do you think?" he asked, barely winded from their
climb.

She looked around at the large, flat area. "I'll have to measure it, and we'll need to have a geological survey done, but I think we have a winner."

Part of the system the town had ordered included adding several cell towers in remote areas. Not only would that help those who were lost call for help, but it would also aid the volunteers by giving them access to the HERO command center and each other.

Cell towers cost about a hundred and fifty thousand dollars each. But because of the difficult location and the extra surveys required, the price of these would be closer to two hundred thousand. But money had been put aside, so Destiny was determined to get the towers in the best locations possible.

She shrugged out of her backpack and pulled out a tape measure. Aidan helped her figure out the length and width of the ledge. She recorded the information on her tablet, then took plenty of pictures and recorded their exact location. Only then did she sit down next to him and take in the view.

They were at about forty-five hundred feet. The air was cooler up here, but still warm. She could see where an old avalanche had taken out the side of a mountain a couple hundred years ago.

She could see trees and sky and mountain, but nothing civilized.

"I feel guilty about sticking a cell tower in the middle of all this beauty," she said.

"It's for the greater good."

"I know, but it's still too bad."

"I don't think the deer or bears will mind."

Aidan stretched out on the ground. He tucked his hands behind his head and stared up at the sky.

He was a good-looking guy, she thought. Fit, intelligent and a successful businessman. Shouldn't she be considering him for her sensible plan? Except she wouldn't. For two reasons. First, there was something about him that reminded her of the guys she'd known who traveled with her parents. Roadies and band members who were there in part because they loved the music but also to get women. Lots of women. And second, she couldn't seem to summon any enthusiasm on the "Aidan as the one" front. When she tried, she only saw Kipling.

She shifted until she was sitting cross-legged and facing him.

"Any news on the candidates for Kipling's second-in-command?" Aidan asked.

"I know there have been interviews. I haven't heard any specifics."

"I gave him some names. Not that Kipling wants anyone else to solve the problem."

She smiled. "You've figured that out about him?"

"That he likes to fix things? Hard to miss it. It's a good quality in someone you work with, as long as you agree with how he wants things done."

"Meaning you'd never work for him?"

"No way. I like being the boss."

"Speaking of the boss," she said teasingly. "Isn't he going to be annoyed that you're goofing off?"

"Nah. He's a laid-back kind of guy. What about you? Anyone going to wonder why you're not working?"

"I need my guide to get back to the car."

Aidan shook his head. "No, you don't. You didn't have any trouble on our hike today. You've spent time in the mountains before."

"The Smoky Mountains. Different from here but just as beautiful."

"I agree. Why'd you leave?"

"I was told college would be a good idea."

"One of the advantages of living here," Aidan told her. "There's a community college and a four-year college in town. I didn't have to go anywhere else."

"Did you want try living somewhere different?"

Aidan's expression sharpened for a second before relaxing. "At one time I did. When I was growing up, it was understood that my older brother Del would be taking over the family business. I was okay with that and had no idea what I wanted to do. Then my first year of college he took off. Suddenly, I was the one everyone thought would take over. So I stuck around."

Family expectations, she thought. Only Aidan had followed through with his. She, on the other hand, had disappointed both her parents with her decision.

"Any regrets?" she asked.

He closed his eyes. "No way. I have a good life. Plenty of time outdoors. I fish and hike and go skiing for a living. Then there are afternoons like this, spent with a beautiful woman. What's not to like?"

She laughed.

He opened his eyes. "What's so funny?"

"That was a very reflexive compliment. You weren't even looking at me."

"I've already seen you. I can compliment from memory."

"While that's probably true, my guess is you, Aidan Mitchell, are a bit of a player."

One corner of his mouth turned up. "I'm wounded."

"Am I wrong?"

"No."

She grinned. "I didn't think so. Let me guess. There are plenty of single tourists who want a hot affair with their hunky guide."

He winced. "It would be better for me if you didn't call me hunky."

"But the rest of it?"

"I do okay. How'd you guess?"

"You remind me of guys who toured with my parents. If it was Wichita, there must be a new opportunity."

"I'm clear on the rules," he said, sounding only a little defensive. "I'm careful."

"I'm not judging," she told him. "I just think it's interesting."

"My mom keeps telling me that one day I'm going to fall in love. That it will be hard and fast, and I won't see it coming."

"You worried?"

"No way. Like I said, I'm careful."

She wanted to tell him he couldn't be careful enough. That if he let his hormones rule his life, he was in for some nasty surprises. But she'd tried telling people that in the past. For the most part they didn't listen. Or they thought she was incredibly strange. Either way it didn't go well.

She looked around at the beauty of the afternoon and wished Kipling were here instead of Aidan. Because she wanted to talk to him, she told herself firmly. Wanting to be with Kipling had nothing to do with the isolated location. She just thought spending some quality conversation time with her friend would be nice.

Nothing more.

Kipling would have thought that ordering a cell tower was a big deal, but apparently not. He printed out the confirmation invoice and walked over to the giant to-do list posted on the only wall not covered by maps of the area surrounding Fool's Gold. With sites determined, all three cell towers had been ordered, and surveying would start by the first part of next week.

Destiny moved next to him. "The tracking equipment shipped," she said, pointing to another item on the list. "It will be here in the next couple of days. Then we can start serious training."

She was standing close enough to get his attention. He knew she wasn't taunting him on purpose. His reaction to her nearness—blood flowing to predictable places, his complete lack of interest in anything but getting her on a nearby desk and then having his way with her—reminded him it was good to be alive. He liked the chase, and in her case, the reward was going to be even sweeter because he planned to show her what she'd been missing.

But that was for later. Today they had a job to do.

"How are the interviews going?" she asked.

Kipling shrugged. "Not great. I haven't found anyone who's going to work."

She looked up at him, her green eyes concerned. "What's wrong with them?"

"One guy was more interested in how much time off he would get than in finding out about the job. Another had no experience."

"You don't have any experience," she said with a grin.

"Which is why we need someone who knows what they're doing. The right person is out there. I'll figure it out."

He knew the value of patience. While his instinct was to simply go for it and deal with the consequences later, he'd learned the hard way that recklessness came with a price. The mountain had taught him that.

Automatically, he glanced out the window. The northeast view meant he could see the mountains clearly. A perk, he told himself, even as the familiar restlessness filled him. The need was there, like it had been for Destiny. Only this need would never be fulfilled.

He would never again feel the wind burning his skin. He would never hover in the air for seconds in time before slamming back onto packed powder and tearing down the mountain. The trees, the crowd, would never again be nothing but a blur as he defied the odds. He would never again be G-Force.

His back hurt, his knee ached and when he woke up in the morning, it took him a good five minutes to get all the kinks worked out. Which meant he was lucky. Damned lucky. But there were moments when he closed his eyes and imagined it was all still there. In his grasp. Until he remembered otherwise.

"Kipling?"

He looked at Destiny, who was watching him intently. His brain replayed the last bit of their conversation.

"My coach drilled certain skills into me," he said as if he hadn't been thinking of anything else. "Don't push the race. Let it come to you. Then plan on flying."

"An oddly mixed metaphor, but if it works..."

"It does." He leaned against his desk. "How are you doing?"

"What do you mean?"

"New town, new sister, indoor plumbing."

She put her hands on her hips. Amusement pulled at the corners of her mouth. "Are you mocking my time living off the land?"

"Pretty much."

"I'll have you know that I learned a lot, and there is much to be said for a simpler life."

"And the indoor plumbing?"

She sat on the desk across from his and laughed. "I'll admit I really, really love it. Hot water, especially. And flush toilets. A brilliant invention."

"Agreed." He studied her for a second, letting his gaze linger over the good parts. "I can't picture you running barefoot through fields, picking wildflowers."

"Probably because I never did. I wasn't staying in some idealized TV world. My grandmother lived simply, which meant she had to do most of the work herself. Fruits and vegetables don't can themselves. And when you're snowed in for a few weeks at a time, there's no running to the corner market."

She smiled as she spoke, as if the memories were good ones. He was glad about that. Given the little he knew about how things had been with her parents, she hadn't had an easy time of it. Kids needed stability. He hadn't realized that when he'd been young, but once he'd moved in with his coach and had seen what a normal family was like, he'd finally been able to relax. He suspected Destiny's Grandma Nell had provided the same escape for her.

"I wish she was still alive," she admitted. "Not just because I miss her, although I do. Every day. But because of Starr. I think she's happy, but I'm not sure. We're connecting more. I'm trying to listen more than I talk, which is actually harder than it sounds."

"What about the things you have in common? She's into music, and it's got to be in your veins."

Destiny drew her braid over her shoulder, then smoothed her hair before tossing it back. "I've been teaching her to play the guitar, and next we're going to move on to my keyboard. She has talent, which helps. She's a quick study. But then she wants to talk about the business, and I'm not the right person. I've always done my best to avoid it, which she can't understand."

"Even singing the way you do? You were never tempted?"

"Not at all. Life on the road is not the fun fest everyone imagines. There's constant pressure to be visible and at the same time to be productive. Which doesn't work for me. I need peace and quiet when I write music."

"You write songs?"

She winced, then flushed. "Pretend I didn't say that."

"Not possible. Can you sing one for me?"

"No. They're private."

Secrets, he thought, wondering why she was so reticent. He didn't know the first thing about how one went about writing a song, but he would guess it wasn't hard for the words to get personal. Wouldn't a songwriter have to pull from his or her own experience? Or at the very least, observation? That would mean exposing a piece of the writer's soul. From what he'd learned about Destiny, she liked emotional distance between herself and everyone else. Which could be part of the problem with Starr.

"You write the songs for yourself?" he asked.

"No. I just write them. I don't have a choice."

Simple words, but there was something in her tone. Sadness, maybe? Resignation?

Without having a plan, he straightened, grabbed her hand and pulled her to him. She rose slowly and stepped into his embrace. Once she was there, he wrapped his arms around her and rested his chin on her head.

"Don't worry," he told her. "I'll keep you safe."

"I don't need protecting."

"Sure you do. Everyone does from something."

"So what scares you?"

"Not being able to take care of the people who matter to me."

Because of what had happened with his father, stepmother and Shelby, he thought, remembering what it had been like to be trapped in a hospital bed a half-world away from his sister. Mayor Marsha had promised to keep her safe and in return, he'd come here and taken over the HERO program.

"You're a really good guy," Destiny told him, her body warm against his. "You sure you don't want to try my sensible relationship plan?"

A sexless marriage? "Not until you try things my way first."

She chuckled, then looked up at him. "That is never going to happen."

"Did you know I competed professionally? Are you sure you want to challenge me?"

She smiled. "I'll take my chances."

"Then game on."

CHAPTER TEN

"My name is Charlie Stryker, and I'm in charge."

Kipling recognized the woman speaking. She was tall and broad-shouldered, with a lot of upper body strength. She didn't move like a pregnant woman, probably because she clearly worked out on a regular basis. She was a firefighter, and Kipling figured anyone would feel a lot better when she showed up at the scene of a disaster. Charlie exuded confidence and competency.

She stood with her hands on her hips. Her gaze was steady, as if she didn't expect trouble, but would handle it if it came along.

"I'm going to divide you into groups. You'll be assigned specific tasks. Let me be clear, this isn't a democracy. You volunteered to help, and help you will. Under my terms."

"You're hot when you're bossy," a male voice called out.

Kipling wondered how long it would take Charlie to flatten the guy, only instead of pummeling him, she flushed.

"Ignore my husband," she told the group of people standing in front of her.

The combination of bravado and blushing was kind of appealing, Kipling thought, thinking this was the damnedest town with the most interesting people.

Charlie explained how the playground sprucing up would work.

"As I was saying, you'll be divided into teams. Each team will be assigned to a playground. You'll have a list of things to do there. Do not deviate from the list. Don't do more than asked. Don't use your own supplies. There are reasons for all this, but it would waste time to go into them, so please, people, do what you're asked, and this will all go smoothly."

She went on to list rules and instructions. Kipling was only half listening as he glanced around at the people who had volunteered to start work at eight on a Saturday morning. There was more turnout than he would have expected. A lot of the people were obviously couples, with wives leaning against their husbands, all of whom were still drinking coffee.

He saw Destiny and another woman. They were listening to Charlie and looking more than a little worried. Which probably made Charlie very happy.

The blonde was pretty enough, but Kipling was only interested in Destiny. But before he could head over, Shelby walked up to him.

"Hey, big brother," she said and hugged him.

"What are you doing here?" he asked.

"Sometimes fixing things is good." She smiled. "Charlie has promised me duties fit for my skill level."

"Which is?"

Shelby grinned. "Basic. Very basic."

"Listen up, people," Charlie said, staring directly at him and Shelby. "Those of you who brought tools are in the first group. You'll be going to a couple of different playgrounds, fixing equipment. The rest of you, line up and I'll put you into your teams. If you have a preference, let me know. We need people with muscles to remove the old mats. Dirty bark has to be raked up and hauled away. Wood needs sanding, and there's plenty of painting for all. Let's move. Daylight's wasting."

"Did she used to be in the army?" Shelby asked idly.

"It sounds like it."

They waited in line. Charlie took one look at him and pointed to her left. "Go with the muscle. It's macho work and should make you happy."

"Yes, ma'am."

Charlie waved Shelby toward a group of women. "Raking and painting."

"Isn't your process a little sexist?" Shelby asked.

"Yes. Do you see that as a problem?"

Shelby grinned. "Nope. Just asking."

Kipling went over to join several other men. He greeted Gideon, one of the partners at The Man Cave. Carter, Gideon's son, was with him.

"Hey, G-Force," Carter said. "I'm with you guys today."

Kipling did his best not to react to the nickname. The one he no longer deserved. "I see that. Impressive." He shook hands with Gideon. "How's it going?"

"Good. Too early for me, but Felicia said it was important to help."

Kipling figured that for a man who worked from ten in the evening until the early hours of the morning, this would be a difficult start time.

"Mom's big on giving back to the community," Carter said with an easy grin. "She says connecting with the core group is biological. That it's a need in all primates. She knows stuff."

"Apparently." Kipling had only met Felicia a few times, but he would guess she was probably the smartest person any of them had ever interacted with. He wondered how she and Gideon had hooked up in the first place. They seemed so different. Of course there were people who would probably be surprised that of all the single women in town, Destiny was the one to capture his attention.

Attraction was always interesting and sometimes complicated.

Thinking about Destiny made him remember Starr. "You're at the summer camp, right?" he asked Carter.

The teen nodded. "My second summer. I've been a buddy to a bunch of new kids. It's pretty cool."

"Do you know Starr Mills?"

"Sure. We hang out some. She's into music and singing, but we've had a few classes together."

"Good. She's new, and I know her sister is worried about her fitting in."

Carter nodded. "Yeah, my mom was worried about that when I moved here. Starr's doing good."

"Checking on the kid sister?" Gideon's expression turned knowing. "Whatever it takes, man."

Before Kipling could respond, they were called to the trucks that would take them to the various playgrounds. Gideon walked with him.

"You hearing anything about the bar?"

"Hearing what?" Kipling asked.

"Complaints."

"No. We're doing well. Business is steady. Why?"

Gideon shrugged. "I hear things. Jo's Bar is pretty close."

"Sure, but a different clientele. They target women, and we target men. There are plenty of both in town."

"It's not that simple," Gideon told him. "But I think we're okay for now."

"You worry too much."

Gideon nodded. "I do. Used to be that's what kept me alive. But I'm sure you're right. That we'll be fine."

"We will. You'll see."

Destiny found that a morning spent painting playground equipment was exactly what she needed to clear her mind. She'd invited Starr along, but her sister had opted to sleep in.

The morning was warming up quickly. The sun was out, and

only a handful of clouds chased across the blue sky. This was a nice way to spend a Saturday, she thought. Until moving to Fool's Gold, she'd never gotten involved in a community event like this. Helping out was actually really fun.

Shelby sat on the other side of the support poles they were painting. They were onto their second playground. As they had moved on from the first one, a couple of trucks filled with guys had pulled up to replace the safety mats.

"How long do you think until Charlie shows up to check our work?" Shelby asked with a laugh.

"I'm not sure, but I'm keeping my brush strokes very even."

"Me, too." Shelby took a deep breath. "This is nice. I usually spend my Saturday mornings in the bakery. It was relaxing to sleep in until six and then be outside."

"I think it's sad that getting up at six is sleeping in for you, and yet I love my morning pastries."

"Someone has to pay the price," Shelby told her. "And I'm willing to do it."

"For that, I thank you."

"In return, you'll find me if I get lost in the mountains."

Destiny nodded, even though she wouldn't be one of the people doing the searching. As of yet, she hadn't been given her next assignment, but it was just a matter of time until she heard.

For once, there would be things she would miss when she left. People, as well as the town. She had a routine here she liked. She enjoyed the girlfriend lunches and the festivals. Even her little rental was growing on her.

She'd made friends, she thought, glancing where Madeline was raking on the opposite side of the playground. Madeline, who'd had drinks with the man who had also taken out Shelby.

Destiny dipped her brush in the can of red paint. "How are things going with Miles?" she asked cautiously.

"I've seen him a couple of times. He's a lot of fun." Shelby looked up and grinned. "Don't worry. I'm heeding your warning. I won't get serious."

"As long as you know he's not a sensible choice."

"Sensible is highly overrated. I know that Miles isn't going to be into anything permanent. I'm open to a fling. Miles and I have talked. He's going to be faithful while he's here and when he leaves, we're done. Normally, I would want more, but there's something about him. I love it when a man makes me forget myself."

"Why?"

Shelby laughed. "Because falling for someone should be unpredictable and fun. I work hard every day. I have a steady routine, which is all good, but sometimes I want more. I want to feel the rush of anticipation. I want to be surprised. I love surprises."

"Only good ones," Destiny pointed out. "Everyone wants to win the lottery, and no one wants to be in a car accident, yet they're both surprises."

"Okay, you're a great person, but sometimes you're a little strange."

"I've been told that before." Destiny rested her brush on the edge of the paint can and stood to stretch her legs. "I've seen plenty of emotional drama in my life. I'm looking for calm."

"You mean boring."

"I'm a fan of boring. I want to know that tomorrow is going to look a lot like today." That the person who mattered most would still be there in the morning. How many times had she awakened as a kid to find her parents hadn't come home? That they'd hopped a flight to New York or Las Vegas. Sometimes they'd remembered to arrange for someone to be around to take care of her. But not always.

She'd been with Grandma Nell over a year before she'd been able to wake up without a knot in her stomach. In her world, surprises were highly overrated.

★ ★ ★

The work crews finished about two in the afternoon. Destiny passed on going to Jo's for nachos and margaritas. She wanted to get home to see Starr. They were supposed to hang out that afternoon. The plan was to practice the guitar, then make dinner together. Not exactly earthshaking, but Destiny was looking forward to them spending time together.

As she crossed the street in front of their house, her leg muscles protested. All the squatting and crouching had done a number on her thighs. She really needed to be thinking about working out, she thought. Or maybe just making sure she got a long walk in every day.

She opened the front door and stepped into the house.

"It's me," she called.

Starr was in the living room, on her cell phone. As Destiny entered the room, her sister turned away. There was something about the set of her shoulders, the way she held her head, that had Destiny freezing in place.

"Uh-huh," Starr said. "Sure. No problem. Bye."

She pushed a button on her cell phone and tossed it onto the sofa.

"What's wrong?" Destiny asked.

"Nothing."

Starr's voice was strangled, and she didn't turn around.

Destiny crossed to her. "Hey, tell me, please."

Starr slowly faced her. Tears filled her eyes. "My dad called. *Our* dad called. He wanted to wish me a happy birthday."

Destiny's whole body tensed as horror swept through her. "It's your birthday? Oh, no. I'm sorry. I didn't know." She wanted to slap herself. How could she have not found out it was her sister's birthday? Talk about thoughtless.

"It's not," Starr told her as she wiped away tears. "It's not my birthday. When I told him, he didn't think it was a big deal."

More tears fell. "He's my f-father, and he doesn't even know when I was born."

Destiny moved in and reached for her. Starr resisted for about a second, then collapsed against her.

"I'm sorry," Destiny whispered, knowing the words were stupid and wouldn't help at all. Not that she could think of anything else to say. "He's like that sometimes. You know it's about him, right? Not you?"

"Because he's the only one who matters?"

"Pretty much."

Starr began to cry, then. "He's my dad. Why doesn't he love me?"

"He does."

"No. I've seen how other dads act. He doesn't care about me."

Destiny hung on tight. "Jimmy Don isn't like other dads. I'm sorry he did that to you."

She continued to hug Starr until the teen finally straightened and wiped her face.

"Thanks," Starr told her, her face blotchy and her eyes red. "It sucks, you know."

"I do."

"Can we still play guitar together?"

"Sure. Later we'll make cookies."

That earned her a slight smile. "I'm not five. You can't distract me with a cookie."

"Maybe not, but I can try."

Starr sniffed. "I need to blow my nose. I'll be right back."

Destiny waited until she was out of the room, then she emailed herself a reminder to get in touch with her father's lawyer. She needed to know a whole lot more about Starr than she did now. Starting with her sister's birthday. Because when that day actually came, Destiny wanted to make sure it was one to remember...in the best way possible.

★ ★ ★

At noon on Sunday Starr got a text from Abby, inviting her to an impromptu sleepover. Destiny talked to Liz, Abby's mom, got confirmation that there would be no boys or unsupervised time and dropped off Starr at four. By six-thirty, Destiny was pacing the floor.

She didn't know what was wrong, but for some reason, she couldn't seem to settle. She cleaned both bathrooms, did a couple of loads of laundry and then tried working on a song from her notebook. Nothing worked. She flipped channels, did a bit of internet shopping and by 7:18 knew she was going to jump out of her skin if she didn't find something to distract herself.

She shoved house keys, her cell phone and a credit card into her jeans pocket, then locked the front door behind her and started for the center of town.

There were still plenty of people walking around. The sun had yet to set, and the evening was pleasantly warm. Most of the restaurants had outdoor patios where happy locals and sun-burned tourists mingled easily. Several people called out greetings to Destiny. She nodded and smiled as she walked but didn't stop. It seemed she had a destination, although she had no idea what it was. Not until she got there.

She came to a stop across the street from The Man Cave. She stared at the sign and at the caveman statue beside the open door before giving in to the inevitable.

Once inside, she felt as if she could breathe more easily. A couple of baseball games played on TVs over the bar. Most of the seats were filled. The crack of balls from the pool tables mingled with laughter. The smell of popcorn and beer, perfume and burgers, welcomed her home.

Maybe it was because she'd grown up in honky-tonks. Maybe it was because being around people made it possible for her to lose herself when she couldn't in the quiet of her house. Or maybe it was the stage at the far end of the room.

The sign said karaoke started at eight every night. Destiny walked to the bar.

"Long Island Iced Tea," she said. "Make it extra long."

The bartender, a woman she didn't recognize, nodded. "You walking?"

Because this was Fool's Gold, Destiny thought. A place where they made sure you weren't going to be drinking and driving before you even started drinking.

"I live less than six blocks away."

"Good to know."

Destiny settled on an empty bar stool. She glanced around the room and figured she knew at least a dozen people, maybe more. Friends. Acquaintances.

Aidan was with Nick, Miles and a couple of other guys. She nodded at them but ignored the wave over. She wasn't in the mood to deal with any of them tonight. Especially not Miles, who'd gone out with both Shelby and Madeline.

She hoped neither of her friends would fall for the man. They both deserved better. He would break their hearts and then move on. Better for Madeline to crush on action star Jonny Blaze and Shelby to find someone a whole lot nicer than Miles. Not that they would listen to her.

She thought about the Hendrix brothers and their unbelievable bet about getting their wives pregnant and her father devastating his daughter with a thoughtless phone call and how she didn't know what she was going to do with Starr when this job ended and how no matter how much she knew that being sensible was the right thing, sometimes she just wanted to let go.

The twisting restlessness inside her grew. The bartender passed her the drink, and Destiny drank deeply. She knew what the alcohol would do. How it would loosen the tight grip she kept on herself. Because of it, she would give in to the unthinkable. Because she had to. Because there was only one way to feel better.

Time ticked by. She finished her drink and ordered another.

At 7:55 she walked up to the karaoke stage. Kipling was there, hooking up the equipment.

He didn't see her at first, which meant she could study him without being caught. She took in the slight hesitation in some of his movements, juxtaposed with his athletic grace. Someone said something to him, and he responded with a quick smile. She knew his eyes were a beautiful shade of blue, that when he kissed her, she forgot she had a plan and that he loved his sister and looked out for her.

If she were someone else, looking for something else, she would already be sleeping with him. She might even be falling for him, which would be worse. But she'd learned to protect herself, so she was careful. Careful about the man, at least. If not careful with the rest of it.

Because tonight she was going to sing.

He looked up and saw her. "Hey, Destiny, what are you—" His expression turned worried. "What's wrong?"

"I'm fine."

"You're not. There's something. What is it?"

She couldn't explain. Not the swirling unease. The sense of not fitting in her skin, of needing something more. Impatience gripped her. Tension made her tremble. There were too many emotions and not enough places to put them.

"I have to sing."

She'd thought he might laugh or grill her, because how could her statement make sense? Instead he put out a hand to help her up on the stage.

"Want to do a set?" he asked.

She nodded. "If that's okay."

He smiled at her. "Let me think. Free entertainment for my guests and listening to you sing more than one song. Yeah, it's kind of okay."

They scrolled through songs together. She selected one by Tumpy Shanks. It was old, but one of her favorites. "Under

the Willow Tree" would be followed by her father's hit "Bar-
stool Blues." She added a few more of her mother's songs, then
"What Hurts the Most," a Rascal Flatts hit, closing with Kenny
Chesney's "Come Over."

She put her drink on the small table by the karaoke machine.
"I'm going to need another one of these in about fifteen minutes," she said.

Kipling touched her arm. "You sure you want to do this?"

"I have to."

"We can go somewhere, if you want. Talk. Drive. Yell at
trees."

Because he saw she was in pain. He knew there was a problem, and he wanted to fix it.

"This is the only way," she whispered. "It doesn't happen
often. Maybe once every couple of years. But when it does, this
is all I can do. At least I didn't have to look very far for a karaoke place. You have one so conveniently located."

"I do what I can." The tone was light, but she saw the worry
in his eyes.

She picked up the microphone. It was a good weight. Solid in
her hand but not too heavy. The lighting could have been better, but this wasn't a professional performance. She scuffed her
boots against the wooden floor, anchoring herself.

Kipling left the stage, and she was alone. Gradually, the room
got quiet as people noticed her. She pushed the button to start
the first song, drew in a breath and lost herself.

"I left you there, under the willow tree," she sang. *"Tears falling,
you always missing me."*

The words came without her having to look at the screen.
She'd probably learned the song when she was four or five. She'd
sung it on tour with her parents.

Song after song, she worked her way through the playlist. She
lost track of time, of how much she drank, of where she was.
She gave herself over to the music, letting go in the only way

she knew how. The only way that was safe. The knot in her gut relaxed, and the restlessness eased. She spent her whole life denying who and what she was. Every now and then she had no choice but to let that part of her out, and tonight was the night. By the time she was done, she was exhausted but at peace.

She put down the microphone, and the bar exploded with applause. She nodded once and walked to the edge of the stage. Kipling was there to help her down.

"You're shaking," he said, putting his arm around her.

"It's okay," she told him.

Instead of leading her to the bar, he took her through the back and into a small office. She sank onto the chair by his desk and watched her hands tremble.

"Have you eaten anything today?" he asked.

"Not since lunch."

"Liquor on an empty stomach. Never a good idea. Wait here. I'll go grab you a sandwich."

She nodded because speaking was suddenly too difficult. When he left, she looked at the clock on the wall and was shocked to see it was after eleven. Had she really been singing for three hours? No wonder she was exhausted.

He returned with a bottle of water and a bowl of popcorn. "I'm closing up soon. The sandwich will only take a couple more minutes. By the time it's done, the bar will be closed, and you can come out."

She drank water, then swallowed. "How do you know I want everyone gone?"

"Because you don't want to talk about what just happened. You don't want to answer questions."

She didn't know how he knew, but he did. He'd guessed the truth, or maybe it wasn't all that hard to figure out. Either way, he was right. She needed to sing, but she didn't want to talk about it. She didn't want to explain.

He left again. She finished the bottle of water, then stood.

The room spun a little. She was still feeling a little unsteady on her feet. Not a huge surprise. She'd lost track of how much she'd had to drink.

She made her way to the door and let herself out into the bar.

The open space was bigger when it was empty. There were still glasses on tables. She would guess the place was usually cleaned before closing but that Kipling had hurried everyone along. For her. So she wouldn't be uncomfortable. Because he fixed things that were broken. Like her.

He walked in from the kitchen, a plate in his hand.

"Eat this, then I'll take you home."

Which all sounded very sensible. And at any other time she would have followed his suggestion. Just not right now. Not with the bar spinning and her heart racing and need building.

She walked up to him and took the sandwich from him and put it on a nearby table. Then she rested her hands on his shoulders, leaned in and kissed him.

She wasn't sure exactly what she was doing. She knew she needed to feel his mouth against hers. She needed to get lost in a different way. One without words. She wanted the heat, the tension, all that she had felt the last time he'd kissed her. Only now, she wanted more than that.

The second his lips touched hers, she parted. He obligingly brushed his tongue against hers. Desire raced through her, igniting sparks all over. She strained to get closer as she realized that the singing hadn't been quite enough. She needed more. She needed him.

She moved her hands down his arms, then to his back. He was lean yet strong. She explored the breadth of his shoulders, the length of his spine. He kissed her more deeply, teasing her tongue with his. She leaned into him, letting her body melt. Thighs brushed. Her breasts nestled into his chest.

She felt everything. The way he kissed along her jaw and licked the sensitive skin below her ear. The warmth of his breath.

The whisper of his fingers against the fabric of her shirt. She didn't know why her senses seemed enhanced, but they were. Maybe it was the Long Island Iced Tea. Maybe it was the man. Either way, she wanted everything he had to offer.

She reached for his wrists and drew his hands to her breasts. His thumbs touched her nipples, and she groaned.

Kipling told himself to slow down. There was no way he was going to do this with Destiny in a bar. While he had every intention of making love with her, their first time was going to be slow. Planned. Romantic. He wanted to make it good for her maybe two or three times before giving in himself. He had a plan.

Only the message didn't seem to be getting from his brain to his dick. Maybe it was a lack of blood flow. Maybe it was how she was touching him all over and offering herself to him. Every kiss seemed to draw him in deeper, and he was a big fan of being drawn in.

The sound of her moans nearly did him in. He felt the weight of her curves, the tightness of her nipples. Self-control snapped. He tugged up her T-shirt and tossed it onto the table behind her. Her bra followed, and he could see the swell of her breasts and the tight, taunting nipples begging to be loved.

He lowered his head and kissed her gently, so gently. She whimpered. He drew the tiny bud into his mouth, and her knees gave out.

He caught her as she fell.

"Again," she breathed, hanging on to him. "Oh, please, do that again."

He sucked in deeply, pulling and flicking his tongue. She groaned. Her fingers clutched his head as if she wanted to be sure he never let go. He shifted to her other breast and did the same. Her breathing increased, and she squirmed against him, then her head dropped back as she moaned.

She was desire incarnate, he thought hazily. All need and hunger. How had anyone made love with her without pleasing her first? If she was this excited when he was touching her breasts, how difficult would it be to bring her to orgasm?

Men were idiots, he thought cheerfully, toeing off his shoes and removing his own shirt. And that was just plain lucky for him.

He pushed the table aside and settled her on the bench of the booth. She pulled off her boots, then helped him remove her jeans and panties. The second she was naked, she brought his hands back to her breasts, which made it tough for him to take off the rest of his clothes. But he substituted his mouth for his fingers and managed to undress.

She stroked his chest and smiled up at him. Her eyes seemed a little glazed, and for a second, he wondered how drunk she really was. Then she whispered, "Kiss me," and he was lost.

Their tongues tangled. The bench was long enough for him to stretch out on top of her. Not doing it, he told himself. Not yet. He just wanted to see how they fit together.

She welcomed the weight of him, shifting and then wrapping her arms around him.

"I knew it would be like this," she murmured against his lips. "DNA always wins out."

"DNA?"

"It doesn't matter." She smiled. "That breast thing really works."

"You liked it?"

"Very much. Who knew?"

"What about the rest of it? What else do you like? How would you like me to please you, Destiny? My mouth, my hands, like this?"

As he spoke, he pushed in gently. Just a little. The tip.

She was hot and wet and tight. Her eyes widened, and her mouth parted. He read the signs as pleasure and pushed in more. A little deeper, a little farther.

Which turned out to be a mistake because he hadn't been with a woman in months and months. That fact became very clear when he felt the familiar pressure building at the base of his cock. Panic flared as his brain searched for a solution to a very imminent problem.

It had been all of two seconds. Seriously? What the hell was he supposed to do now? Pull out and come all over her leg like some teenager? Or simply push in all the way and come like some teenager? Either way he was going to be humiliated.

He swore. "I swear, it's not usually like this," he told her. "I'll take care of you in a second, okay? It's just—"

His hips gave an involuntary flex. He pushed in.

Three things happened at once. Destiny put her hands on his shoulders and said, "Kipling, I'm—"

He felt something between him and the deep, wet place he most wanted to go. Instinctively, he pushed harder, and the barrier gave way. And he climaxed.

He pulled out as fast as he could, but it was too late. Foreboding grew as he looked down and saw blood on his penis. Pieces of a very surrealistic puzzle fell into place. He shook off the obvious solution and searched for another explanation.

There was no way. It wasn't possible. She was in her late twenties. She was beautiful. She was—

"You're a virgin?"

CHAPTER ELEVEN

"Was," Destiny said automatically, telling herself that in some strange, twisted way, the circumstances were completely fitting. Why wouldn't she lose her virginity in a bar? She was her parents' daughter, after all. Destiny couldn't escape her destiny.

She giggled at the ridiculousness of it and thought maybe she was a little drunker than she'd realized.

Kipling scrambled to his feet and stared at her. "You're a virgin?" he repeated. "No. You can't be. "

She sat up and tried to figure out how she felt. A little sore and, to be honest, disappointed. After all this time, all her plans and hopes to not be like her parents, she'd done it. She'd had sex with a guy in a bar. And while the kissing had been fun, and she'd really liked how she'd felt when he touched her breasts, in the end it hadn't been all that interesting.

Sex, like many forbidden things in life, was all hype. Her parents had broken up marriages, abandoned their children and tried very hard to destroy themselves over that? Three seconds of pressure with a bit of pain thrown in? She'd rather go eat a brownie.

What about the earth moving and all that crap people sang

about? The intense, life-changing moment? Talk about anticlimactic.

"Destiny."

Kipling's voice was sharp. Maybe a little panicked.

"I'm fine."

"You were a virgin?"

She nodded and stood. The room only swam a little, which was probably a good thing. She was going to have to—

She glanced down at herself and realized she was naked. Totally and completely naked. In a bar. What had she been thinking?

"My clothes," she said.

Kipling handed her her underwear still rolled up in her jeans. She pulled them apart and slipped on her panties. While she stepped into her jeans, he collected her T-shirt and bra then started getting dressed himself.

"We have to talk about this," he told her.

"No, we don't. I'm fine. I'm an adult. I did it. We did it." All that waiting, she thought. "I'd wondered, and now I know."

He slipped on his shirt. "It's not that simple."

"Sure it is. Don't worry. I'm perfectly fine."

"You're not. You can't be."

She slipped on her boots and made sure she still had her keys, cell phone and credit card. Her credit card.

"I never paid for my drinks."

"I'll take care of it."

"You don't have to pay for them."

He grabbed her by her upper arms. "We have to talk about what happened."

She felt the first throbbing promise of a headache. "Tomorrow," she said. "I'm not feeling well."

Kipling hesitated, as if he were going to push back, then he nodded once. "Tomorrow. For sure."

She wasn't sure if he was promising or threatening, and right now she didn't care.

He led the way to the front door, then locked it behind them. The walk to her house was accomplished in silence.

When they stood on her porch, she did her best to smile and sound perky. "I'm completely okay. I'm as much responsible for what happened as you are. I have no recriminations. You need to let it go."

His expression was unreadable. "We'll talk tomorrow."

"I'll count the hours."

She let herself in the house and went directly to her room. Seconds later, she was in her pj's and about a minute after that, she was sound asleep. Her last conscious thought was *virgin, smirgin. It was no big deal at all.*

Destiny woke to the mother of all hangovers. Her head had grown two sizes in the night, her body ached and there was a nagging sense of something having gone very wrong. Not that she could think clearly.

At least Starr was still at her friend's and had a ride to camp. Destiny's only responsibility was to survive the next couple of hours. Hydration and aspirin, she thought as she crossed to the bathroom. Then she would feel better.

The previous night was more than a little fuzzy. She remembered feeling out of sorts and how the singing had made it better. There had also been way too many Long Island Iced Teas.

She turned on the shower, then brushed her teeth while the water got hot. She dropped her pj's to the floor and was about to step into the shower when it all came crashing back.

The kissing. The touching. The sex.

"Oh, my God! I had sex with Kipling."

She stood there, one leg raised to step over the edge of the tub. Memories returned in vivid color and 3D detail. His body against hers. The way he'd stroked her. How nice it had all been and how at the end, she couldn't, for the life of her, get what all the fuss was about.

She was both embarrassed and resigned. She'd wondered, and now she knew. She supposed she'd experienced a rite of passage. To be honest, now that she'd done it, her sensible plan made even more sense. Why would anyone want to do that more than one or two times in a life?

She stepped into the steamy water and let the heat of it soak into her muscles. It was for the best, she told herself as she washed her hair. There weren't any more mysteries. She was just like most other women her age. At least when she did meet the right man, she wouldn't have to have the awkward "I'm a virgin" conversation. Because she'd sure shocked Kipling.

She smiled as she thought of his wide-eyed stare. She could almost feel sorry for him. She was old enough that there was no way he would have been expecting that particular surprise. Briefly she wondered if it had made the experience different for him, but knew there was nothing she could do about it.

She still couldn't figure out why people did the things they did for sex, she thought later as she dressed. It simply wasn't all that special. But then many things in life were surprising or puzzling. This was just one of those.

She got her backpack and texted Starr a quick "good morning," before heading out to Brew-haha. She wasn't much of a coffee drinker, but today called for the biggest coffee in the history of the universe, followed by about a gallon of water. That should get her on the road to feeling better. Oh, and she would make sure not to drink for weeks and weeks.

She walked the few blocks to the coffee shop. As she waited at the light, she saw a man in the park. There was nothing unusual about that. What made this sighting memorable were the odd feathers he was holding and the striped paint on his face. Plus, he kind of looked like he was doing some odd version of Tai Chi.

She walked into the store and found everyone there watching the man in the park.

"What's going on?" she asked.

Patience, the owner, shook her head. "Near as we can figure, Ford is trying to perform an ancient Máa–zib fertility ritual."

"Oh, right. For the pregnancy bet."

Patience started toward the cash register. "You know about the bet?"

"Yes. Men are so strange."

Patience laughed. "They are. Why doesn't he simply get her pregnant the regular way? With sex? Oh, well. Not my problem. What can I get you?"

"A large latte to go," Destiny said automatically, even as part of her brain started keening and rocking back and forth.

Get pregnant the regular way? With sex? Like the sex she'd had the previous night? Sex with absolutely zero protection?

She handed over her money and nodded as Patience talked, but Destiny couldn't do anything but try to keep the spinning world in focus. Her chest was tight, her body cold, and panic began to swallow her whole.

Pregnant? Pregnant? No and no. She couldn't be. They'd only done it one time, and she'd been a virgin. Didn't she get a free pass or something? She'd never been all that interested in biology, but surely she'd read something like that.

"Destiny?"

She blinked and saw Patience holding out a to-go cup.

"Sorry. Too many Long Island Iced Teas last night," she said with a nervous laugh. "I'm still foggy."

Patience nodded knowingly. "I've been to that particular party myself." Her eyes widened. "Were you at The Man Cave? Did you sing? I'd love to hear you sing again."

"Next time," Destiny said, knowing there wasn't going to be a next time. Not for the singing or the drinking or the sex. When she got restless, she would take up jogging or go split logs.

She knew how to split logs, and that would be a whole lot safer than what she'd done the previous night. The worst that would happen with a misplaced ax was she would chop off her foot.

She called out, "Have a good day," and hurried toward the exit. She needed to drink her coffee and get her heart rate back to normal.

Pregnant? There was no possible way.

Having reassured herself, she sipped her hot coffee and walked toward her office. The day was pretty, and if she ignored the memories crowding in around her, she would be fine. Better than fine. She would be—

She rounded a corner and ran smack into Kipling. When she started to stagger to the side, he grabbed her by her upper arms and steadied her.

"I was coming to see you," he said.

I was planning on avoiding you. Not that she said that aloud. Instead she managed what she hoped was a friendly, "Oh."

They stared at each other.

His hands were still on her arms, and she could feel the heat of his skin, along with the pressure of each individual finger. He had nice hands, she thought idly. Large and capable. He'd had his hands on her body. He'd seen her naked. OMG, the man had seen her naked.

A shrill sound built up inside her, but Destiny forced it down. Calm, she told herself. She was calm. Later, she would look up meditation on the internet and start practicing for sure. Because no matter what, she would not turn into her screaming, plate-throwing, emotionally intense parents. One sexual encounter did not a crazy person make. She was stronger than her DNA, stronger than her hormones, stronger than whatever she needed to be stronger than.

Kipling pulled her toward a bench. She thought about bolting, but knew he would only follow. If they were seen running through town, people would talk, and she really didn't want the speculation. She sat.

He settled, angled toward her. His blue eyes were dark with worry and concern.

"I'm fine," she told him, hoping to short-circuit the conversation with reassurances. "Completely and totally fine."

"I don't believe you."

He looked good, she thought absently. Tired, as if he hadn't slept much the night before. There were shadows under his eyes. But still, there was something about him. The shape of his mouth, maybe. It was nice, and she'd enjoyed kissing him. Those little neck nibbles had given her goose bumps. And when he'd put his big hands on her breasts and licked her nipples, she'd—

Stop it!

She screamed the command in her head. She was a sensible, rational person. Sensible, rational people didn't think the word *nipple* at 8:15 in the morning. Ever.

"I didn't know if I should call you, or come by," he admitted. "You shocked the hell out of me last night."

She sipped her coffee. Okay, they weren't not going talk about what had happened. She could deal. They would discuss it and put it behind them.

"Last night," she clarified.

"Yeah, last night. We have to talk about it."

Yes, she'd figured that part out herself. "Because of the sex."

He stared at her. "It's more than that, Destiny. You were a virgin. You should have said something."

"I didn't know what to say," she admitted.

"How about, 'Kipling, this is my first time'?"

"In retrospect, that makes sense," she admitted, not sure when she would have mentioned the fact. Any sentence with the word *virgin* in it was going to make things awkward. "I had a lot to drink, and I wasn't thinking. It all happened so fast."

He tensed. "About that," he began, then paused.

She waited.

"I haven't had a girlfriend in a while. You know...first the accident and then my recovery. I was in the hospital and rehab for months. Then I came here."

She sipped her coffee. "I think I knew all that."

He rubbed his face. "I'm talking about my performance. It isn't usually like that."

"What part?" It really *had* happened so fast, she thought. Or maybe it was that it had happened hazy. "The whole thing is kind of a blur, to be honest. I don't drink very much, but with the singing and all. I just wanted to get lost in the music."

He opened his mouth then closed it. "What? What are you talking about?"

"I'm not sure. I'm sorry you were in the hospital for a long time after you were injured."

He swore and stood. "That's not what I want to talk about."

"You're the one who brought it up."

She couldn't be sure, but she thought maybe he was grinding his teeth together. He swore again, then sat back on the bench.

"About us having sex," he began. "I didn't know you were a virgin. The way you'd talked before, I thought you'd done it, and it hadn't been very good."

"Oh. No, I hadn't done it. Because of the plan. I was saving myself for marriage."

Emotions flashed across his face. She couldn't read them exactly, but she could tell he wasn't happy.

"Just because I didn't want to have sex with anyone," she added quickly. "You don't have to feel bad. It wasn't for significant spiritual reasons. I just saw what happened all around me. People making really bad decisions because they were having sex or wanted to have sex."

"Sex is the root of all evil," he said.

"Right!" She smiled. "So waiting made sense. In a way, you've done me a favor. Now when I meet the right guy, I don't have to have an awkward conversation. I mean I'm twenty-eight. It was time."

He stared at her for a long time. "You're more calm than I expected."

"I like calm. The highs and lows never end well. Better to stay emotionally steady. It's easier."

"So you're not upset?"

"No. It's odd, I'll admit. I'm kind of embarrassed. You saw me naked."

"You look good naked."

The unexpected compliment made her blush and feel a little proud at the same time.

"Thank you. Um, you do, too."

"About what we did last night."

She held up her hand to stop him. "I'm okay, Kipling. But I don't want to talk about it anymore. It happened. Now we move on."

"Because you're still looking for Mr. Sensible? So you can have a nonphysical connection and raise a family?"

When he put it like that, she felt ridiculous, but she nodded, anyway. Because she'd put a lot of thought into her plan, and she knew she was right.

He reached for her free hand. "Destiny, last night didn't go the way I'd planned. I don't want you thinking that's all there is. Sexually."

She pulled her hand free and stood. "I know. It's fine. Thank you for worrying. It's no big deal. I promise. We'll go on as if this never happened. You'll see. Just put it out of your mind."

Kipling let Destiny walk away because he honest to God didn't know what to say to her. She defined unruffled. He would guess that most women in her situation would be shrieking or crying or threatening him with a knife. She was acting like it was no big deal.

But it was. It had to be. These days, very few women got to

be her age without having had at least one serious boyfriend. And with that kind of relationship came intimacy. But she hadn't done that. Twenty-four hours ago she'd been a virgin. Now she wasn't, and it was his fault.

Talk about a problem that needed fixing, he thought. How was he supposed to make things right?

He shifted so he could rest his elbows on his thighs and dropped his head to his hands. Maybe it would be better if she *was* threatening him with a knife. At least he could understand that. But her total acceptance had him baffled.

Unless it was a facade. But she seemed so sure. Was she fooling herself? If he kept thinking in circles and worrying, was he going to turn into a woman?

Nearly as horrifying, he'd left her unsatisfied. Now he was the kind of jerk guy he'd been so smug about. And while that problem could be fixed, he wasn't sure where to start. Or what to say.

He stood and looked at his watch. He had a meeting with Mayor Marsha in a few minutes to interview another candidate for his second-in-command. Work now, Destiny later, he told himself. Because while she might have accepted what had happened, he was still trying to take it all in. And once he had it figured out, he was going to fix it. All of it.

He walked to City Hall and took the stairs up to the mayor's office. Her assistant waved him in.

"Right on time," the mayor said, greeting him with a warm smile then gesturing to the chair by her desk. She was dressed in a purple suit and pearls. "Our candidate is filling out some paperwork as we speak. I have a good feeling about her."

"The résumé is impressive," he said, thinking about the file he'd reviewed over the weekend. Cassidy Modene, age thirty-nine. She'd grown up in Wyoming, had worked for the Wyoming State Parks. She trained horses for search and rescue missions, and worked with search and rescue dogs. "She brings more to the table than we're looking for."

Mayor Marsha nodded. "You're thinking of the horses and the dogs."

"I am."

"There seems to be some extra grant money, so I thought we might expand our mission statement."

He wasn't sure which comment to address first. The steady influx of money or the dogs and horses. In an era of decreasing funds for local governments, Mayor Marsha had started a new and expensive program. Was there a secret money stash somewhere? Did she have rich benefactors? Or was it best that he not ask?

As for the dogs and horses, he was interested. "We'll have more resources," he said. "I'm not sure how they'll fit in with the software we have."

"I'm sure you can speak to Destiny about it," the mayor said confidently. "Her company seems to pride itself on providing custom solutions."

He chuckled. "Special tracking collars on the dogs?"

"Something like that." Her gaze turned speculative. "I assume you wouldn't have a problem working with a woman."

Kipling started to laugh. This time yesterday he would have assured the mayor that he was very good with women. Now he was a whole lot less sure of that. But the older woman wouldn't want to hear about his personal issues.

"None at all," he promised, thinking that as long as he kept things professional, he was fine with women.

"I thought not."

Her assistant knocked once then opened the office door. "Cassidy's ready if you are."

Mayor Marsha stood. "Send her in."

Kipling rose and followed the mayor toward the latest potential candidate for his second-in-command job. While he'd studied her résumé, meeting her in person would tell him a lot more about whether or not she would be a good fit.

Cassidy Modene was about five six with short, spiky blond hair and hazel eyes. She wore a dark blue suit and plain navy pumps. Used to sizing up opponents at a glance, he saw that she was strong and athletic. Not surprising, considering her occupation. She looked capable.

She shook hands with both of them. She wore a plain gold band on the ring finger of her left hand. As the cuff of her sleeve moved with the motion, he caught sight of a rose tattoo on the inside of her wrist.

"Mrs. Modene. Thank you so much for coming to see us here in Fool's Gold," Mayor Marsha said, leading the way to the sofas in the corner.

"My pleasure. It's a nice little town."

They all sat. Kipling respected how the mayor had maneuvered them. He was next to her on the sofa, with Cassidy perched on the edge of a club chair. Two against one? He was comfortable with his expertise, but hiring wasn't it. He'd learned a lot from each of the interviews he'd participated in and knew this one would be no exception.

The good mayor lulled with seemingly idle chitchat before effortlessly shifting into more meaty conversation. Often with no warning. She'd gotten one apparently excellent candidate to admit he was more interested in time on the slopes than doing his job. Kipling wondered if Cassidy had any similar secrets to spill.

"You grew up in Wyoming," Mayor Marsha said.

"Yes. So I'm used to small towns." Cassidy flashed a smile. "I'm not sure what I would do in a big city. I like the outdoors."

"I noticed the rose on your wrist. Any emotional significance?"

Cassidy's eyes darkened. "It's in honor of my mother."

Mayor Marsha didn't say anything. Kipling thought Cassidy would keep talking to fill the silence, but she didn't. *Score one for the recruit,* he thought.

"Is your husband willing to relocate?" the mayor asked.

"Jeff's in his last year of twenty with the navy. He told me he wanted me to find him a nice place for his second act. We're thinking Fool's Gold might be it."

Mayor Marsha nodded. "Well, then, tell us about your search and rescue dogs."

CHAPTER TWELVE

Kipling's knowledge about what went on in a gynecologist's office could easily fit on a three-by-five card and leave room for a recipe. But he'd made the appointment and now found himself in the offices of Cecilia Galloway, MD.

The good doctor was probably close to seventy, with short, steel-gray hair and glasses. She was tall, large-boned and when she raised both eyebrows as if asking why he was here, Kipling had no idea what to say.

"It's not about me," he told her.

"I'm relieved. The last time I examined a man, I was in medical school. While I'm sure none of the parts have changed, I doubt I remember how to take care of them." Dr. Galloway nodded encouragingly. "How can I help you, Mr. Gilmore?"

"Kipling. And, ah, I'm here about a friend of mine. She, ah…" He wondered how much he should say. While he was part of the problem, technically Destiny didn't know he was here, and he had a feeling she wouldn't approve.

"I doubt there's anything you can say that I haven't heard a dozen times before," Dr. Galloway assured him. "Just take a deep breath and blurt it out. That's usually the best way."

"Right. I have a friend. And we—" No, that wasn't right. "The virgin thing," he began, then wished he hadn't. "After sex…"

He cleared his throat and started again. "If you can deflower a virgin, can she be reflowered?"

The woman sitting across from him blinked. "Excuse me?"

"Can she be made a virgin again?"

He had to give her credit. The doctor's expression barely moved, although he thought he saw the corners of her mouth shift down, as if she didn't approve of their conversation.

"How old are you, Mr. Gilmore?"

"Thirty-two."

"Perhaps if you were with more age-appropriate women, this wouldn't be a problem."

"What? No. Shit. Is that what you're thinking? No. She's not young. She's in her late…" He realized he shouldn't be talking about Destiny in specifics. "She's not a teenager at all. Not for several years. I'm not into young girls."

He stood and walked to the window, then turned back. "Look, it's not what you think. I didn't know, okay? She talked about not being interested in sex, and I thought she'd been with a bunch of jerks who never gave her an orgasm. But it turns out she was a virgin. And I hadn't been with anyone in months. Like almost a year, so it was quick, and there was this barrier, and I tried to stop because I kind of guessed what it was but it was too late and then it was over and…"

He swallowed. "Can you put it back?"

Dr. Galloway's lips were moving for sure, but they didn't look disapproving anymore. If anything he would say she was trying not to laugh.

"I see," she said slowly. "I'm pleased to know you're not preying on young women."

"I'm not. Ever. That's awful."

"Yes, it is. So about your friend. That barrier you felt is the hymen, and while it can be sewn back, I don't recommend it. From what you said, she hadn't been avoiding sex for religious reasons. There's no disapproving family to punish her?"

"No."

"Then let it be. Did you run out on her? Leave her crying?"

Kipling flinched. "You really hate men, don't you?"

"Not at all. I'm simply trying to discover the kind of man *you* are. From what I can see so far, you're a good one. So here's my advice. Talk to her. Find out why you. Why that night. As for the orgasm she didn't have, fix it. I assume you know how. If you don't, I have some brochures."

He held up both hands. "I know how. No brochures. Please."

Dr. Galloway smiled. "It will be fine. Although I do recommend that next time you learn a little more about your partner before having sex with her. Did you—"

Her phone buzzed, capturing her attention. "Excuse me. I have to take this."

"Sure. No problem. Thanks for your time."

He ducked out while he could and got out of the office without lingering. Once back on the sidewalk, he wished it was a whole lot later in the day because he needed a drink. As that wasn't possible, he walked the few blocks to Destiny's office.

She was at her computer, typing intently. For a second, he allowed himself the pleasure of looking at her. Long, wavy dark red hair tumbled over her shoulders. She had on a T-shirt and jeans, with hiking boots. Not sexy, not glamorous, but just looking at her was enough to get him thinking.

Not that they were going to do that anytime soon, he reminded himself. There were a few things that needed to be cleared up first.

She glanced up and saw him.

"Hi."

"Hi, yourself. How are you feeling?" he asked.

She frowned, as if confused. "Fine. Why? Do I look like I'm getting sick?"

"No. I wasn't talking about that. The other night—"

She leaned back in her chair and groaned. "Not that again. Kipling, we talked about it. You have to let it go."

He sat in the visitor's chair and leaned toward her. "I don't, and I won't. Destiny, losing your virginity is a big deal. I don't know why you chose that moment or me, but that part is done. What I'm concerned about now is making it right."

Emotions flashed through her green eyes. "It can't be un-done, and I wouldn't want to undo it. I like that I'm not a vir-gin anymore."

"Right. It's less complicated when you meet your calm Mr. Uptight."

"You don't have to say it like that," she grumbled. "Like you think I'm an idiot."

"I think you're underestimating the power of an intimate, sexual connection."

She rolled her eyes. "Right. It's powerful and exciting and makes life worth living." The words were at odds with her bored tone. "I've heard it all before, and I don't care."

"That's because you didn't have an orgasm."

"I'm not interested. It was fine, Kipling. Really. Let it go."

Something that wasn't going to happen, he thought firmly. "I wasn't prepared, and I messed up," he told her. "I owe you. If, after that happens, you still believe that sex is dangerous and bad, I won't mention it again. I swear."

She sighed heavily. "Why is this so important to you? I don't need fixing."

"No, you need teaching." He thought for a second, then de-cided to try reaching her from a different angle. "You were amazing on stage that night. Your singing, the vocals. You have real passion when you perform."

Instead of reacting with pride, she slumped lower in her seat. "I know. It was horrible."

"No, it was brilliant and powerful. How come you don't want to do that every day?"

"It's exhausting and requires me to be vulnerable. There's rawness in singing like that."

And no way to protect herself, he thought. Based on the little he knew about her past, he understood that she'd grown up feeling unsafe. As if her world could shift or crumble at any moment.

"You're not that kid anymore," he said gently. "You would be able to control what was happening around you."

"Not enough. Better to avoid the risk."

"Life without living is boring. It's beige. What's the point? You have a gift, Destiny. A chance at the dream."

More emotion flashed in her eyes. This time he had no trouble reading the annoyance.

"Don't talk to me about my dreams. You don't know anything about them. This is my choice. I don't want to be like them. You have no idea what it was like. No idea about what happened. It was different with Grandma Nell. Life made sense there. It was quiet. We lived by the rhythm of the seasons. With nature. That's what I want."

"Nature isn't quiet," he told her. "It's violent and beautiful. Most of all, it's uncontrollable. You're denying who you are on so many levels. You have a passionate nature. If you ignore that, you ignore who you are. You still have a chance."

"Kipling, I..." She stared at him. "Are we still talking about me?"

"Of course. I'm the expert here. Living the dream—there's nothing better. I know what I'm talking about. You still can."

"And you can't."

Blunt but true, he thought, ignoring the stab of longing for what had been. For *who* he had been. "I had a good run, and I mean that in all senses of the word."

"I'm sorry," she said softly. "I get what you're saying. That I should be grateful. I still have a chance. The thing is, I don't want it."

He didn't think she was telling the truth. Not on purpose but because she was afraid.

"I'm not your problem," she pointed out. "Let it go. I only want to talk about business now."

He nodded because he didn't have a plan. Not yet, anyway. But he would figure one out, and then he would fix the problem. Not just because he'd taken her virginity, but because it was the right thing to do. And maybe, just maybe, because a part of him wanted to. Very much.

Destiny did her best to get lost in her work. She'd completed the mapping, and the information had been fed into the tracking program. Their next step would be to start practice searches.

She had plenty to do, but kept finding herself thinking about Kipling. Avoiding him wasn't an option—they had a job to do. So far he'd kept things professional. But when they were in the same room, she felt him watching her. Not in a creepy, scary way, but as if assessing the situation. And that made her nervous.

She wanted to tell herself that she was imagining things, only she knew she wasn't. He was a man who liked to fix things, and explaining that she didn't have a problem wasn't going to be enough to dissuade him. The sex thing had really thrown him, although for the life of her, she couldn't figure out why. They'd done it; she was fine. Let's move forward. But, no. He wanted her to have an orgasm.

As if that would change anything, she thought as she headed into Kipling's office. Seriously, how good could it be?

Determined to act like the professional she was, she pushed all personal thoughts aside when she saw a pretty, thirtysomething blonde with spiky hair sitting at the desk across from Kipling's.

Rumor was, the second-in-command he'd hired was a woman. Destiny had been eager to meet her.

The woman looked up and smiled. "Destiny Mills?" she asked as she rose and offered her hand. "I'm Cassidy Modene. I've done a lot of research on your STORMS program, and I'm excited to work with it."

"Welcome to Fool's Gold," Destiny said, shaking her hand. "When did you start work?"

"This morning." Cassidy grinned. "I'm the optimistic type, so I'd already packed up everything I own in my truck. It helps that I'm not much of a pack rat. Having a husband in the navy has taught me that. Mayor Marsha and Kipling offered me the job, I accepted and here I am. My horses will join me in a few weeks. My husband, Jeff, should be here by the end of the year."

"I heard the program was expanding to include horses and search and rescue dogs. The tech guys back in the computer lab are quivering with excitement at the thought of all the modifications they're going to have to make. They do love a challenge."

"I'm with them on that."

The two women sat by Cassidy's desk. Destiny wanted to ask where Kipling was, but told herself it didn't matter. It wasn't as if she'd been looking forward to seeing him or anything. He was a colleague. Their conversations were always interesting, and she liked the verbal challenge of dealing with him. Nothing more.

Even so, she found herself asking, "Kipling's not in yet?"

"He stopped by City Hall for a quick meeting with the mayor. He'll be back shortly."

Destiny nodded as if the information was mildly interesting and nothing more, then went through the basics of the STORMS program with Cassidy. They moved to the big map on the wall.

"There's a lot of rugged terrain in the area," Cassidy said as she traced the city limits. "My horses will be a help. They can go farther and longer than anyone on foot. Plus carry gear."

Destiny nodded as she typed into her tablet. "You're right. With more supplies, the searches aren't as limited geographically. If they have a way to set up camp, they can stay where they are for the night and start fresh in the morning. That gives us a lot of advantages. Also, there's an easier way to transport injured people to a helicopter pickup site."

Cassidy turned to her and grinned. "Speaking of helicopters, I've met Miles."

"I thought you only arrived in town a couple of days ago?"

"I did, and he works fast. We met at The Man Cave. He's a charmer. Me being married and a few years older didn't seem to bother him in the least." Cassidy laughed. "Stupid man. I set him straight."

"Good for you."

Cassidy turned back to the map. "He's not my type, that's for sure. I've been in love with my husband since the second I met him. But I have to respect Miles's ability to go for it."

"He's a player."

"Like I said, not my style. Fool me once and all that. Seems like a fun town, though," Cassidy added. "I'm looking forward to exploring and getting to know people."

"Everyone is friendly. There's a really great group of women," Destiny said. "I'd be happy to introduce you, if you'd like. I've gone to lunch with them a few times already. It's a fun way to meet people and find out the real scoop."

Cassidy grinned. "I do love small-town gossip. It's a flaw, but one I can live with."

Before Destiny could respond, her cell phone rang. She pulled it out of her cargo pants pocket and glanced at the screen. The area code was local, but the number unfamiliar.

"Hello?"

"Destiny?"

"Yes."

"Hi, I'm Dakota Andersson. I run End Zone. I'm sure it's

nothing, but Starr never showed up this morning, and no one called to let us know she was staying home sick. I wanted to follow up with you and make sure she was all right."

There was a lot of information in those few sentences. That the camp took its responsibilities seriously. That they made sure the kids were where they were supposed to be. And that Starr was missing.

Destiny went cold all over. "She's not sick," she said slowly. "Not that I'm aware of. We talked this morning. She said she was getting a ride to camp with Abby. She was very clear about that. I know because I know Abby and like her. I've met her mom and everything."

On the other end of the call, Dakota paused. "She's not here. We've checked twice. Starr never arrived."

There was an edge to panic. A sharpness. Destiny had never felt it before. Not like this. Not with a combination of horror and fear. Anything could have happened. Something had. But what? Where was Starr?

"How can we help?" Dakota asked, obviously expecting Destiny to take the lead. To handle the situation.

In the back of her mind she was aware that given her job description she was possibly the best person to find a missing teenager. But honest to God, she didn't know where to start. She felt hot and cold and knew she was seconds from throwing up.

The office door opened, and Kipling stepped inside. Destiny lunged for him, grabbing his arm and squeezing hard.

"Starr's missing," she said, her throat tight as her heart pounded in her chest. "She never showed up to camp."

Kipling grabbed her phone and identified himself. He spoke calmly but quickly. When he hung up, he handed back the phone and took her hand.

"You have my cell number," he told Cassidy. "Phone me if you hear anything."

"I will."

He turned to Destiny. "Starr has a cell phone, right? Call her."

With trembling fingers, Destiny did. "It went straight to voice mail."

Then he was pulling Destiny out the door, toward his truck.

"Where are we going?" she asked. "I don't know where to start. She hasn't been here very long. I thought she was fine. What if something awful happened? What if we can't find her?"

"We'll find her. It hasn't been that long. She can't have gotten that far. Call the mom. See if she took Starr up to camp. We'll go by the house to make sure she's not there, then go up the mountain and talk to her friends."

Right. A good place to start. Destiny got into the truck and fastened her seat belt. After scrolling through her contact list, difficult to do with her hands shaking, she pushed the talk button and waited for the call to connect to Abby's mom, Liz. Two minutes later she had her answer.

"Starr lied."

The words weren't real. At least they didn't feel real. They couldn't be. How could Starr have done this? Lied to Destiny about being taken to camp, then disappeared? How could her sister be gone?

They arrived at the house and hurried inside. Starr wasn't there. Destiny followed Kipling back to his Jeep. Her eyes burned as the fear thickened. She could barely think, barely breathe.

"I don't know her well enough," she said, fighting tears. "It's only been a few weeks. I should have tried harder. I was busy with my job and other stuff. I left her alone too long. I wasn't there for her."

Kipling kept his gaze forward as he drove up the mountain. "How long have you known your sister?"

"Six weeks."

"Not long enough to screw her up. Destiny, this isn't your fault."

"I'm responsible for her. There's no one else to blame."

"How about all the stuff that happened before she moved in with you?"

She thought about the call from their shared father, celebrating a birthday that wasn't Starr's. And the boarding school her sister didn't seem all that excited to return to. And her longing to get involved with music, while Destiny resisted as best she could.

"You're saying there's plenty of blame to go around," she whispered. "Fine. I'll have that conversation when we find her. But right now all that matters is getting her back."

They arrived at the camp in record time. Kipling had barely slowed before Destiny jumped out and headed for the main office.

Dakota Andersson was waiting for her with two of Starr's friends. Both girls looked scared.

"I'm sorry," Abby said, tears filling her eyes. "She said she wanted to go to Nashville. She's taking the bus. We both gave her money."

Dakota put her hand on the girl's shoulder. "I've already called the sheriff's office. They're sending a patrol car to the bus station. Small towns have some advantages. Only one bus has gone out this morning. I'm expecting they'll find her waiting at the station."

Destiny felt the ground shift beneath her feet. "Nashville?" Because Starr was running away. That was how bad things were. She'd taken in her sister, had agreed to be her guardian and less than two months later, Starr would rather take her chances on the streets than live with Destiny.

How had everything gone so wrong so fast?

Destiny didn't know if she should scream, cry or take up drinking. She could make a case for any of those actions, along with several others.

Dakota's prediction had been right. Starr had been found on a bench in the bus depot. She'd missed the earlier Greyhound that went to Los Angeles and was instead heading to San Francisco. From there, she'd told the deputy who'd found her, she was planning on taking a plane to Nashville.

She'd had five hundred dollars in cash, a small suitcase and her guitar. Destiny couldn't get over the terrifying thought of an innocent fifteen-year-old girl on her own in the world.

Kipling had driven them both home and left them to work it out. He'd promised to drop by later, to check on them. Destiny had wanted to beg him to stay—she didn't know what on earth she was supposed to do or say. But she'd let him go and now had to deal with the aftermath herself.

She and Starr sat across from each other in their small living room and tried to figure out what to say. She supposed the good news was that nothing awful had happened. Maybe they'd both learned a cheap lesson. She just wasn't sure what it was.

She studied her sister. Starr stared at her hands or the floor. Her red hair hung down, covering her face. Or maybe keeping the world at bay, Destiny thought.

The room was quiet. Somewhere a clock ticked. A car drove by. Aside from that, there was nothing. Not even the sound of their breathing.

Indecision pulled at her. What was she supposed to say? How did she make this right? She supposed the bigger issue was she hadn't known there was a problem—certainly not one that warranted running away.

She drew in a breath. "Starr, I—"

Her sister's head snapped up. Her green eyes narrowed. "Yeah, I lied. Get over it. You would have done the same if you were me. What was I supposed to do? Just wait for you to get tired of me? I'm not going back to that boarding school. You can't make me."

So much anger. So much energy. And so much pain. Destiny felt her heart flinch as she realized how Starr had been suffering. And she'd never guessed.

"You think I don't know," her sister continued, coming to

her feet. Her hands were tight fists at her sides. "I know. It's not hard to figure out. Nobody wants me. Not you, not my dad." Tears spilled from her eyes. "He doesn't even know when it's my birthday. I'm his kid. How come he doesn't know that?"

Destiny stood and crossed to her. She tried to pull Starr close, but her sister shrugged away.

"Don't pretend you care now," the teen snapped.

Destiny took a step back. "I care. I took you in. I brought you here. I thought we were doing well together."

"Oh, sure. It's great. You're counting the days until school starts and you can get rid of me. We talked about your job before. About how it was better for me to go back to boarding school. Because you can't wait to get rid of me."

While that wasn't true, Destiny had been thinking she would only have Starr in the summers. "My work," she began, only to realize that wasn't the point. "Can we talk?" she asked. "Just sit and talk?"

Starr wiped away her tears and sank back onto the sofa. Destiny took the chair opposite and tried to figure out what to say.

"You scared me," she began, thinking it was the truth. "When Dakota called from camp and said you'd never arrived, I was so afraid of what had happened."

"I didn't think they'd call," Starr grumbled.

"So you'd have all day to get away? And then what? Didn't you think I'd totally freak out?"

Her sister shrugged.

"Starr, you have to know I care about you."

"Do you?" the teen asked. "Do you really? Can you honestly say you were thrilled when you got that call from the lawyer? Because you'd just been sitting here thinking if only you had some kid sister you'd never met, then your life would be perfect?"

"I was surprised, but I didn't hesitate. I wanted you to come live here."

"Whatever. I don't believe you. You don't care about anything, ever. You're like a robot. You never get mad, you never get happy. You're the same all the time. Regular people don't act like that."

People who never wanted to deal with the mess of highs and lows did, Destiny thought grimly. Because she knew the price of feeling too much. Only until right now, she'd never considered that there was a price to trying not to feel anything. The price of Starr not knowing she belonged.

"I'm sorry you think I don't care," she said quietly. "I do. I care a lot."

Her sister's mouth pulled into a straight line. Disbelief radiated from her. "Sure you do."

Irritation battled with concern and started to win. "You're going to ignore the truth because it's not what you want to hear," Destiny snapped. "Just like you were going to run away without thinking about the consequences. You're fifteen. You're not ready to be on your own. Life is complicated. You can't hide from your problems. They follow you wherever you go."

"You should have let me figure that out on my own. That would have made it easy for you, and isn't that what matters?"

"You're not making any sense."

"You know what doesn't make sense?" Starr demanded, glaring at her. "You. You don't make sense. You tell me not to run away, but you're doing it every day. You run away from your talent, from who you are. I've heard you sing, Destiny, and you're better than all of us. But you won't perform. You won't even admit that you have any ability. What's up with that? I want to write songs and sing and have music in every part of my life. You want to hide away from it."

"This isn't about music," Destiny told her. She could feel her sister's pain, her confusion, and didn't know what to do about it. Kipling had been right. Starr had been delivered to her a nearly grown person. Whatever was going on, Destiny was only part of the problem. But she had to be all-in for the solution. "It's about us."

"There's no *us*," Starr snapped.

"I'd like there to be. You're my sister, and I want us to be a family."

"Until school starts. Then you want me to go to boarding school. Well, I'm not. Not ever. And you can't make me. I'll just run away and live on the streets until I'm old enough to get my trust fund money. I can do it, too. I can go to where you can't find me."

Not if today was any indication, Destiny thought with irritation. Starr was fifteen and didn't know how to take care of herself, let alone survive on the streets. What if she *had* gotten on the bus and had disappeared? A thousand horrible things could have happened to her.

Images flashed through her brain, each more awful than the one before. Starr could have been beaten or raped. She could have been terrorized by some crazy person. Taken drugs, gotten sick. She could have been hurt and suffered, and she could have died.

Unexpected tears filled Destiny's eyes. Fear returned and with it determination.

"No," she said loudly, then repeated the word again. "No. You're not running away. I will not lose you. Do you hear me? I don't care what it takes, but by God we are going to make this work. I'm not giving up on you, and I'm not giving up on us. You're my sister. You're my family. Our parents are totally screwed up, and that means we're messed up, too. But so what? We have each other."

Starr stared at her. Color stained her cheeks and for a second, there was hope in her eyes. Then it bled away.

"You're just saying that so I won't run away. You don't mean it."

"I love you, child. I have from the day you were born. I was there.

Did your mama tell you that? I was the first one to hold you. I'm still holding you, and I'm never letting go."

The memories came back to her. Of being ten and standing in Grandma Nell's modest living room. She'd been scared and alone, and she'd had no idea where she belonged. Not with her parents, who had long since moved on with their lives. Not anywhere else.

But Grandma Nell had welcomed her. It was possible the other woman hadn't wanted a troubled ten-year-old thrust upon her. Even her own granddaughter. But she'd taken her in and had always made her feel special. She'd homeschooled her, loved her, and when it was time, sent her back into the world.

More tears formed. Destiny wiped them away. She knew what she had to do—knew what was right. Maybe she'd always known, but she'd been avoiding the truth. Which was wrong of her.

"I'm sorry," she said slowly. "So sorry, Starr. I do want us to be a family. You're right. I assumed you were going to go back to your boarding school in September, but only because I thought you liked it. But if you don't, then you're staying with me."

Green eyes so much like her own widened. "What about your job? You move, like, every three months. You said that was a problem."

"I know. It is, but we'll just have to figure it out." She thought about her job and the moving around and how she never settled anywhere. Maybe because settling meant the risk of belonging. She wanted relationships on her own terms. Starr had just reminded her that didn't happen very often.

She opened her mouth and shocked herself by saying, "I guess I'm going to have to quit my job and find another one where I don't have to move around. We'll have a permanent home. A house. With a yard."

Just like normal people.

Destiny held her breath and waited for the internal shriek.

Only there wasn't one. There was a bit of apprehension at the unknown but also a sense of maybe it was time. Maybe the reason she hadn't been able to find the right guy and start her family was because she was never in one place long enough. But her future plans aside, what mattered now was her sister.

"Starr, I love you. I don't think I've said that before, but I do. You—"

There was more to say, but her sister was flying toward her, tears running down her cheeks. Destiny barely had time to stand and brace herself before her sister flung herself at her and hung on as if she would never let go.

She hugged her back. As they held each other, she realized that while she didn't know how she was going to make it work, the details didn't matter. They were together. They would always be together. Starr needed her and just as important, she needed her sister.

CHAPTER THIRTEEN

Kipling watched Destiny carefully. She was different tonight. More fragile. He hadn't realized how much he took her confidence and control for granted. They were a part of her and without them, she seemed almost broken.

She sat at the far end of the sofa, her bare feet tucked under her legs. Her hair was long and loose, her skin pale.

She was beautiful simply because she was breathing, but his need to be close to her had a whole lot less to do with sexual desire and was a whole lot more about protecting. He wanted to find and slay whatever dragons taunted her. Only it wasn't that simple. She'd been shattered by something he couldn't attack or defeat. She'd been undone by her own heart.

He reached across the couple of feet separating them and touched her hand. She shifted her arm so their fingers could entwine and gave him a smile that didn't reach her eyes.

"Thanks for coming by," she said quietly. "I'm sorry I'm not better company."

"I'm not here to be entertained. I wanted to check on you."

He'd called a couple of times, then dropped by after dinner. Starr had already gone to bed. Destiny had explained the teen had been too nervous about running away to sleep much over the past couple of nights.

"You should yell at me," Destiny told him. "I deserve it."

"No, you don't."

"I do. I didn't do enough when Starr arrived. I didn't make her feel welcome or safe. I thought she was happy at her boarding school. I wanted her to go back because it would be easier for me."

He shifted closer and angled toward her. "Hey, beating yourself up doesn't fix anything."

"I hurt her." Big green eyes filled with tears. "I'm a terrible sister."

"You took her in. You gave her a home."

"A temporary one." She swallowed. "That's not good enough. I don't know why I didn't see that from the start. She needs something permanent."

Which was a problem, he thought. Given Destiny's job description. "You're quitting."

She looked at him. "How did you know?"

"It's the right thing to do. You said it. Starr needs something permanent, so you're going to provide it. What are you going to do?"

"I honestly have no idea. I'm still in shock about all of this. I can't believe she was so unhappy, and I never knew. I guess I only saw what I wanted to see. Plus, it's not like we've known each other very long. I am so in over my head."

"So get help."

One corner of her mouth turned up. "Is this you fixing things?"

He held up his free hand. "No way. You're above my pay grade by miles. Get help from someone who does know what they're doing. It's like being an athlete. You hurt something, so you get it fixed. Surgery, physical therapy, whatever it takes."

"You mean family counseling? I never thought of that." She

gave a short laugh. "With our family history, we could be an entire case study. A therapist. It's a good idea. Starr needs someone she can trust to talk to. I know she has me, but I'm sure she needs to talk *about* me to someone. And I need to be able to share my feelings."

He deliberately kept quiet—letting her work it out herself. He suspected that for most women he knew, the talking about Starr role would be handled by a girlfriend. But Destiny kept the world at bay. He understood some of the reasons. Others he could guess at. Funny how from the outside, being rich and famous seemed like a dream come true. But for those living it, the situation was anything but.

She drew in a breath. "Thanks for listening."

"Anytime."

"And for helping earlier today. I panicked. I don't get it. I'm the one who understands the search criteria. I'm the expert. But when I needed to take charge, I crumbled."

"You weren't dealing with an exercise or practice session. It was family."

She shook her head. "Grandma Nell would be so disappointed in me."

He stood and pulled her to her feet, then drew her against him. She stepped easily into his embrace. He wrapped his arms around her and breathed in the scent of her.

"She would tell you that loving someone is never wrong," he told her. "She would tell you that giving up is the only unforgivable mistake. Except she'd have a cute Southern accent."

Destiny laughed, then started to cry. He continued to hang on, rubbing her back and murmuring softly that it was going to be all right. And for reasons he didn't question, she believed him.

Destiny and Cassidy arrived at Jo's Bar for lunch. Destiny was looking forward to time with her friends. She was emotionally exhausted, and she longed for the support she knew she would

find at the table. The past forty-eight hours had been an emotional marathon. Starr had run away and returned home. They'd
agreed they were going to be a family, and Destiny had given
notice at her job.

There were dozens more decisions to be made. Were they
staying in Fool's Gold? What was she going to do with her life?
The list went on and on. But for the next hour or so, all she
wanted was to hang out with people she liked and laugh a little.
Nachos would be good, too.

She tried to remember the last time she'd felt this way about
a group of women in her life. Maybe in college, she thought.
How sad. All her refusal to connect with the people around her
had gotten her was a lonely, solitary existence. No support, no
love, no sense of belonging. What had she been thinking?

"So this is a regular thing?" Cassidy asked as they walked
into the bar.

"Sort of. Texts go out and whoever can make it shows up."
Destiny saw a couple of her friends had already claimed a large
table. "There they are."

Madeline and Felicia waved them over. Destiny introduced
Cassidy, then sat next to Madeline.

"How are you?" Madeline asked. "We are going crazy at
Paper Moon. A new delivery of wedding gowns came in. People probably think that they arrive laid out in huge trunks and
are stuffed with tissue and look fantastic. The truth is they're
shoved into impossibly small boxes and have to be hung up and
steamed. For hours." Madeline rotated her shoulders. "I hurt
everywhere. I need carbs."

Destiny leaned over and hugged her friend. "Thank you."

"For what?"

"Being normal. I needed normal today." A reminder that life
went on, and that every crisis was different. Some small, some
huge, but all demanding.

"Would ironing and steaming help you feel better? Because I have lots of that to offer."

"Say the word," Destiny told her. "And I'll be there."

Larissa joined them, along with Patience from Brew-haha. Jo took orders for drinks then explained the day's nacho special and left them to talk.

Felicia leaned toward Cassidy.

"I heard you have trained horses and dogs you're going to be bringing to town."

Patience's eyes widened. "Trained how? Like for entertainment? Because Lillie and I could totally get into that. I love the festivals, but there aren't enough performing animals." She sighed.

"We have Priscilla," Felicia said. "Although I suppose she doesn't actually do anything out of the ordinary."

"She's an elephant," Madeline said. "I think she wins by showing up."

Cassidy blinked a couple of times, as if having trouble following the conversation. "Okay," she said slowly. "Not circus animals. My horses and dogs are working animals. They help with search and rescue."

"HEROs." Patience nodded knowingly. "I love that," she sighed.

Felicia turned to her. "You're in an unusual mood today. And you've sighed several times. That's significant." Her brows drew together. "Although my statement makes no sense. A sigh is simply an involuntary or voluntary response to—"

"I'm pregnant."

The table went silent for two beats before exploding into laughter and congratulations.

Patience beamed. "I know," she said. "I'm surprised, too. Well, not surprised. We've been trying. But for a while we weren't sure we wanted more kids. I think Justice was thinking I didn't want another baby. But I do, and he does, and now we're pregnant."

Destiny added her best wishes to the conversation, even as she found herself wondering about her own situation. A couple of days ago, she would have heard the news and known she would never meet Patience's baby. That by the time he or she was born, she would have moved on. But all that had changed. Not for her seeing Patience's baby, but in the future. She was settling down. Which meant at some point she would have long-term friends. Friends who would get married and pregnant and have babies, and she would be there to be a part of all of it.

She was doing the right thing for her family. Because she wanted to. And that felt good.

Jo brought over several bottles of champagne and one glass of sparkling water garnished with lime. Everyone in the restaurant toasted Patience's good news.

Later, when they'd finished lunch, Cassidy headed back to the office she shared with Kipling while Destiny walked out with Felicia. The two women turned toward the park.

"I'm feeling especially insightful today," Felicia said. "So I'm going to ask you a question. Is everything all right? You appeared more quiet than usual at lunch."

"I'm okay. Just dealing with some family stuff."

Felicia pointed to one of the benches facing the lake. "Want to talk about it?"

Destiny started to say no, but found herself nodding instead. When they were seated, she paused, not sure where to begin.

"You know about my family," she said after a couple of seconds. "Who my parents are."

"Yes. They're country singers. I enjoy country music. It tells a story. I've learned a lot about life from country music. Your parents both have excellent musicality."

"Ah, thank you." Kind of a strange compliment, but she knew

Felicia meant well. "Starr is my half sister. We share a father. A couple of months ago, my dad's attorney contacted me."

Destiny told her about taking in Starr and how things hadn't gone well. She finished with the teen running away and how they were committed to being a family.

"I have experience with a child running away," Felicia said. "Although Carter was pretending. Still, I've never been so afraid in my life. It's not an experience I want to repeat."

"Me, either."

"I've researched teenaged behavior in an effort to handle future situations, but there doesn't seem to be any one school of thought. And many of the theories are contradictory." She shook her head. "This is why I prefer hard sciences. I want a fact to be a fact. Unwavering. People aren't like gravity."

Destiny nodded, thinking that wasn't an analogy she would have used, but it was actually true.

"Carter was thirteen when he came to live with us. He was so normal and centered in himself. I respected and admired that. He's taught me a lot about people and life. Watching Ellie's brain develop with each new experience has taught me even more about what it means to be human. What I can tell you is loving the child in your life is never wrong. That you're going to make mistakes. You can't help it. We're human. But how you deal with the mistakes makes all the difference."

"I'm getting that. I wasn't there enough for Starr. I thought sending her back to boarding school was the right thing when it was really just the easiest thing for me." Destiny hesitated, thinking of her conversation with Kipling. "I'm thinking of finding a family therapist."

"We did that," Felicia said.

"Really?"

Her friend shrugged. "Psychology is a discipline I'm ambivalent about. There are too many variables. But Gideon had been through so much, and I lacked experience in a traditional family unit, and Carter had lost his mother the year before. We needed help. Therapy brought us together. A caring but disinterested third party aided us in establishing house rules and processes that have helped us create a strong connection. I can give you her name, if you'd like."

"I would like that. Thank you."

Felicia smiled at her. "Starr is a very sweet girl. I think you're going to find a closer relationship with her very fulfilling."

"I do, too."

Later, when Destiny had returned to her office, she found herself feeling lighter. As if the weight of all she carried had been lifted somehow. She supposed, in a way, it had been. Friends were helping her carry the burden. Friends who would offer advice and be there when she needed them.

Something she'd never had before. And by choice. How foolish, she thought. Look at all she'd been missing.

Nick passed Kipling a bottle of water, then retreated behind the bar. Kipling looked around at the results of his handiwork and had to admit, he'd done a hell of a job. The Man Cave was everything he'd imagined. From the decor choices to the chalkboard menu, it was all male. While the ladies would always be welcome, this was a place where a guy could come with his buddies, get a beer and a burger and watch the game in peace.

He looked at the other men sitting around the table. He and his business partners had agreed on biweekly meetings for the first couple of months they were open. Then, once things were flowing smoothly, they would change to monthly meetings.

So far there hadn't been anything unexpected to discuss. The crowd was steady, the complaints minimal. Nick did a good job managing everything. Kipling glanced at his watch and figured he could be out of here in an hour. Which worked out well for him because he wanted to go see Destiny.

Things with her and Starr seemed to have settled down. She'd found the name of a therapist she wanted to use, and the first appointments were made. Which meant she wouldn't be as consumed with her sister. That fit in nicely with his plans. Because he still owed her an orgasm.

The problem was how to get there. Not the logistics of it. He was confident that when the time came, he could get her over the edge. His issue was more about how to get to that time, so to speak. It wasn't as if he could simply make an appointment to drop by and do the deed.

Sam Ridge walked into The Man Cave and strolled over to the table. Everyone greeted him. He sat down, and Nick brought him a soda.

"You're the last dog in," Gideon told him. "Let's get this meeting started."

Kipling leaned back in his seat and waited for the accolades to pour in. The business ran smoothly, the nightly karaoke was a hit, and it had all been his idea. He'd seen a problem, and he'd fixed it. Some days it was good to be him.

"We have a problem," Sam said.

Sam was a retired NFL kicker who worked at a local PR firm in town. He was the financial wizard of the group, so he oversaw the money part of the business.

"What's that?" Ford Hendrix asked.

"Receipts are down."

"Not possible," Kipling said. "We're busy every night."

"Less busy than we were." Sam flipped open his tablet and turned it to face the others at the large table. "We had a good opening week, but since then business is declining."

"We're not new anymore," Kipling pointed out. "But I still see a crowd here."

Josh Golden, a former champion cyclist and Tour de France winner, shook his head. "It's not anything we're doing wrong. It's Jo."

The other men nodded. Kipling frowned. "Who's Jo?"

"Jo Trellis, you know, from Jo's Bar," Sam said.

"That woman bar? No way." Kipling motioned to the room. "We have nothing in common. That place is geared to women. It's why we all talked about opening The Man Cave. To have a place to go to watch sports. One where we didn't have to deal with shopping and pink walls."

"They're mauve," Ford said, then shrugged. "It's different than pink."

"Whatever." Kipling studied his partners. "You're serious about this?"

"It's a big deal," Gideon told him. "We should have discussed this with Jo before we opened. Without her support, we're screwed."

"How do you figure?" Kipling asked. "There's enough business for both of us."

"Technically," Josh said. "But it's not that simple. We're all married, and if our wives want us supporting Jo's Bar instead of The Man Cave, that's what we'll do."

"But you all own this business. You discussed that with your wives, didn't you? They agreed?"

The men exchanged looks.

"In theory," Ford told him. "But now that it's here, Jo's not happy. Her place is a big part of their lives. She's a friend. She's always there when they talk about stuff."

Kipling felt as if he'd stepped into an alternate universe. "I don't get it. Each of you complained there was no place for a guy to go out with his friends in this town. We brainstormed ideas and came up with The Man Cave. We're equal partners. We put in money. And now you're telling me you're scared because Jo isn't happy?"

Sam nodded. "That about sums it up."

"How is that possible? You used to play football."

"What does that have to do with anything?"

★ ★ ★

By the next morning, Kipling was still pissed at his partners. They'd had a problem, and he'd fixed it. Now they were whining like little girls. Seriously, they were proving the need for a place men could go and be men. Talk about a bunch of wimps.

He grumbled the whole way up Mother Bear Road to the site where he, Cassidy and Destiny would have their first practice search.

Lucky for him, he was by himself in his truck. Cassidy had gone ahead to "get lost" in the woods. The plan was for her to head about a half mile in and wait. He and Destiny would calibrate their equipment and look for her. If they hadn't found her by eleven-thirty, she would head back in.

He pulled into the small parking lot by the meadow and saw that Destiny was already there. When he spotted her standing by her car, studying a map, he felt the tension inside him ease.

Destiny turned as he approached and parked, and when he stepped out of his truck, she smiled at him. That started a whole new kind of tension heating, but he ignored it. At least for the moment.

"Hi," she said as he approached. "Ready for our first test run?"

She looked good, he thought. More relaxed than she had been the last time he'd seen her.

"As ready as I can be. How are you?"

"Better. Starr and I are still figuring out our relationship, but it's going well." She tilted her head. "Thank you for helping me. I'm not sure how I would have gotten through it all without you."

"Glad I could help."

They stared at each other for a second.

There weren't any cars on the nearby road. The only sounds came from birds and the gentle breeze rustling the trees. He knew he was up in the mountains, but being here today didn't bug him. There wasn't any snow. Plus, having Destiny around seemed to make him feel better about everything.

His gaze settled on her mouth. It was full and free of makeup or gloss. He could count the pale freckles on her nose. When he inhaled, he caught the scent of soap and maybe a hint of her, without any other distractions.

He didn't have a plan beyond finding Cassidy, so he wasn't expecting to step forward and put his arms around Destiny. Yet when he did, he liked how she felt as she moved against him. He liked the heat of her body and the feel of her back and hips against his hands. She was strong, but soft in that way women had about them.

He went slow, wanting to give her time to adjust, to pull back if she needed. Because Destiny wasn't as experienced as he'd thought, and he was determined to make things good for her. But he also had a burning need to kiss her.

Destiny let the feeling of safeness surround her. There was something about being close to Kipling that set everything to rights. Maybe it was his determination to fix things. A characteristic that could have been annoying, but oddly wasn't. She liked how he took charge. As if he knew what to do next. Because half the time, she was faking it.

His gaze was intense, almost predatory. But he didn't move closer to try to touch her beyond holding her. Funny how just being held by him had her stomach churning. Strangled little tingles zipped through her body and made it difficult for her to catch her breath.

She had her hands on his upper arms. Slowly, she moved them to his broad shoulders. She could feel the muscles shifting under his skin.

Everything about the moment felt nice. Right. And when he finally lowered his head to press his mouth against hers, she leaned in that last little bit to help things along.

His lips were warm and firm but still tender. She liked the way they fit together. The way he moved back and forth but didn't deepen the kiss. She liked her thighs nestling against his, her breasts lightly touching his chest. She felt *treasured*. A ridiculous word, but there it was.

She moved her fingers against the cool, silky strands of his hair. He stroked the length of her back, stopping just at her hips. And still he kept their kiss chaste.

The soft pressure teased as he moved from her mouth to her jaw, then down to her neck. Once there, he nibbled gently. Goose bumps erupted as she shivered slightly. Her breasts began to ache, and she remembered how much she'd enjoyed him touching them before. That night.

They'd been naked, she thought as he shifted to the sensitive skin just behind her ear. She felt the nibbles again, followed by a quick dart of his tongue. Her breathing increased just a little, and more memories filled her mind.

How he'd looked. The feel of him on top of her. It had all been really, really nice. When he'd sucked on her nipples—that had been the best.

Heat and pressure seemed to build inside her. There were unexpected aches. Her breasts swelled and between her thighs, she felt a strange heaviness. Not pain, exactly, but a restlessness that had nothing to do with needing to sing and everything to do with the man who held her.

"Kipling," she breathed.

Before she could tell him what she wanted—not an easy task, considering she had no clue—he kissed her again.

The second she felt his lips on hers, she parted. She wanted, no, she *needed* him inside her. Needed the dance of tongue against tongue.

He didn't disappoint. He plunged into her mouth as if he required the connection as much as she. She met him stroke for stroke, straining for more. At the same time she leaned against him, wanting their bodies touching everywhere. She arched her hips and found her belly flat against an unexpected hard ridge.

For a second she was confused, and then she got it. He was aroused.

She'd done that! She'd given Kipling an erection. Elation joined passion and gave her a thrill of female power. Not sure what to do, she kissed him deeply. At the same time she rotated her hips, pressing her belly hard against him.

His hands dropped to her hips and held her in place. Fingers dug in, and she heard a low groan. She wasn't sure if it came from him or her and knew it didn't matter. The aching, heating, straining became clear in a single word. *Desire.*

She wanted Kipling. Wanted him the way they'd been together in the bar. It didn't matter that the ending had been weird and, well, disappointing. She wanted to do it again. Very much. Which made no sense.

For a second, she thought about them taking off their clothes right here, on the grass. The sun would be warm on their naked bodies. They could take more time and—

Kipling drew back. "For someone who was recently a virgin, you do pack a punch."

He was breathing hard, and his eyes seemed a little glazed. Destiny was too shocked to notice much more. Because as she watched, he was moving farther away.

"We're done?" Done with the delicious kisses and thrilling touching?

He gave her that sexy smile of his. "We're here to work. Cassidy's going to wonder why we're not looking for her."

"Oh."

Right. They had a job to do. They were on a well-traveled highway. What was wrong with her? They couldn't get naked here and do *that* on the side of the road. What was she thinking?

She had a bad feeling the problem was a lot about not thinking.

"You're right," she said, turning away to grab her equipment.

Only instead of walking, she seemed to stumble a little. As if her legs weren't working right. And now that she was paying attention, she felt flushed and disoriented. Was she getting the flu?

She spun back to face Kipling. "It's you," she told him. "You did this to me."

"Did what?"

"I don't know. Something. I'm not right."

"You're right enough for me." His expression was annoyingly self-satisfied.

Why would that be? Kipling wasn't—

She froze. "You fix things. You think there's something wrong with me." More pieces fell into place. "You want me to have an orgasm. You're trying to change my mind about sex. You want me to like it."

The last sentence was more accusation than statement. "You're drawing me in." She squared her shoulders. "It's not going to happen. I'm stronger than any biological urge."

He didn't look the least bit discouraged by her tirade. If anything, his smile widened. "Is that so?"

"Absolutely."

"You're not at risk?"

"Not even a little."

"Good. Have dinner with me Friday. At my place." When she would have spoken, he held up his hand. "Not one article of clothing will be removed. You have my word."

How disappointing.

Destiny didn't know where the thought had come from, but she ignored it. "Fine. I'll come over for dinner and you'll see. Now that I know what you're up to, I'm going to be strong. Like a rock. I have absolutely no interest in sex at all. Not with you. Not with anyone."

Kipling walked to the back of his truck and lowered the gate. He handed her a backpack.

"Famous last words," he said. "Now let's go find Cassidy."

CHAPTER FOURTEEN

"Try this," Destiny said and played the chord on her guitar. "The rhythm is off, so it's harder to follow. I asked Dad once why he wrote it that way, and he didn't have an explanation. I think he was drunk."

Starr giggled. "He used to drink a lot. I've read some stuff online about what he was like."

"Not everything you read about Dad is true," Destiny told her. "There are a lot of stories that people make up. I guess because it sells magazines or allows the teller to pretend to be close to someone like Jimmy Don Mills. There have been a couple of unauthorized biographies written about him. One of them is mostly accurate, if you want to read that."

"I'd like to."

Starr tried the chord again, this time singing along with the song.

"Good," Destiny murmured.

She hoped that focusing on the music would prevent her sister from seeing the awfulness of the conversation. No teenager should have to read a biography to learn about her father. Not when the man was still alive and more than capable of spending time with her. But that wasn't Jimmy Don's way. He was in Europe for a couple more months, and after that, he was heading to Asia. Places where he could be adored by screaming fans.

In her head she understood that he needed to feel relevant. And for all she knew, money was an issue. Their father had often lived large. He'd always been generous—she had the trust fund to prove it—and sometimes that generosity got the better of him.

"And in the night, I remember my denim promises. And think of you," she sang, joining in with her sister at the end of the song. "Good. You've been practicing."

Starr smiled. "Plus, I'm learning a lot at camp. The classes help. I'm learning to play the keyboard."

"When camp's over, we can get you an instructor in town," Destiny offered. "I'm happy to teach you what I know, but I never studied music."

Starr rested her arm on her guitar and shook her head. "I don't understand that. You're so good. You were nominated for a Grammy when you were, like, eight. You could have had a career a thousand times over. Why didn't you want to be like your parents?"

Two weeks ago Destiny would have dismissed the question or at least tried to change the subject. Now she knew that the best way to connect with her sister was through honest, caring conversation. Not that she was an expert, but two sessions of family therapy had already taught her a lot.

"Living on the road isn't anything I would enjoy," she began. "You don't get to see much of the places where you play. You perform, drive all night, then set up the next day. If you're lucky, you have a few hours to walk around town."

"How did you go to school?"

"If I was on the road with my parents, I didn't. Or they brought along a tutor. Sometimes they left me at home, and then I went to regular classes."

Starr picked out a few notes on her guitar. "But you never

belonged, right? Living like that, it would have been hard to make friends."

"It was."

"Do you think that's why you move around now? Because you don't know how to be in one place?"

An unexpected and insightful question, Destiny thought. "I don't know," she admitted. "Maybe I've been reliving what I know."

Starr glanced at her then looked away. "Do you get lonely?"

"Sometimes. When I do, I play music or write a song. It's different here," she admitted. "I have friends in a way I never have before. People let you in."

"I know, right?" Starr smiled. "Like at camp. I'm just one of the group. It's nice to belong."

"It is. We're going to have to figure out where we're going to live. I have my place in Austin, but it's a rental and too small for us. I haven't really had a home base in a long time. I meant what I said. I've given notice with my company. We'll get a house or something."

Starr stared at her. "You're really quitting?"

"Of course. You need to be settled. High school is a really important time."

"You didn't go to high school."

"I know, and sometimes I think it would have been good for me. A rite of passage, so to speak." She shrugged. "We don't have to decide right away. You can think about it."

"What if I want to stay here? In Fool's Gold." Starr bit her lower lip then spoke in a rush. "We both have friends here, right? And the schools are really good. We like the town, and you're dating Kipling, so that could work out."

Her tone was hopeful, her eyes huge. Destiny drew in a breath. Stay. She'd never stayed anywhere before and even after realizing she would need to have a permanent home for Starr, it had all been more theoretical than reality.

There were pluses to staying, she thought. As Starr had pointed out, they had friends. A community. She liked what she knew about the town. It was big enough to have things to do but not so large that they couldn't belong. They could find a cute house—maybe one of the older ones in an established neighborhood. Fix it up together. Not that she knew anything about remodeling, but they could learn together.

As for Kipling, they weren't dating. They were friends. And they'd had sex. And she was having dinner at his house. But that wasn't dating, was it? Because he was not part of her sensible plan. There was no way Kipling was interested in a sexless marriage and to be honest, around him, she didn't want one, either. So how could they have a meeting of the minds with all those hormones getting in the way? Not that he was asking or anything. They were friends. It wasn't love or anything close to love.

"Destiny?"

"Sorry." She shook her head in an attempt to clear her head. "Fool's Gold works," she told her sister. "I'm happy to stay if that's what you want."

"Really?" Starr put down her guitar and threw herself at Destiny. They hugged, then Starr bounced back to her cushion and grinned. "That is so cool. Because I've been thinking I want to start a band."

"What?"

"A girl band. Guys make everything complicated. We'll play music and write songs, and it's gonna be great."

Destiny fought the beginnings of a headache. "I don't know what to say," she admitted.

Starr laughed. "You'll get used to the idea. In the meantime, I need to start writing songs, and I don't know how. How do you do it?"

Destiny was still caught up in the *girl band* comment, and it was hard to switch gears. She decided that her concerns, aka terrors, about Starr being in a band were probably best left for a family therapy session and instead told her sister, "Wait right here."

She walked to her bedroom and collected her battered notebook from her nightstand, then returned to the living room.

"This is how I do it," she told her sister as she sat next to her. "I'm old-school. If you want to try working on the keyboard directly, there are a lot of programs that can help you with that. I write the lyrics first, then find the melody. Sometimes they come together, but not often."

She flipped through the pages until she found her favorite song in progress.

"This is what I'm working on. It's close, but not right yet."

Starr leaned over Destiny's shoulder. "'We can't even trust, and we don't know how to live,'" she read, then picked up her guitar and played a couple of chords. "What did you have in mind?"

"I don't know." Destiny strummed with her then flipped the page. "Here's the melody I've been playing with. Can you read the music?"

Starr looked at the notes then played them on her guitar. Destiny closed her eyes and listened. After a couple of seconds she realized what was missing.

"How about this?" she asked, changing one of the chords and flipping back to the lyrics. *"From across the room, the distance is clear. I see you through the heartbreak, you see me through the fear."*

Starr nodded and joined in. *"The time we spend together, the life that we could find. You could be my best regret, I could be your peace of mind."*

Her sister stopped. "Did you mean this as a romantic ballad? Because, in a way, it's sort of about us."

Destiny glanced at the page. "I didn't see that before, but you're right."

Starr flushed, then glanced down at the page. "What if you change the end to this?"

Two hours later, they'd finished the song. Destiny ordered

a pizza, then sat next to Starr while they waited for the delivery. She had her tablet set up with the external microphone for them to record their final version. When they were done, Destiny laughed.

"We have a hit."

"You think? I didn't help much. It's your song."

"It's our song," Destiny corrected. "You're good at collaborating. We should do this again."

"I'd like that."

Kipling took the steaks out of the fridge and set them on the counter. Destiny was due over any minute, and he wanted to give the steaks an hour or so to warm up before he put them on the grill.

He had the fixings for salad. She'd told him she would bring a potato dish, along with dessert.

He still wasn't sure how the evening was going to go. While seduction was on his mind, he'd made a promise not to remove any clothing. He grinned as he walked toward the living room. Not that keeping her dressed would get in the way of seducing her. Despite his embarrassing first performance with her, he had skills.

But tonight was about more than that. Because the truth was, he liked being with her. Just talking. Or laughing. She was interesting and funny, and when he was around her, the world was a better place.

The doorbell chimed right on time. He opened the front door to find Destiny holding two glass dishes, both covered. One was a bowl and the other rectangular. Although he was a lot more interested in the woman carrying them than any contents.

"Hi," she said, her smile just a little tentative.

"Come on in."

He stepped back to let her enter, then took the large bowl from her. "What did you bring?"

"Roasted Potato Salad and S'mores Bars. Did you know there's a Fool's Gold Cookbook? I found it at Morgan's Books the other day, and I've already made a couple of recipes. They're really good."

She was nervous. He sensed it in the speed of her words and the way she kept looking at him then glancing away. He liked that she was a little off guard. It evened things up. Because looking at her left him damned close to speechless.

She'd traded in her usual jeans or cargo pants and T-shirt for a strappy summer dress. It was fitted to the waist then flared out to just above her knees. The pale green color was pretty against her skin.

Her hair was loose and wavy, and she'd put on a little makeup for the evening. All good signs in his book. While the "d" word had never been used, Destiny was acting like this was a date.

They walked into the kitchen. She put down her dish. He slid the potato salad into the refrigerator then turned to face her. She'd set her dessert on the counter.

He moved close, took her hands in his, then leaned in and kissed her lightly on the lips.

"You look beautiful," he murmured against her mouth.

"Thank you."

"Tonight is going to be fun."

"I hope so."

He flashed her a smile. "Trust me."

She met his gaze. "I do. I trust you, Kipling."

He'd been with a lot of women over the years. When he'd been young, he'd taken advantage of all the invitations thrown his way. As he'd gotten older, he'd been more interested in quality than volume, but women had always been available.

He'd been charmed, blown away and knocked sideways by different women, but he couldn't remember any of them giving him such a kick to the gut with a handful of words.

He wanted to tell her that she was right to trust him. That

he would protect her, be there to take care of things. Only they were having dinner, not getting married. It was the town, he told himself. Or the way she looked in her dress. Or how big her eyes got when she looked at him.

"Lemonade okay?" he asked.

"Lemonade?"

He held in a grin. "You were expecting something else?" Because wine was a lot more traditional. But he hadn't wanted her worrying about the evening and how it would progress. Not serving alcohol went a long way toward allowing her to relax.

He stepped back and poured them each a glass, then led the way out onto the patio.

The barbecue was at the far end. There were a couple of lounge chairs by the back door. She took one, and he settled in the other. They clinked glasses.

"How's Starr?" he asked.

"Better. We've had a few therapy sessions." She smiled. "It's not like I thought."

"You're not lying on a sofa, talking about your feelings?"

She laughed. "No. We sit upright and talk about problems, then the therapist offers really practical suggestions on how to approach them. Starr is going to have chores she has to do every week and get an allowance. We've made a list of house rules and punishments." There was wonder in her voice.

"Is that good?"

"It's strange, but yes, I think it's good. Normal teenage responsibilities. Starr has consistency. We both know what's expected and what the consequences are if she breaks a rule. So I don't have to worry about being the bad guy. We've negotiated everything in advance, so she's a part of the decision-making process."

He thought about how things had been when he'd been a kid. How his father would lash out for no apparent reason, and the consequences were often destructive.

"My parents could have used a system like that," she continued. "There weren't any rules. What I could and couldn't do changed from day to day. A lot of my friends were envious, but it wasn't as fun as it sounded."

"You never knew if you were okay," he said.

"You're right. I don't want that for Starr. I want her to feel safe." She turned toward him. "You left home when you were pretty young, right? To ski?"

"Uh-huh. I lived with my coach and his family, and there were lots of rules. Breaking them was not an option."

"Like what?"

"Everything from keeping up with my schoolwork to exercising to what I ate to getting enough sleep. I had to be in peak shape to compete." He winked. "My body is a temple."

She laughed. "Of course it is." Her mouth twitched. "I was going to make a vestal-virgin joke, but that's probably not a good idea."

"It is if you want to talk about it."

"Vestal virgins? Not really."

"Your virginity."

She sipped her lemonade. "Not my favorite topic."

Nor his, but there were things to be said. "I'm sorry I hurt you."

She turned to him. "You didn't. I mean it hurt a little, but it wasn't a big deal. The pain." She sighed. "Now that I'm learning how to be in a family unit, I can see that you were right before. When you said I should have told you. I wasn't thinking straight, so that was part of it. And the other part is…" She hesitated. "I wasn't embarrassed exactly. But I knew being a virgin at my age made me different. Of course, a lot of things make me different."

She looked away as she spoke. As if unsure about his reaction to what she was saying.

"Why would you worry about that? You're beautiful, talented, caring. Why would you think you don't fit in?"

"I didn't exactly have a normal childhood. I don't play well with others."

Several things occurred to him at the same time. First, she'd totally ignored his compliments. Because she wouldn't believe them? Had the little girl shone less brightly than her famous parents? Second, he thought she played just fine with others. Especially with him. And he'd like to have a lot more playtime. But that wasn't what they were talking about.

"Do you want to play with others?" he asked. "Your no-sex rule is pretty extreme."

"I know. It's just the things I saw. People make really bad decisions because of sex. They do things that aren't rational or right. Avoiding the whole problem seemed the best solution."

"But for every person who acts out, there are thousands who manage to have a sexual life and act responsibly. It's like saying you've seen one kid have a tantrum in the grocery store and you didn't like it so you're not going to have children."

"What is it about men and logic?" she asked, smiling at him.

"Go with your strength."

"I still think sex is the root of all evil."

"You know it's not," he said gently. "People act badly. Sex is just the delivery system."

"Is this you trying to seduce me?"

He chuckled. "No. When I seduce you, there won't be any question about what's going on."

"I plan to resist."

He forced himself not to react when every part of him wanted to celebrate the victory. Because resisting wasn't anything like saying no. She hadn't asked him *not* to seduce her. Which meant she wanted him to. At least on some level.

"You're a complicated woman," he told her.

"Is that good or bad?"

"It's excellent."

★ ★ ★

The evening went by quickly. Starr was spending the night with Abby, so Destiny didn't have to watch the clock. Still, she was surprised to find that by the time they'd finished dinner and dessert, it was after eleven. She'd arrived at six. How on earth had it already been five hours?

Kipling was easy to talk to, but still. Shouldn't they have run out of things to say? Apparently not, she thought as she reluctantly put her napkin on the table.

"It's late. I should go."

She watched him as she spoke, hoping he would tell her to stay. Or get that sexy, predatory look and pull her into his arms. Instead he glanced at the clock, then nodded.

"I'll walk you home."

"Uh, thanks."

Disappointment surprised her with its intensity. So much for his plans to seduce her, she thought as she stood and carried her plate to the kitchen. Of course he'd promised nothing would happen tonight, and he'd been telling the truth. He was a man of his word. That was a good thing. Only she couldn't help wishing he'd been just a little bad.

"Don't worry about the kitchen," he told her. "I'll clean up when I get back."

He led the way to the front door. She reluctantly followed. They stepped out into the night.

The sun had set a few hours before, but the evening had yet to cool off. Heat radiated from the sidewalks and streets, giving off that "it's summer" kind of warmth. The air smelled of cut grass and blooming flowers. Most of the houses were dark. She could hear crickets and her own breathing, but little else.

Kipling walked next to her. Close enough that they were obviously together, but not so close that they touched. She found herself wanting to move closer, to have her arm brush his. Which was confusing. What had happened to her sensible plan with a sensible man and a meeting of the minds kind of relationship? In something like that, there was no need for arm brushing. And yet that was what she wanted.

And kissing, she thought wistfully. A little kissing would be nice. With tongue. And maybe a bit of groping. Because she missed the feel of his hands on her breasts. And his mouth. She would like to feel that again.

"The stars are pretty," she said in an effort to distract herself from her wayward thought. "I like that you can see them here."

"Me, too. I miss the stars when I'm in a big city."

Because he would have seen them when he was in the mountains.

Funny how she never thought of Kipling's previous life. He had a slight limp and a few scars, but otherwise could have been anyone.

"Do you miss it?" she asked without thinking. "Skiing?"

"Every day."

She glanced at him. "Because it wasn't your choice to be done?"

"Some, and because I can't go back. I could probably make my way down a mountain if I had to, but it wouldn't be pretty. I'd have to go slow, not take risks."

He'd lost a part of who he'd been. She'd never considered that. Not just the fame and the accolades, but the very essence of what made him who he was. It would be as if she couldn't sing again or appreciate music.

"I'm sorry."

One shoulder raised and lowered. "I deal."

"More than that. You've made a whole new life for yourself. It's impressive."

They'd reached her house. He walked her to the porch, then turned to face her. "Don't make me into a hero. I'm just some guy, getting by. There are real heroes out there. Pay attention to them."

Words designed to make her admire him more, she thought, stepping closer and anticipating their good-night kiss. She hoped he would take his time and linger. That he would tease before he brushed his tongue against hers. That there would be—

He leaned in and lightly kissed her cheek. "Thanks for a great evening."

She stared at him. "Um, sure. I had a good time."

She waited.

He smiled.

And then he walked away.

Destiny scrolled through the screen on her computer because the alternative was throwing it across the room. And it was never a good idea to take out personal emotion on a defenseless, innocent machine. Especially not one as expensive as her computer. But she wanted to throw something.

Kipling hadn't kissed her. There'd been no tongue, no bodies straining. What happened to seducing her? Had he changed his mind? Decided she wasn't worth the trouble? Why was he acting like that? She wanted to stomp her foot. And maybe pout.

Instead, she took a deep breath, then another and returned her attention to the screen in front of her. Information from the practice search was displayed. She could adjust updates from minute-to-minute to hourly. She and Kipling had found Cassidy in forty minutes. Not record-breaking, but still a good first try. Next time they would make the search more difficult, and Cassidy would be a searcher. Their third or fourth simulation would include volunteers.

They were on schedule, and her training would end in another four or five weeks. Normally, she would already be discussing her next assignment. But not this time. She and Starr were staying in Fool's Gold, and Destiny honestly had no idea what she was going to do with herself.

She had a computer science degree, but wasn't excited about

pursuing another job in the field. She wasn't a tech kind of person. What she'd liked about her facilitating work was helping people. But it wasn't like she had a bunch of transferable skills.

She knew she was very lucky. Money wasn't an issue. Thanks to her trust fund, she could live frugally without working. Mostly because, except for paying for her college education, she'd never touched a dime of it.

But she wasn't going to be comfortable just sitting around. And living frugally while raising a teenager didn't seem possible. She wanted to get a house with Starr, and a mortgage required a job.

Still, she had time on her side. There was a local employment agency in town. She could go there and take those tests that tell you what you're good at. She doubted dabbling at songwriting and singing karaoke would offer much in the way of job opportunities.

She returned her attention to the screen and continued to study the results of their first practice search. She wanted to get through the report before heading home. She'd nearly finished when Cassidy walked into her office and sat in her visitor's chair.

"This is the weirdest place ever," the blonde announced.

"Good weird or bad weird?"

"Mostly good. I just took an exercise class at CDS."

Destiny frowned. "Where's that?"

"The bodyguard school."

"Oh, right. I've heard about it. How was the class? One of my friends swears by what they do there."

"It was a killer. The instructor is Consuelo Hendrix. She's tiny but tough. This is only my second class, but after the last one, I hurt in places that I didn't know had muscles."

"Which you loved," Destiny said.

Cassidy grinned. "You know it. Anyway, I signed up for twice-a-week classes. When I went today, her husband, Kent, was participating, but there was something about the way he was watching her. It was very strange."

"He's not a serial killer," Destiny told her. "He's in the middle of a bet with his brother."

"What? That he can survive one of her classes?"

"Nothing that simple. The guys have a competition about who can get his wife pregnant first. I don't think Consuelo and Isabel know about it. My guess is Kent was keeping an eye on her. In case she is pregnant."

Cassidy blinked. "What did he think he could do? She's teaching a class. Someone in as good a shape as her should be fine continuing with her regular routine. Unless there's a problem. And he doesn't even know if she's pregnant yet."

"I know. I'm simply sharing what I've been told."

Cassidy leaned back in her chair and groaned. "Weirdest little town ever."

Before Destiny could respond, her cell phone rang. She looked at the screen and saw the caller ID.

"Hey, Starr," she said by way of greeting. "You beat me home."

"I didn't stay to practice. Um, I know you usually work until five, but, uh, someone stopped by the house."

Destiny's first thought was that the person in question was Kipling. Or maybe that was wishful thinking. Because she would very much like to spend the evening with him. Only her sister's tone was more cautious than Kipling warranted, and she would have just said his name. "Who?"

Starr cleared her throat. "Your mom."

CHAPTER FIFTEEN

Lacey Mills had to be in her late forties, but she looked thirty-five and dressed like what Kipling imagined would be appropriate for a beauty queen from the 1960s. With her big hair, tight dresses and high heels, she made Dolly Parton look prim. Lacey's hair was red instead of platinum, but it was still big. All poufy, with lots of curls. What was that saying? The bigger the hair, the closer to God? Kipling figured Lacey and the Almighty were on a chummy basis.

He'd stopped by Destiny's office on the pretense of asking about the program, but really to see her and to gauge her reaction to their date. Or rather how the date had ended. Because he'd been pretty sure she'd expected a little action. Which was exactly what he wanted. Better that she be anticipating than he be pushing. That way, when he made his move, she would be receptive.

But instead of leaping to greet him, she'd been wide-eyed and pale as she'd hung up her cell phone. Her announcement that her mother had arrived unexpectedly had stirred both his curiosity and his protective instinct. He'd offered to be the fourth person at the table for dinner, and she'd instantly accepted.

Now he found himself mixing drinks in Destiny's small kitchen while Starr hovered next to him, obviously not sure if she should join the other women in the living room or not.

"She's really famous," Starr whispered. "And pretty. I mean, like, she's pretty on TV and stuff, but I wasn't sure what she'd look like in person. She's just as pretty. But small. I thought she'd be taller. And it's interesting that she and my dad both have red hair. That's unusual."

Lacey was a few inches shorter than her daughter. They shared their beautiful green eyes and red hair, although he suspected that Lacey's golden highlights were store-bought.

"Did you see her makeup?" Starr asked, her voice still low. "I wonder if she'd teach me how to do mine."

"I'm sure she'd like to show you a few things," he said as he added both sweet and dry vermouth to the ice and gin in the shaker.

Lacey had been very clear with her order.

"A gin martini, two kinds of vermouth and cold. I need it cold."

She'd smiled at him, a practiced, seductive smile he was sure had brought stronger men than him to their collective knees. But he was immune. Sure Lacey was beautiful and, despite Starr's disappointment in her height, larger than life, but his attentions had settled elsewhere.

"The liquor's in the freezer," Destiny had told him.

"I'll figure it out."

Now he shook the mixture and wondered what Destiny was thinking. From what she'd told him, she had a complicated relationship with her parents.

"I need olives," he told Starr. "They're probably in the refrigerator."

She checked inside and found a small jar of pimento-filled olives. He poured the martinis, added an olive, then poured a soda over ice for Starr, Destiny and himself. He wasn't sure drinking around Destiny's mother was a good idea, and Destiny had requested soda.

"Do I get an olive?" Starr asked with a quick smile.

"Do you want one?"

She wrinkled her nose. "Not really."

She found a tray, and he put all the drinks on it then carried it back to the living room. Lacey took her martini, closed her eyes and sipped.

"Perfect," she drawled. "And cold. Aren't you clever?"

"I've always been good with martinis." He handed Destiny and Starr their drinks before settling on the end of the sofa.

"I'm sure you're good with many things," Lacey told him.

He ignored any innuendo in the comment. He had a feeling that flirting was as automatic as breathing for the country singer.

"Did you drive in?" he asked.

"To town?" Lacey asked. "Goodness, no. I took my jet to the local airport." She turned to her daughter. "I have to say, I like this town a lot. It's so pretty. And the festivals."

"How do you know about the festivals, Mom?" Destiny asked.

"I read about them on the plane. I like to know about where you're living." She smiled at Kipling. "My little girl moves around all the time. A job here, a job there. Some places are nice, but others..." She shuddered.

Her attention shifted to Starr. "Now you're just the prettiest thing! I'm sorry about your mama. You're staying with Destiny now?"

Starr swallowed. "Um, yes, ma'am."

"She's steady. You listen to her, you hear me? Destiny's always been a rock."

"Yes, ma'am."

A rock? Kipling thought of Destiny singing onstage at The Man Cave. How she'd poured all her emotions into her music. She was calm on the outside, but underneath the facade was plenty of passion. He wondered how much of her rocklike nature was learned because she'd had to be the adult in the room. So far Lacey had been plenty nice, but she didn't strike him as someone overly interested in anyone's viewpoint but her own.

Lacey turned her attention to him. "Kipling, you seem familiar to me. Why is that?"

"I was an Olympic skier."

Her brows rose. "That's right! At Sochi. G-Force." She smiled. "You won gold medals and then you had a crash. You seem to be getting around all right. Good for you." She turned to her daughter. "You found someone famous. That makes me so happy. People respect a man with a little danger in his past. Now that we're all caught up, I know you want to hear about my new album. It's being released in the fall. My label wanted me to do my greatest hits but I said no. I want to cover some wonderful old songs. We argued, but I won."

"I'm sure you always do," Kipling said.

Lacey fluttered her lashes. "Why yes, I do."

"She's not what I expected," Starr whispered, later that night.

Destiny sat on her sister's bed. "She never is. My mom is more like a tornado than a person. It's best to keep an eye on how she's tracking and then get out of the way."

Starr laughed. "She's nice, but a little scary."

"Same thing."

Starr pulled her knees up to her chest and wrapped her arms around her legs. "How long is she staying?"

"A couple of days. She usually visits when I'm on assignment." Often without warning. Destiny had learned to expect the visits, but not plan for them. Lacey had her own schedule and rules. She'd taken over Destiny's room without bothering to ask if that was okay, yet would probably get up and make them all breakfast.

"You can talk to her about the business if you'd like," Destiny said. "She loves to talk about her past and how things have changed in the music industry. You'll learn a lot from her."

"You won't be mad?"

"No. Not at all."

Starr would keep her mother distracted, and that was a good thing. Because when left alone for too long, Lacey came up with crazy plans. Like the time she'd tried to talk Destiny into going on tour with her.

"Oh, and talk to her about songwriting. She's good, and she loves to write with other people."

Starr's mouth dropped open. "Really? You think she'd do that with me?"

"Yes."

"Why don't you write with her?"

"We end up fighting too much."

And every songwriting session ended with Lacey telling her that she'd wasted her life and her talent. That she would never feel fulfilled if she didn't honor her gifts. Which wasn't ever anything Destiny wanted to talk about.

Funny how Kipling had said nearly the same thing, only that had been easier to hear. Maybe because of what he'd been through. And because she trusted him. He couldn't do what he most loved because of the accident. She knew that was hard for him, but he'd accepted the inevitable and got on with his life.

She'd tried to do the same. At least the getting on with her life part.

"Lacey wants me to be like her," she added. "I guess it's a mom thing. But it's never going to happen."

Starr nodded, then rested her chin on her knees. "My mom used to say I was just like her. Only I never wanted to be. You know, the drugs and everything. I don't want that."

"Do you worry about it?" Destiny asked.

"I don't know. Sometimes. I don't want to take drugs and

have that be the only thing that's important. I want to sing and write music. I want to be proud of myself."

Destiny shifted so she could pull her close. "I hope you already are. You're a great person, and I'm proud you're my sister."

"Thanks. I love you, too."

Her sister said something else, but Destiny only nodded. She needed a second to let the words sink in. Because they made everything worth it. They were sisters of the heart, and that was never going to change.

Destiny knew the foolishness of avoiding the inevitable, so two nights later she dropped Starr off at Abby's, swung by Angelo's for takeout then returned home to spend an evening alone with her mother.

Lacey sat crossed-legged on the living room floor with the contents of several shopping bags spread out around her. Her hair was loose, her shirt embellished and her jeans tight. Lacey had always understood the importance of being true to herself.

"No store went untouched," Destiny said as she took in the Fool's Gold T-shirts, key chains and mugs, along with stacks of clothing, shoes and books.

Lacey laughed and reached for her martini. "I like to support the local economy. There's a clothing store called Paper Moon with some pretty snazzy things. I spent a fortune there. The rest of it is just for fun." She sniffed. "That smells wonderful. What did you bring us?"

"Lasagna and garlic bread. A salad so we can pretend we're being healthy."

"You're my favorite oldest child. Did you know that?"

Lacey rose gracefully, the martini she held not spilling a drop. She crossed to Destiny and hugged her tight, then released her and went to the kitchen.

"When does Starr get home?"

"She's staying with a friend. It's just us tonight."

Her mother laughed. "My favorite way to spend an evening. You're so sweet to me, hon. I'm starving and craving some girl time."

Destiny set the bag of takeout on the counter, then washed her hands before setting the table.

"Want one?" her mother asked, pulling a pitcher of martinis out of the refrigerator.

"No, thanks."

While Lacey was visiting, Destiny would drink water. Because she knew her mother was imbibing for two. Or possibly twenty. She supposed she had the same concerns that Starr did. There were parts of her mother's personality she didn't want to embrace, although Destiny knew she was just as guilty of using alcohol as a crutch. That night at The Man Cave, she'd needed the Long Island Iced Tea to allow herself to perform. Something she should probably discuss with her therapist.

Her mother would tell her that singing in front of an audience was in her blood. It wasn't that she got nervous, she thought as she put plates and flatware on the table then collected the food. It was more about giving herself permission.

Lacey sat down, and Destiny passed her the lasagna. She inhaled deeply. "Smells delicious. Remember when I used to make you mac and cheese? From a box, of course. That's as much as I could cook. I wasn't a traditional mother."

"You wouldn't be Lacey Mills if you were."

"And I want to be Lacey Mills."

"My mom, the superstar," Destiny murmured, thinking how her parents had both awed and frustrated her when she'd been little. She supposed they still did.

On the other hand, she'd gone in a completely different direction, basically turning her back on their lifestyles. They'd both made it clear they wanted her to go into the family business, and she hadn't.

"Are you disappointed in me?" Destiny asked before she could stop herself. Because Lacey would be nothing if not honest.

"What? No. Don't be silly. You're my daughter, Destiny. I love you."

"I love you, too, Mom. But that's not what I asked. I'm not like you."

Her mother put down her fork. "If you're talking about the music, then I would have liked you to be more like me. We could have toured together. We would have had so much fun. It gets lonely so it's nice to have a friend along. But, honey, you have to do what's right for you."

Lacey picked up her martini and took a sip. "It's our fault. I see that now. When you were little, we dragged you all over the place. Some children would have thrived in the chaos, but not you. You always liked a routine. Being settled. When my mama told me she was going to take you, well, I cried for a week. But I knew it was the right thing to do."

Lacey's green eyes filled with tears. "I missed you, but I did what was best for you. I hope you know that."

"I do."

"And now you've taken in Starr. It's all about taking care of family."

"You don't mind that she's Daddy's daughter with someone else?"

"What? No." Lacey took a bite of lasagna. "Jimmy Don was never meant to be with just one woman. We were young and in love, and then you came along. A magical time. But our marriage never would have lasted. We're too much alike. People in love should complete each other. Complement each other."

"Are you in love?" Destiny asked.

"Not right now, but I hope to be again." Her mother sighed. "It's the best feeling in the world. Finding the one. Although I've never believed in forever, as you know."

Destiny picked at her food. "Don't you want that, Mama? Someone you can count on to always be there."

"Maybe. But then I'd have to give up all the others. And there are plenty." Lacey grinned, then her smile faded. "I don't want you to worry about how I feel about you. You're a joy to me. I hope you'll find that joy with your sister. Did you adopt Starr?"

"I'm her legal guardian."

"Maybe I should adopt. Aren't there lots of orphans running around?"

There it was, Destiny thought, fighting irritation. The shift that would make her crazy. It would be followed by sharp words and a fight and the sense of being stuck in a never-ending loop of emotional conflict. Talk about exhausting.

"I'd need two," Lacey mused. "So they could keep each other company."

"We're talking about children, not puppies," Destiny said calmly.

"The same principles apply."

"You can't mean that."

"There are differences, I suppose," Lacey allowed. "You can't take children to the pound if they get on your nerves." Lacey smiled. "Although I do think I would look especially adorable with a couple of babies at my feet."

"You're always looking for distractions, Mama. What's so bad about being you that you're always looking to be someone else?"

Lacey froze, her glass halfway to her mouth. She stood suddenly and nearly ran to the living room. Seconds later she was back, her cell phone in her hand.

"Say that again," she ordered. "What you just said."

"That you distract yourself with ridiculous schemes that never—"

"No, that's not it. I need the exact sentence. Or rather you do. There's a song in that energy, Destiny. Tell me what you said, and I'll email you the MP3 file of it."

Destiny considered banging her head against the table but figured there was no point. Her mother would never change.

"What's so bad about being you that you're always looking to be someone else."

Lacey tapped on her phone. "Got it. God, you're talented! I've always known that." She picked up her martini. "You should talk to Richard."

"I don't think so." Destiny had nothing to say to her mother's business manager.

"He knows people."

"We all know people."

"Oh, you know what I mean! You want to talk about me trying to be someone else? Let's talk about you denying who you are. I'm not disappointed in you, Destiny, but I am worried. One day you're going to wake up and realize you've been avoiding the truth about who you are. The sooner that happens, the sooner you honor your talent, the happier you're going to be. What does your young man say about all this?"

She had to mean Kipling. Destiny thought about telling her he wasn't her young man, only Lacey wouldn't believe her, and even Destiny wasn't quite sure if it was true or not. They were friends and they'd had sex and when she was around him...

"You have it bad," her mother teased. "You have the look in your eyes. Isn't it nice to be in love?"

"I'm not in love with him. I like him. He's a good man, and I can count on him."

"How's the sex?" Lacey held up a hand. "Never mind. I'm your mother. It's an awkward question, and I take it back. If my mama had asked that about Jimmy Don, I would have plumb died right there. For what it's worth, I like him, too. He's a handsome devil."

Lacey leaned back in her chair and laughed. "You two could certainly produce some pretty babies." Her eyes widened. "That's it, Destiny! That's what I need. Grandbabies. Then I get all the fun and none of the work. You get on that right away. You hear me?"

"Yes, ma'am."

The words came automatically, but Destiny's brain had hopped three subjects and taken a sharp left. Babies. Babies came from sex. She'd had sex with Kipling, and they hadn't used any protection.

None of which would have bothered her because it was her first time, and surely the body would protect her or something. Only it had been over three weeks, and she hadn't gotten her period yet. Math might not be her strongest subject, but even she could add up one night of doing it, three weeks of being late and get that they might very well make a baby.

Kipling looked up from his paperwork. "You could have come to me for the money, Shelby. I would have given it to you."

Shelby covered her face with her hands. "Don't make me feel guilty for asking. I wanted to do this myself. I wanted to stand on my own." She dropped her hands and glared at him. "I mean it, Kipling. You don't get to say how I live my life."

While he understood her point, he couldn't get past the fact that they were family. Of course he would give his sister the money to buy into the bakery. But she hadn't asked. Instead, she'd gone to the bank for a loan.

"If they hadn't needed someone to cosign, would you have told me about this?" he asked.

She hesitated just long enough for him to get his answer.

"I only want what's best for you," he told her as he grabbed the pen and scrawled his name.

"Kip, don't be mad. I'm sorry. I appreciate all that you do for me. It's just sometimes I want to be my own person without having to always be asking you for things. Can you understand that?"

"Sure." He handed her the paperwork.

She took it but didn't leave. "You're upset."

"I'm not the bad guy. I haven't done anything wrong. I want to help you in every way I can. If that means cosigning your loan, then I've done it. Go buy into the bakery."

"You still love me?"

Some of his hurt and anger faded. "Shelby, you're my sister. I'll always love you, no matter what. I signed the paperwork, didn't I?" Because the act was always more important than the words.

"I love you, too. Thanks for doing this."

He nodded, and she left.

Kipling settled back at his desk but couldn't seem to get interested in the spreadsheet on his computer. He sort of understood what his sister had told him, but he still thought she should have come to him rather than a bank. He also thought she was making a rash decision about buying into the bakery so soon after moving to Fool's Gold, which he'd already told her. It was probably the reason she'd gone to the bank in the first place.

He closed the spreadsheet and clicked on his email. He had one from Gideon saying he was getting lots of pushback from women on The Man Cave. Something else Kipling didn't want to think about. He saved the email then stood and paced restlessly in his office.

There were too many things going on, he thought. Problems he couldn't fix. The issue with The Man Cave and Jo's Bar frustrated him. There'd been a need. He'd filled the need, and now he was the one in the wrong.

Couldn't the men in this town stand up to their wives and girlfriends? There was plenty of business for both locations. Tourists would have options on where to go. Why was that bad?

As for Shelby—not much he could do there. He'd done his best, and now she had to make her own decisions. And live with the consequences. Because if he was right and it all went—

The door to his office opened, and Destiny walked in. Kipling immediately relaxed. Not only was she a nice distraction from all the things he couldn't control, being around her grounded him, too. Something he couldn't explain but was willing to accept.

"Hey," he began, then paused.

She was upset. He could see it in her eyes. Emotions churned. She was flushed and tense. He crossed to her.

"What's wrong? How can I help?" Fixing her problem would go a long way to make them both feel better.

She stared at him and laughed. Only the sound was more strained than happy.

"You've already done enough," she said. "Did you know my body doesn't care that I was a virgin? I looked it up online. Something I should have done before. But I figured I got a free pass. Just one. Or maybe some kind of protection from my hymen or something. But, no. There's nothing."

She wasn't scaring him exactly, but she sure wasn't herself. The emotions he'd long suspected she buried had finally broken through, and it wasn't the thrillfest he'd been hoping for.

"Destiny," he said calmly. "Catch your breath and then tell me what's going on."

"I'm breathing fine." She exhaled to demonstrate. "See. This is me breathing. As for what's going on, nothing new. Nothing that hasn't been going on for weeks now. I'm pregnant. I saved myself all these years because I wasn't sure. Because I wanted to make a rational decision. I wasn't going to become my parents who, by the way, actually *did* wait until they were married to have sex and get pregnant. My mom told me this morning. Who knew?"

Pregnant? Destiny was having a baby? His baby? Kipling took in the news. Mentally, he turned it over in his mind, not sure how he felt about it. He liked kids. He'd been hoping to have kids. He could make sure he was always there to fix things for a kid. Yeah, he could do this. A child. He felt himself start to grin. A mini G-Force.

"I don't get it," she said, her voice rising just a little. "There should be a one-time protection mechanism. Like a do-over. But no. Virgins get no special allowances. Instead, there are consequences. That's what gets me. I believe in consequences. I'm a huge fan. I live my life to avoid ever having to worry about them. But there we were, on the bench in the bar, doing it, and I'm pregnant."

"Are you okay?" he asked.

"No!" The word came out as a shriek.

She visibly drew in a breath. "No," she repeated more quietly. "I'm not okay. I'm just getting things together with Starr. We don't even have a permanent place to live. We've decided to stay in Fool's Gold, but it's not like I have a job lined up. Or even a plan. What am I supposed to do with my life? And now there's a baby?"

She walked to the window then turned back and glared at him. "This is so your fault. Before I met you I was a calm and rational person. Now I'm *pregnant*. And I have feelings. Like before, after our dinner? I wanted you to kiss me but you didn't, and I was upset. What's with that? I've gone my whole life not needing to be kissed. Things are a whole lot more calm when there's no kissing, let me tell you."

He leaned against the desk and held in a smile. Oh, yeah, this was the Destiny he'd long suspected was hidden inside. The passionate woman who sang with body and soul.

"Don't look at me like that!" she told him.

"Like what?"

"I don't know. With amusement and pride. I'm not a puppy."

"I never said you were."

She stomped her foot. "I want to throw something! Do you know what that means? I really am my parents. I've worked so hard to not be them, and here I am, wanting to throw a plate at your head!"

He crossed to her, grabbed her by her upper arms, hauled her against him and pressed his mouth against hers. When he drew back, he stared into her green eyes and knew exactly how to solve the problem.

"Marry me."

CHAPTER SIXTEEN

Destiny sat on her bed. The part where she'd left Kipling's office and walked or possibly run home was kind of a blur. She remembered him proposing. She was pretty sure she'd told him no, burst into tears and then run off. But maybe the fact that she couldn't exactly remember meant she'd politely thanked him for his generous offer then had sedately strolled away.

Or not. And remembering was highly overrated, anyway.

She reached for her guitar. Her fingers found chords. She wasn't looking for a song, but the act of playing allowed her to relax.

On the bright side, Lacey had left that morning. The whirlwind visit had ended with her mother promising to return in a couple of months to see how things were going with Starr. Destiny had a feeling that once word of her pregnancy spread, Lacey would become a regular in Fool's Gold.

She had to admit, that wasn't necessarily a bad thing. Having a baby was scary. Knowing her own mother would be around was nice.

She continued to play, thinking that now that she was pregnant, wine was out of the question. Which meant she was going to have to curl up with a glass of milk and some cookies later. Dairy was good for her, wasn't it? And if she had raisin oatmeal cookies, they were practically a fruit and a whole grain.

Nutrition aside, she'd had a life and a direction. Maybe a slightly strange one, but a life that was hers all the same. A life that was basically laughable now. Wasn't she ridiculously old for an unplanned pregnancy? Shouldn't she have known better? All the running from her genetics and her family had landed her in a situation even her mother had managed to avoid. Single and pregnant and nearly thirty.

She kept watching the clock and when it was time, she put down her guitar and walked into the living room to wait for Starr to get home.

A few minutes later the teen flew into the house. The second she saw Destiny, she started talking.

"There's a musical. They're putting on a musical the last week of summer, and I want to audition for one of the lead roles. Do you think I can do it?"

"Of course. You have a beautiful voice."

"I'm so scared," Starr admitted with a laugh, as she dumped her backpack on the floor by the sofa. "What if I freak out?"

"You'll know the music," Destiny told her. "Why don't I talk to Kipling? Maybe he can open The Man Cave some Saturday afternoon so you and your friends can practice with a microphone and a few family members in the audience. Less pressure than an audition, but in a safe environment."

"That's an awesome idea. Thanks. I was going to ask you what song you think I should sing. They gave us a list to choose from."

"We can look them over tonight."

"That would be great." Starr wrinkled her nose. "What's up? You have a scrunchy face."

"What?"

"Your face is all scrunched up. Something happened."

Destiny figured things were bad when she couldn't fool a fifteen-year-old. "Have a seat. We need to talk."

Starr's happiness faded as her mouth straightened. She sank onto the sofa. "Is it bad?"

"No. I'm not sick, you're not sick. We're staying in Fool's Gold. It's something else." She settled next to her sister.

How on earth was she supposed to come clean? She was going to sound like an idiot. Which she was, in a way.

She tried to smile but had a feeling it came out more as a scary grimace. Still, Starr stayed where she was and didn't shriek or anything.

Destiny opened her mouth then closed it. Simple was better, she decided, then went for it. "I'm pregnant. Kipling is the father."

"Oh, wow." Starr stared at her. "I knew you two were, like, going out, but I didn't know... Wow, so are you keeping the baby?"

"Yes." She hadn't considered not keeping it. "I am. So I guess you're going to be an aunt."

Starr grinned. "You're right. That's cool. I can help. I don't know anything about babies, but I can learn."

Destiny didn't know anything about babies, either, but didn't think saying that out loud would make either of them feel better.

"Kipling proposed to me."

Starr grabbed her hands. "Did he? That's wicked! When are you getting married? Because that's what people do, right? Get married and have babies? It makes them a family."

Destiny started to tell her, no, they weren't getting married. That lots of people didn't get married. Then she remembered that Jimmy Don had never married Starr's mother. Jimmy Don was the kind of father who hadn't married her mother or taken her in when she'd needed a place to go. He hadn't even remembered her birthday.

Destiny squeezed her hands. "It doesn't make them a family," she whispered. "It's the loving that does that, not being married."

"But getting married helps."

Talk about an unexpected twist, Destiny thought helplessly. Kipling wasn't her idea of a sensible choice. There was too much chemistry between them. Sure he was kind and caring, and he would always be there to support her. She liked how he could have had a huge ego based on his previous career and fame, but he didn't. He was practically ordinary.

But the sex thing concerned her. Strong emotions were nothing but trouble. She didn't love him, and he didn't love her, so that was a start, she supposed. But was their friendship enough to sustain a marriage? Even more to the point, had his proposal been a knee-jerk reaction to the news, or had he meant it?

Because until she'd stared into her sister's face, it had never occurred to her to say yes. And now, it seemed, she might not have a choice.

Kipling had decided not to push Destiny. He knew she'd been avoiding him, but time and geography were on his side. Not to mention the fact that they had to work together. Finding out she was pregnant was news that would take a while for him to absorb. He was still dealing with it himself. But them getting married wasn't an option. She was having his baby, and he was determined to be a part of his child's life.

But she was still making her way, so he didn't seek her out. They had a second search scheduled, and there was no way she wouldn't show up. So he'd loaded up his gear, driven to the search area and waited.

She arrived minutes after him. When she stepped out of her car, she had on her usual jeans, T-shirt and hiking boots. Her hair was pulled back in a simple ponytail. She wasn't wearing makeup.

That was his Destiny, he thought with a smile. Honest. The

shadows under her eyes were a testament to the fact that she hadn't been sleeping. He would guess finding out she was pregnant had messed up a lot of things in her life.

"Hi," she said cautiously when she saw him. Her expression was wary.

"No."

She blinked. "No what?"

"No, I'm not going to talk about our personal business at work."

"Oh." She visibly relaxed. "Okay. Good. Are you ready?"

He held up his tablet, with tracking software installed. "I am."

The rules were similar to what they had been for the first search. Cassidy had gone about a mile or so in from the main road. She would keep moving away from them for about a mile, then turn in a different direction and start walking in wide circles. A classic pattern for someone who was lost.

If this test went well, then they would expand the practice sessions. Volunteers would pose as the missing person, Kipling and Cassidy would run the search and Destiny would move to observation only. After each practice search, she would run the debrief.

"Where do you want to start?" Destiny asked.

He knew she was talking about their test and not her pregnancy. He pointed to the path. "We'll take the obvious road first."

They were each equipped with GPS tracking devices that would feed real-time data to the computer program. Destiny put in the data they had, including Cassidy's approximate start time and the fact that she was being classified as a hiking novice. For their purposes today, she was.

Kipling watched Destiny work. She was quick and efficient then told him they could move out. He motioned for her to lead the way.

For the first few minutes, they didn't talk. He walked easily, his injuries not bothering him today.

He and Destiny followed the path for a quarter mile before it branched out in two directions. He pointed to the left. There was no way of knowing which way Cassidy had chosen, but that was part of the fun.

The underbrush was thick, the air sweet with flowers and a light breeze. It was already warm and would get hotter as the day progressed.

Funny how a year ago he'd been lying in a hospital in New Zealand, drugged and broken, talking to Mayor Marsha about taking a job in a place he'd never heard of, and now he was here. A lot had changed. He'd given up skiing for good and while some days he had regrets, most of the time he was able to deal with what had happened. Had it been his choice? No. But he'd managed to move on. Sure he still wanted to battle the mountain, but he never would. He could accept that and live happily, or he could be bitter forever. The choice was his.

Somehow in the past couple of months, he'd started moving toward the former. Maybe it was time healing or maybe it was Destiny. Being around her made him feel better about everything.

It wasn't love. He wasn't willing to reduce what they had to empty words. Instead, he found himself wanting to be there for her. To take care of her. He knew she felt the same way. Destiny believed in action. Look at how she'd stepped up with Starr. They didn't need love. They had each other and mutual respect. Even more important, they were going to have a child.

"We'd do well together."

Destiny swung around to face him, nearly tripping as she turned. He reached out and steadied her.

"This is us not talking about it?" she asked.

"I changed my mind."

"You don't have to marry me," she told him.

"I want to."

"Why?"

"Because we're having a baby. We're both traditional enough to want to be part of a family. We could make that happen."

He had no idea what she was thinking. She didn't look away, and she didn't say no.

"I have Starr."

"I know. She's part of the deal. Having us get married will give her a sense of stability. You won't have to do everything yourself. You can depend on me, Destiny."

Her mouth twisted. "You're not going to try to convince me you love me?"

"No. I will tell you that we have a lot in common. I understand why you keep your passions buried, and I'm okay with that. But when you have to let loose and throw a few plates, I'm good at ducking."

"I would never throw a plate."

"You talked about it."

"Not the same as doing it." She drew in a breath. "You're going to want sex, aren't you?"

He did his best not to smile. "Yes, I am."

"A lot?"

"It depends on your definition of a lot."

She nodded, as if she'd expected the answer. "I'm not going to like it, but you can do it whenever you want. I won't say no."

Now he did smile. "Thank you for that."

She had no idea what she was getting into, he thought humorously. Giving him as much access as he wanted. Once they were married, he would make sure she found out what all the fuss was about. Based on what he'd seen so far, Destiny was hiding more passion than even she was aware of. Unleashed, she would be unstoppable. And he couldn't wait to get in the way.

"If you still want to marry me," she said with a sigh, "then I'm saying yes. For the baby and for Starr."

"Good. Sooner is probably better than later. Say toward the end of this week?"

She nodded. "Then we should probably get back to finding Cassidy."

He pointed to the path. "I'm right here behind you."

Destiny hadn't expected that a wedding could be pulled together in less than forty-eight hours, but it turned out it could. The fact that there were no guests helped. As did holding it in Mayor Marsha's office in City Hall, with only the bride, groom, Shelby and Starr attending. Bailey, the mayor's assistant, and Shelby were the witnesses. Before Destiny could catch her breath, she was married.

When Mayor Marsha smiled and said, "You may now kiss your bride," Destiny realized she felt nothing. She was totally numb—both emotionally and physically. Kipling's lips barely registered. After, when everyone congratulated her, she was pretty sure she smiled and said the right things, but it was all happening from a great distance.

The next couple of hours passed in a blur. Shelby was going to stay with Starr for the night while Destiny and Kipling had a mini honeymoon at Ronan's Lodge. Destiny was aware of packing her overnight duffel and hugging her sister. There was a short drive to the lodge and the business of checking in. Then she was standing in the middle of a pretty hotel suite wondering what on earth she'd been thinking. About all of it.

The living room of the suite was bright and nicely decorated. A happy combination of sophisticated and comfortable. Beyond the open door, she could see into the bedroom. Technically, all she could see was the bed, but that was enough. Because she knew what was coming next.

The price of her one moral misstep gleamed on her left hand. A simple gold band. One Kipling had surprised her with during the ceremony. Because she hadn't thought about rings. Or much else. In fact, since saying yes to his proposal, she hadn't thought much at all.

He caught her gaze and walked over to her, then took her left hand in his. "I want to get you a different ring," he told her. "But I'll need your help in picking it out. I figured this would be a good start. Classic usually works."

"This is fine. I don't need anything else."

He smiled. "It's not about what you need, Destiny. It's about what's right."

Nothing was right, she thought. Sure, she was married and pregnant and she had her sister, so she was well on her way to the perfect family she'd always wanted. But everything was oddly distant. As if she was experiencing her life through a thick pane of glass. Or underwater. Or from another planet. She could see what was happening, hear it, even touch it. But it wasn't real.

Her attention shifted to the large bed and how it loomed in her future. Dear God, they were going to have to do it, weren't they?

"If we do the sex thing now, can we let it go for the next couple of days?" she asked, not quite looking at Kipling as she asked the question.

"Would that be better for you?"

"Yes. Then I wouldn't be so worried thinking about 'is it now?'"

His mouth twitched. "Sure. Let's get it over with."

Which sounded way too easy, she thought. "And then we're done for a couple of days?"

He nodded. "I promise I won't ask for sex while we're staying at the hotel. If you want it, you're welcome to tell me and then we can do—" he released her hand and made air quotes "—the sex thing."

"Very funny." As if she would be the one initiating *that*. "Okay, give me a couple of minutes, then come in."

She picked up her duffel and walked into the bedroom. After

closing the door behind her, she moved around the bed without looking at it then went into the bathroom.

Once there, she wasn't sure how to prepare. She brushed her teeth, then changed into a simple cotton nightgown. The only one she had. She was more of a T-shirt over panties kind of sleeper.

She agonized over her underwear then figured that leaving them on was wishful thinking on her part. She tucked them under her other clothes then returned to the bedroom. After folding down the covers, she stretched out on one side of the bed and rested her head on the pillow.

"Come in," she called.

The door opened. Kipling walked in and paused to look at her. One eyebrow rose.

"Ready to make the ultimate sacrifice?" he asked.

She couldn't quite read the tone in his voice. Humor, maybe. Although she couldn't figure out why he thought this was funny.

She nodded. "I am."

He moved toward the bed. He'd taken off his shoes and socks but left on the rest of his clothes. Which was nice. Seeing him naked would have been jarring.

His dark blue eyes locked onto her face. She noticed he needed a haircut, but that he'd shaved recently. Probably for the wedding, she thought. He was the kind of man who would shave for his wedding.

He got in on his side and moved toward the middle. After patting the center of the big bed, he waited until she slid a little closer.

She'd thought he might say something or maybe simply get on top of her and do his thing. Instead, he brushed his fingers across her cheek before gently kissing her.

The feel of his lips on hers was both familiar and arousing. She knew about the kissing—liked it, in fact. So it was easy to close her eyes and relax. His mouth moved against hers. Back and forth. He settled one hand on her waist, which momentarily distracted her, but when he didn't move it, she could focus on the kissing again.

The room was quiet, the bed comfortable. They were alone, and no one would be bothering them. Not that she was looking forward to what they were doing. Only she couldn't help thinking about having his hands on her breasts. That was the part she liked.

His tongue brushed against her lower lip. She parted to let him in then sighed when she felt the first quivery spark ignite in her belly. She wrapped both arms around him, resting her hands on his back. He was broad and strong, she thought absently. Masculine. He would always keep her safe.

Their tongues danced and teased, touching, retreating, stroking. Her breasts began to ache, and she felt her nipples straining against the fabric of her nightgown.

Kipling shifted slightly, moving to kiss along her jaw then down her neck. He brushed his lips against her collarbone then dipped lower to the scooped neckline of her nightgown, but didn't go beyond the fabric. The hand on her waist stayed exactly where it was. He returned his attention to her mouth and kissed her again.

She rolled toward him as she ran her fingers up and down his back. The kiss deepened. With every stroke of his tongue against hers, she felt herself melting. At the same time a particular tension emanated from various points on her body. Her breasts, which ached more each second, and between her thighs. There was an odd heaviness. An almost pulsing.

Images filled her mind. Of how he'd touched her before. Of him pushing inside her. She wanted that again, she thought hazily. She'd said she would do the sex thing, so why was he taking so long?

He broke free for a second time and kissed his way down her neck. This time he moved past the edge of the nightgown. He hovered over her breasts for a heartbeat, then two. Anticipation filled her, making her want to grab him by the shoulders and pull him down.

At last he lowered his head and took her right nipple into his mouth.

She exhaled sharply as she felt the warm, moist heat of his mouth envelop her through the thin cotton. His tongue swirled against her tight, sensitive skin. Nerve endings danced with joy and sent ribbons of heat shimmering down to her belly.

She was still in her nightgown, but the gauzy fabric didn't get in the way at all. She felt the flick of his tongue then pulsing pleasure when he sucked, the coolness of the air on the damp material as he shifted to her other breast.

She wasn't sure how long he went between them. First one then the other. When his mouth was on one breast, his hand was on the other. She learned there was a difference between what he could do with his tongue and his fingers, but both were very, very nice.

At some point she'd rolled onto her back, although she couldn't say when. She'd moved her hands from his back to his shoulders and head. She trailed her fingers through his hair, and when he sucked a nipple in deeply, she groaned and dug into his shoulders.

The room had become very warm. She stirred restlessly, feeling the need for something more. She moved her legs against the sheet, squeezed her thighs together, but nothing helped. Relaxed muscles tensed, although she wasn't sure why.

Kipling moved on the bed. She opened her eyes and saw he was removing his white long-sleeved shirt. She watched greedily, wanting to see his chest. He tossed the shirt away and, without thinking, she put his hands on the sculpted muscles.

His skin was warm and smooth. She saw his nipples were slightly raised.

"Does it feel the same?" she asked as she brushed her fingers against one of them.

He grinned. "I don't know how it feels for you, but I like it."

The anatomy was interesting, she thought. Similar but different.

He leaned in and kissed her as he tugged at her nightgown. She pulled it up to her waist, then he drew it off her.

Funny how a few minutes ago the thought of being naked would have made her nervous. Now all she could think about was that he was going to touch her without the impediment of fabric, and how good that was going to be. She sank back onto the mattress and wrapped her arms around him. He smiled then kissed her.

Her eyes closed as she lost herself in his mouth on hers. His hand returned to her breasts. She sighed as he cupped her curves. This was so nice, she thought. She could—

His hand was moving. Down her rib cage, across her belly, before settling on the top of her thigh. Because he was going to touch her *there*.

Destiny wasn't sure how she felt about that. She was still kind of tense and hot, but also nervous. But the kissing was good, and when he didn't move right away, she relaxed. Because so far everything he'd done had felt nice. Not earth-shattering like everyone said, but still pleasant. If this was sex, and it was important to him, she could certainly see doing it every month or so.

He let his hand travel up her thigh, back to her stomach then make the return trip. So slow and easy, she almost didn't notice. The second time, he went all the way to her breast, where he stroked her nipples. The restlessness returned, and she shifted.

When he went back down again, somehow her legs opened a little, and he rested his fingers against her girl parts. Not pushing or actually touching, just kind of resting.

He broke the kiss.

"I want you to tell me if you don't like what I'm doing," he said softly. "If it hurts or makes you uncomfortable."

She opened her eyes and found him watching her. His dark blue gaze was intense.

"If you want to tell me to go faster or slower, that would be good, too."

"Why would I do that?" she asked.

He smiled. "There will be a point when you're going to want to give instructions."

"I doubt that."

The smile turned into a grin. "Trust me."

"Okay."

He moved his hands against her, pressing down some. Warmth seemed to radiate from wherever he touched. An odd warmth that made her want to strain toward him.

"What do you know about anatomy?" he asked. "About this area in particular?"

"The usual stuff."

He lightly kissed her. "Close your eyes."

She did as he requested. His fingers parted her, then he touched her intimately.

That one night at the bar had been different. He'd been inside her, but he hadn't touched her. Not like this. Not with fingers that seemed to find every nerve ending she had and set it tingling.

He pushed a single finger inside her, and she instinctively pressed her hips toward him. She liked the feeling of fullness. The in-and-out motion made her strain a little. She parted her legs even more. He stroked inside her, pushing up, and in and—

The good became great as he found some nerve knot or something. Her breath caught as he moved his finger back and forth against sensitive inner skin.

"G-spot," he murmured.

"I thought that was a myth."

He moved his finger again. "You tell me."

She would if she could breathe, she thought, tilting her hips to give him more access.

He pulled out, and she nearly whimpered. But before she could complain, he placed three fingers on the very center of her and moved in a slow circle.

"Clitoris."

She would have said something, only she couldn't speak. Nothing they'd done had prepared her for the waves of heat and need rushing through her.

She was helpless, she thought, sinking into the sensation of him circling and circling, the pace not changing, yet the tension inside her building.

She wanted to whimper. She wanted to beg. Every part of her only cared about that small core. About what he was doing to her body.

Her breathing increased as he touched her over and over. He moved a little faster. She strained toward something she couldn't see, couldn't touch, couldn't—

She exploded, flew apart into a zillion pieces, into the very essence of what she had always been. She might have gasped or screamed or been totally silent. She had no way of knowing. She could only be lost in the powerful waves of pleasure reducing her to base metal before allowing her to reassemble into a metamorphosed version of herself.

When she could think again, when she could breathe and speak, she opened her eyes and found Kipling watching her. One corner of his mouth turned up.

"*That* would be an orgasm."

CHAPTER SEVENTEEN

The house was pretty. Two stories with a partially finished basement. Four bedrooms upstairs, lots of windows to let in light and a big backyard. Destiny knew she should be checking out storage space and the size of the kitchen. Did the layout work for her, and would the place need paint? There were considerations when one purchased a home for the first time. But honest to God, she simply couldn't think straight. Not with her body still quivering and tingling with aftershocks.

Someone should have been a lot clearer about the whole sex thing.

Kipling walked back into the kitchen and smiled at her. "The yard is nice. Big enough for a swing set and a dog to run around. There's a big tree with good-size branches. What do you think about a tree house?"

He had such a nice mouth, she thought, watching him as he talked. And the way he moved. Every now and then there was the slightest hesitation. From his accident. He had scars, too. On his legs and hips. One circled halfway around to his back.

She knew that now. She knew other things, too. Like the scent of his skin and how his gaze sharpened when he entered her. She knew that he liked it when she made noise when she came. She knew the sound of his voice as he urged her on.

He walked over and pulled her against him. "Tired?" he asked.

"A little."

Neither of them had slept. They'd spent the night making love. After her first climax, she'd been stunned. Blown away. Pick your description, she thought, still amazed by what had happened. Then he'd slipped inside her, and she'd climaxed again.

They'd gone to dinner, then returned to their room to make love over and over again. She hurt everywhere, but the ache was worth it. Every step reminded her of what they'd done. Of how he had pleased her.

He stroked her hair then lowered his mouth to hers. She leaned into him, parting her lips immediately. As his tongue tangled with hers, she was already unbuttoning the front of her shirt. When it was open, she unhooked her bra then grabbed his hands and put them on her breasts.

His kiss turned greedy, then he pulled away. "Hold that thought. I want to check the front door."

Because they were alone in the empty house. The local real-estate agent had simply handed them keys to the handful of houses that were vacant and for sale. Apparently, word that they were looking for something they could close on quickly had spread.

Kipling hurried out of the kitchen. Destiny put the time to good use. She unfastened her jeans and toed out of her shoes. By the time he returned, she was naked.

Kipling took one look at her then shook his head. "You're going to kill us both."

She grinned. "I doubt that."

He crossed to her and grabbed her by the waist, then settled her on the built-in desk. She reached for the fly of his jeans and freed him.

He was already hard. She parted her thighs, and he pushed home. She wrapped her legs around his hips and drew him in deep.

It only took them a thrust or two to find the right rhythm. Even as he returned his mouth to hers, he was also cupping her breasts. She ran her hands over his chest and back, then shifted closer, pulling him in deeper.

He filled her completely. Nerve endings were already screaming for the hot friction. At minute one, she was breathing hard. At minute two, she was nearing her climax. At minute three she opened her eyes to find him watching her.

In and out. He moved hard and fast, pushing her closer and closer.

"Yes," he breathed, his gaze locked with hers.

He could see her getting closer. They'd both figured that out last night. As she strained toward her release, he went deeper. It was just enough.

She felt the first telltale internal shudders. Her orgasm swept over her, claiming her. She shook and groaned, all the while looking into his eyes. Letting him see it all.

He didn't break rhythm, not even once. She felt him shaking as he held back until she was done. When she'd quieted, he squeezed her butt and pushed in one more time. She watched his face tighten as he climaxed inside her.

They stayed like that—connected and united—until their breathing slowed. They kissed each other slowly, lazily, letting their bodies return to a more resting state. He withdrew and then helped her dress.

After fastening her bra, he reached around and cupped her breasts. Wanting shot through her. She could never get enough of him, she thought, not sure if that was good news or bad news.

Something about his body and her body created an irresistible dynamic.

She pulled on her T-shirt then faced him.

"I am turning into my parents," she murmured, stepping into his embrace.

"I've yet to see you throw a plate, so I don't think so."

She laughed. "I'm sure the plate throwing will be next. But the sex thing. I had no idea."

He touched her chin. "It's not usually like this," he admitted. "Usually it's less intense. And less frequent. Even at first." He smiled. "This is unexpected for me, too."

For a second she wondered if it was more than that. If her reaction to him were as much about her brain as her body. Because when she thought about all the things good in a man, Kipling checked every box. But he also scared her. He was a really good guy, *and* he made her blood race. Kind of an irresistible combination. Which was exactly what she'd been trying to avoid.

He put his arm around her then turned her so she was facing the kitchen. "Want to talk about the space?" he asked.

She laughed. "I like the built-in desk."

"It's convenient." He kissed the top of her head. "Okay, we're going to be adults about this. We're house hunting. Does this one work for us?" He motioned to the open area just beyond the island. "There's room for a table and chairs there. The playpen could go there."

Playpen? Kipling continued talking, but Destiny couldn't listen anymore. She pressed her hand against her stomach and let the reality settle over her. She was pregnant. Yes, she'd known that before, but it hadn't been real. It probably still wasn't. But here she was, married, looking for a house with her new husband. Because they were having a baby together. Plus, she was responsible for her teenage sister.

It was a lot for anyone to take on. She could have staggered under the weight of all of it, only she wouldn't because she wasn't alone. She had Kipling at her side.

Destiny hesitated before walking into Jo's. While she usually looked forward to her standing weekly lunch date with her friends, today she was more than a little apprehensive. She had a feeling that announcing her recent and very unexpected marriage was going to shift the focus of the conversation.

Still, there was no avoiding what had happened. She'd gotten pregnant, and now she was married. Not exactly her master plan, but she was dealing. Being responsible and adult, if one ignored hot sex in an empty house. Fortunately, she was as good at ignoring the obvious as the next person.

She drew in a deep breath then pushed open the door and smiled when she saw several of her friends sitting at a table.

Shelby and Dellina waved her over. Madeline turned and grinned then pointed to the empty chair next to her. Cassidy was there, as well. A couple of empty chairs remained, indicating they were expecting a big crowd.

"I'm trying to convince everyone to come with me Friday night to see the new Jonny Blaze movie," Madeline admitted as Destiny took her seat. "Say you'll come. It's going to be great."

Shelby wrinkled her nose. "Violent movies aren't my thing."

"This isn't real violence," Madeline told her. "It's cartoony. Death is very tidy, and then we move on."

"You're weird," Cassidy said cheerfully. "I like that about you."

Madeline beamed. "Thank you. How are you enjoying Fool's Gold?"

"It's great. Everyone is friendly." Cassidy wrinkled her nose. "Maybe too friendly." She turned to Destiny. "I've had to tell your friend Miles to back off a couple of times. Hello, married, and so not interested in anyone but my hunky husband."

"I'm sorry," Destiny murmured and glanced at Shelby. The other woman had gone pale.

Now Shelby stood. "I'll be back in a bit. Order without me."

Destiny followed her to the doorway. "Is it Miles?"

"Yes. I need to talk to him about a broken promise."

Destiny kind of didn't want to know what that was about. "Should I come with you?"

"No. I can yell at him all on my own."

Larissa and a very pregnant Taryn walked in and joined them. Destiny hesitated, but Shelby turned and waved for her to go back to the table. Destiny walked with Taryn, eyeing her, wondering if she would look as uncomfortable when she was that far along.

From the back, Taryn looked sleek and slim, but from the side and front, she was huge. Just her stomach—not her face or shoulders or legs. Other women Destiny had known had gotten heavier all over. It was a more balanced look, but would require more weight loss later.

She supposed her doctor would tell her what was the healthy amount to gain. Speaking of which, she needed to find a gynecologist and schedule a visit.

Cassidy pulled out a chair for Taryn. "How are you feeling?"

"Huge. It's awful. Biology sucks."

Cassidy patted her arm. "That's my brave little toaster. Always keeping your feelings to yourself so you don't upset those around you."

"Bite me."

Cassidy laughed.

Jo came by and took drink orders.

"You taunt me, and it's mean," Taryn said, glaring at the specials board on the wall. The first one was a berry margarita. "I swear when this kid is born, I'm going to get drunk for three days."

"You're not," Cassidy said cheerfully. "You're going to be breastfeeding."

Taryn glared at her. "Don't start with me. You think you're all skinny and tough, but I could take you."

Cassidy's amusement grew. "Like I'd take on a pregnant woman."

Taryn sighed. "Fine. Four months after this kid is born, I'm getting really, really drunk. Until then, make me that stupid herbal iced tea drink. It's not completely gross."

Jo glanced at her. "Love the endorsement. I've been thinking of doing some TV advertising. I should have you as my spokesperson."

"Very funny," Taryn grumbled. "And I'm sorry. I'm huge. I can't sleep. My feet are swollen, and none of my good shoes fit. Kill me now."

Everyone laughed, then continued with their drink orders. Destiny glanced at Taryn then back at Jo. "She made the herbal iced tea sound so good, I'll try one."

"You'll love it," Jo assured her then turned back to Taryn. "I have a new salad. Fresh, organic and locally sourced. High protein with some quinoa."

Taryn made a gagging sound. Jo chuckled and walked away.

"It's her way of expressing love," Madeline said. "Jo takes care of people, and we love her for it."

"I know," Taryn said with a sigh.

"The salad sounds delicious," Larissa admitted. "I think I'll get it."

"You would," Taryn grumbled.

"I agree with her," Cassidy added.

Destiny had a feeling she was saying that to bug Taryn. The two women seemed to have made good friends fairly quickly. Not a likely friendship, but one that seemed solid.

Conversation swirled around her. Talk about upcoming festivals, the great weather, the crazy things tourists had done. The usual stuff. Jo returned with the drinks, took their lunch orders then left. Destiny knew she was running out of time.

Not sure what to say, exactly, she put her left hand on the table. Light glinted from her gold wedding band. She stared at the ring, searching for the right words. In the end she figured she would just blurt it out. Simply say—

"OMG, is that real?" Madeline asked. "Destiny Mills, are you wearing a wedding ring?"

The table went silent as everyone turned to look at her. Or, more precisely, her hand.

She felt herself flush. "I, ah..."

Taryn poked at the ring. "It feels real to me."

Destiny cleared her throat. "Kipling and I got married a couple of days ago. I know it's quick, but there are reasons. One reason. I'm pregnant."

Everyone stared at her. Eyes widened, a couple of mouths dropped open.

"That was fast," Taryn said, then winced. "Sorry. I meant that to sound less judgmental."

"Good for you," Cassidy said. "Kipling's a great guy. When did this happen? And where?"

"Yes, we need details," Larissa added.

"Congratulations." Madeline gave her a hug. "He's dreamy, and you two are so cute together. And a baby! That's wonderful. Does Starr know? Is she thrilled?"

"She says she is," Destiny told them. "She keeps going on and on about being part of a real family. Plus, she's super excited about having a baby niece or nephew."

"I get that," Larissa said. "If it were just me in my family, I would have run away. My parents are fantastic, but intense." She smiled at Destiny. "You're lucky to have found each other so quickly. I was in love with Jack for ages and never figured it out. My mother had to tell me. Talk about humiliating."

"Jeff and I knew from day one," Cassidy said with a wink.

"He said hi and I said hi, then we were staring into each other's eyes. By the end of the first week, I'd moved in with him, and when we hit the six-month mark, we were married." She sighed. "I do love a good love story."

Taryn sniffed. "Me, too. Damn hormones are turning me into a girl."

Madeline leaned toward her. "Taryn, honey, you *are* a girl. You knew that, didn't you? Because if you didn't, someone needs to have a little talk with Angel."

"Very funny."

Jo arrived with their lunches. "Congratulations," she said. "I heard the happy news. That man moves fast. Opens a bar in town after only being here a couple of months and takes half my business. A few weeks later, he's married with a kid on the way. Talk about being born under a lucky star." The other woman shook her head. "Sorry. That came out wrong. I really am happy for you. Lunch is on me."

Destiny looked at her. "Thanks."

Jo left. Madeline touched Destiny's arm. "Don't worry about Jo. She's fine."

Destiny nodded, thinking Jo seemed more upset about The Man Cave than enthused about the wedding. Taryn tasted the healthy salad and declared it edible. Cassidy pressed for details about the wedding, and conversation moved on to other topics. Destiny relaxed as she realized she'd had no reason to worry at all. Friends didn't judge. They were accepting and supportive.

She might be pregnant and dealing with a lot of changes, but she wasn't alone. She had Kipling, Starr and these women to help her. After all the years of mostly being on her own, she had to admit it felt good to be connected.

Saturday Kipling pulled into the driveway of Destiny's rental. They'd agreed he would move in with her until they closed on the house they'd bought. His place wasn't any bigger, and Starr was already settled here. It didn't make sense to move her twice.

The process of comingling their belongings would take a few days. He was bringing over a few things today and would officially move in with his furniture next weekend.

He carried boxes into the house. "Starr, it's me," he called.

The teen didn't respond.

He'd phoned her earlier to let her know he would be dropping by. Destiny was out running errands, but Starr had said she would be home all afternoon. He walked down the hall and found her bedroom door open and the room empty. Maybe she'd gone out and left him a note, he thought, retracing his steps then heading to the kitchen.

He glanced at the kitchen table and didn't see anything. Before he could figure out what to do next, movement caught his attention. He looked out the big window over the sink and saw Starr and a boy sitting on the bench seat on the patio.

The kid was familiar, Kipling thought. Gideon's son. Carter.

The two teens were talking intently. They looked cute, he thought indulgently as he walked toward the back door to let them know he was here. His hand settled on the doorknob. Carter and Starr leaned toward each other. He opened the door as they kissed.

Kissed?

Kipling was outside in a heartbeat. "What the hell are you two doing?" he demanded.

The teens jumped apart. Carter sprang to his feet and stood between Kipling and Starr. A protective posture that would have been admirable if Kipling weren't so pissed off. They were fifteen. That was too young for kissing, wasn't it? Sure, kids these days did stuff, but not on his watch.

"Starr, does your sister know Carter is here?"

"Don't yell at her," Carter told him.

"I'm not yelling," Kipling growled.

Starr looked around Carter. "You kind of are." She looked more intrigued than scared. "It was just a kiss."

"You're fifteen."

"We know that," Carter said. "We're allowed to kiss."

"No, you're not." He moved toward the boy. "What you're allowed to do is get the hell out of this house."

"What?" Starr demanded, coming to her feet. "You're not the boss of him. Or me. Just because you married my sister doesn't mean you're in charge. Destiny wouldn't be upset."

"Want to bet?" Kipling asked. He pointed at the door. "You get out of here."

Carter didn't move. "Not until you promise you won't hurt Starr."

"What? Hurt her?" He swore. "Starr, go to your room until Destiny gets home. Carter, get your ass out of here. You hear me?"

Carter and Starr exchanged a look, then they both nodded. There was a whispered conversation as they walked to the back door. Kipling followed. Starr went down the hall, and Carter left the house. Kipling looked at the clock and wondered how long it would take Destiny to get home.

Destiny got home as quickly as she could. She'd abandoned a nearly full cart at the grocery store, something she'd never done in her life. But Kipling had sounded more worried than she'd ever heard him.

He was waiting for her on the front step when she pulled up.

"They were kissing?" she asked as she got out of her car. "I can't believe it."

"Neither could I."

"Starr said Carter was stopping by, but I didn't think anything of it. They're friends."

"Good ones."

Just then a truck came barreling around the corner and skidded to a stop in front of the house. Gideon got out and stalked toward them.

"What the hell were you thinking?" he demanded.

Destiny had met the other man a couple of times, in social situations. He was bigger than she remembered, and a lot more menacing. Kipling immediately stepped between her and Gideon.

Felicia scrambled out of the passenger side and hurried to her husband. "Gideon, we talked about this. Your anger may or may not be justified. I, too, want to punch in Kipling's face, but we need to get the facts." She paused and smiled tightly at Destiny. "Hi. We have a problem."

There was an understatement, Destiny thought. "One we have to figure out."

"I know what I saw," Kipling growled and glared at Gideon. "Your son was over here, without permission, kissing Starr. She's fifteen. If I hadn't walked in, who knows what would have happened."

Destiny wanted to say she had faith in her sister, but she also was a product of her wonky genetics. Destiny knew exactly how powerful sexual urges could be.

Felicia sighed. "Teenage hormones are formidable. Sexual desire can override judgment at any age, but when the parties in question are their age, it's foolish to expect rational behavior."

Gideon turned to her. "I love you. You're right, and I still want to rip him apart."

Kipling took a step toward him. "Go ahead and try."

Destiny grabbed his arm while Felicia got in front of Gideon.

"You're not helping," Felicia said firmly.

"I don't care about helping."

"But you do care about Carter."

Gideon stared at Kipling. "You had no right to yell at my son."

"I told him to get out. If Starr was your daughter, what would you have done?"

"Stop it! Just stop it!"

The voice came from behind them. Destiny turned and saw Starr standing on the front porch. Tears filled her eyes.

"You don't have to fight over this. It was just a kiss."

Destiny hurried to her sister. "We're worried about you."

"It was just a kiss," Starr whispered again. "Stop fighting like this. Stop yelling. What's so bad about what we did? Haven't you ever been in love?"

"You can't be in love," Gideon said flatly. "You're too young."

Felicia touched his arm. "Actually there are studies that suggest age isn't—" She pressed her lips together. "Perhaps this isn't the time for that kind of information."

Love? Destiny had trouble inhaling.

Starr turned to Kipling. "You're in love, right? So you know what I mean."

He stared blankly. Starr frowned.

"You have to be in love," she said. "With Destiny. You married her."

Destiny had never heard such a loud silence. It grew and expanded until it was all that existed. It was like standing onstage and not remembering the words to a song. No, it was much worse than that. Humiliation burned hot, becoming shame. She wanted to run away but couldn't move. It was one thing for her to know that her marriage to Kipling had been a practical decision, but another to have that very unromantic fact shared with the world. While she'd never said they were in love, people had assumed, and she'd let them.

Gideon and Felicia glanced at both of them then at each other. Starr's breath caught.

"You got her pregnant, and you don't even love her?" Starr surged toward Destiny. "Did you know?"

"We can talk about this later," she murmured.

Starr stepped back. "Sure. I'll be in my room."

She went inside. Felicia cleared her throat.

"We'll talk to Carter about kissing Starr. That perhaps they're both too young."

Kipling nodded. "I'm sorry I yelled at him. It was a knee-jerk reaction."

"You have the jerk part right," Gideon told him. "See that it doesn't happen again. And I'm out of The Man Cave. Find another partner."

They got in their truck and drove away.

Alone once again, Destiny found she couldn't look at Kipling.

"I need to take care of Starr," she said. "Why don't you give us some time to work through this?"

She thought he might fight her, but instead he nodded and left. She went into the house.

Starr was waiting for her in the living room. She had Destiny's guitar in her hand. Without saying anything, she handed it over then retreated to her room and closed the door.

Destiny sat on the sofa, her guitar next to her. She stared at the instrument, the implication clear. She would need the music because the only way to process her emotions was through a song. Only she was fine. Completely and totally fine.

Kipling didn't love her. That wasn't news. They got along. They were friends, and when she'd gotten pregnant, they'd made a sensible decision about their future. Everything was fine. Technically, it was what she'd always said she wanted.

He was a man who liked to fix things. She was his current project. There were worse fates.

She picked up the guitar and strummed the strings. Soft music filled the room. Love was a complication she'd never wanted or needed. To be the center of someone's life—who needed that? Obviously, Kipling wasn't in love with her. If he was, he would have said something. Or even hinted. But he hadn't. He'd looked shocked. Maybe even horrified.

So he didn't love her. That was fine, right? It wasn't as if she loved him, either. Loving Kipling meant caring about him more than she cared about herself. It meant imagining life with him for years and years and being happy that of all the men she could have gotten pregnant with, she'd chosen him. Loving him meant being grateful he was in her life and trusting him to help her with Starr. Loving him meant that she knew for certain that forty years from now her heart would still beat faster when he walked into the room.

She realized the room had gotten a little blurry and blinked. Tears rolled onto her cheeks. She brushed them away, but more replaced them. Her throat tightened, and she fought against a sob. Because the truth had been there all along. She'd just never noticed. Somewhere along the way, she'd fallen in love with Kipling and as far as she could tell, he had no intention of loving her back.

CHAPTER EIGHTEEN

Kipling knew that his week was about to get a whole lot worse. He sat at one of the tables by the bar and watched the rest of his partners take their seats. They were all there. Josh Golden, Raoul Moreno, Kenny Scott, Jack McGarry and Sam Ridge. The Stryker brothers: Rafe, Shane and Clay. Only Gideon was missing. Probably because he had already pulled out of the partnership.

Rafe, Josh and Kenny exchanged a look, as if they'd talked things over ahead of time, then Kenny turned to Kipling.

"We understand what happened with Carter," he said. "If it was one of our daughters, we'd feel the same way. But the problem is bigger than you and Gideon going at it."

"Kudos on taking him on," Raoul added. "You know Gideon has Special Forces training, right?"

Kipling hadn't known, but didn't see how the information made any difference. He wasn't going to stop protecting Starr because his opponent was dangerous.

Rafe shook his head. "If we could stay on topic…"

"I wasn't off topic," Raoul told him. "I was just saying, it took balls."

"Big ones," Kipling said. "Now why are we having this meeting?"

The partners exchanged a look that confirmed they'd all been in contact. Kipling was going to be the last to know, which meant the news wasn't good.

"The women are upset," Kenny said with a shrug. "The Man Cave is doing steady business. Not what we were at the opening, but still enough that they're worried about Jo and how this is affecting her. Now personally I think she can take care of herself and her bar, but it's not my decision. It's Bailey's."

Kenny Scott was a big guy. Tall, muscled and a former NFL player. If Kipling had to pick the one person who wouldn't be pushed around by the woman in his life, he would say it was Kenny. And he would be wrong.

"Let me see if I understand you," Kipling said calmly. "We opened The Man Cave because there wasn't a place in town for a guy to go and have a beer. Jo's caters to women, and the restaurant bars aren't the same. So we created this place together to solve a problem. Now you're telling me you want out because it's working?"

The other men shifted uneasily in their chairs.

"It's not that simple," Rafe began, then nodded. "But yeah, that's about right. Look, the bar is great. I like it here. When I have a potential buyer in town, this is exactly where I want to bring him. But Heidi doesn't like it. She and Jo are tight."

"Jo talked to all your wives?"

Everyone nodded.

"And because she's upset, you're pulling out?"

"No," Sam corrected. "Jo's great, but I'm doing this for Dellina."

The phrase "pussy whipped" came to mind, but Kipling knew there was no point in stating the obvious.

"Then go," he said. "The business will survive without your support. I'll make arrangements to buy you out."

"No rush," Rafe told him. "Start-ups need cash. You can pay me back last."

"Me, too," Jack said. "I just need to be able to tell Larissa that I'm out."

"What he said," Raoul added. "Except it's Pia, not Larissa."

In a matter of minutes, they were all gone. Kipling stood by the bar and wondered what the hell had just happened. Two days ago he'd totally screwed things up with Destiny, and now this?

Nick walked in from the back, his expression sympathetic.

"I take it you heard them," Kipling muttered.

"Enough."

"I thought we were doing something here. How's the business doing, anyway?"

"Receipts are down. The tourist trade is steady, but it's not enough. This isn't exactly a place to bring the kids, and the majority of folks coming to town have families. So we need the locals to survive. If the women tell their husbands to boycott, we're screwed."

"You've lived here all your life. Any suggestions?"

"Talk to Jo."

Kipling had already figured out he was going to have to. "And say what?"

"I don't know. She's a woman. Apologize."

"That is not happening." He thought about putting his fist through the bar, only the bar was solid wood. So it would win.

"I'm not the bad guy in all this," he told Nick, only to remember the look in Starr's eyes when he'd been unable to say he loved her sister. Because while thinking about that was hell, it was still easier than thinking about how he'd hurt Destiny.

"You're not," Nick agreed. "But you still have to fix it. Or we're going to have to close."

Kipling walked Toward Jo's Bar via his sister's bakery. He wasn't sure what to think about what had just happened, let alone what he was supposed to say to the mysterious and powerful Jo. He figured Shelby might be able to offer advice.

When he got to the bakery, the teen at the counter waved him toward the back. He found Shelby standing over a couple dozen unfrosted cupcakes. But instead of smoothing on toppings, she was staring at the far wall. Her shoulders were slumped, her expression sad.

"What?" he said, concerned. "Tell me what's happened."

She jumped, as if he'd startled her, then she wiped her cheeks and shook her head.

"Sorry, big brother. There are problems you can't fix."

"I can fix this one."

"I doubt it."

"Tell me."

She rolled her eyes. "It's about my love life. Or lack thereof. Men are jerks, someone hurt my feelings and then he left town. Before you ask, no, you can't fix it." She gave him a shaky smile. "I love you like a brother, and you have to let this go."

He glared at her. "Tell me."

"No. I was seeing someone who was seeing a bunch of other women at the same time, and now he's gone. It's for the best. I'll move on. I'll find the right guy."

Kipling was at her side in a heartbeat. "Did he—"

The sadness fled as tenderness filled her eyes. She hugged him.

"No," she whispered. "He never hit me." She straightened and touched his face. "Kipling, not all guys are like our dad. Some are jerks with their words and actions, not their fists. You can't protect me from everything. I appreciate that you try, but please, let this go. I'm okay. Or I will be. It's a good lesson. I need to stop falling for flashy, charming men. I need to find someone solid, who will love me for me."

"Someone sensible?" he asked, thinking of Destiny and her ridiculous plan. She didn't want love. She'd been clear on that. No strong emotions for her. So she should be happy that he wasn't in love with her. Only she hadn't looked happy, and in the past two days, she hadn't taken any of his calls.

"Not exactly sensible," Shelby admitted with a smile. "I want something more romantic than that. But someone steady. Someone I can depend on." Her smile widened. "Who isn't my brother. This isn't something you can—or should—fix. Not every problem has a solution. Just let me heal and get on with my life."

"That's a clear message."

"Good. What's going on with you?"

"Not much."

"How's Destiny?"

"Great."

"I'm glad you two are together. She's so right for you."

An unexpected statement. "How do you figure?"

"Because she's caring, and you need someone to look out for you. Her family is a little wild, which means there will always be a crisis, and you like to take care of people. You have the same world view." She laughed. "I don't know. You fit. I like seeing the two of you together."

Kipling kissed her forehead. "Thanks, kid. I'll see you soon. Let me know if you need my help."

"Always."

He left. Shelby's words echoed in his head.

He'd thought he'd slept with Destiny because she was hot and that he'd married her because she got pregnant. Was there more to it than that? Shelby's description of their relationship made him wonder if there was more going on than he'd realized. But first he had to see a woman about her bar.

"Let me know when you want to hike in, and I'll come with you," Cassidy said.

"It's not your responsibility," Destiny told her then looked back at the screen.

"We're in this together. Besides, I like hiking."

"Thanks."

The last session with the volunteers had shown her there were blank areas in several of the search grids. While she and Miles had mapped as much as they could from the air, there were still several areas she had to cover on foot. She'd thought she'd gotten them all, but apparently not. Which was why she stayed on-site as long as she did.

She logged off her computer and collected her bag.

"You're working late?" she asked Cassidy.

Her friend shook her head. "Nope. I have a date with Jeff over Skype in an hour. The lighting is better here than at my place." She grinned. "I know, I know. After nearly twenty years of marriage, why on earth would I care about how I look, and yet I do."

"Young love," Destiny teased.

"Exactly." Cassidy sighed. "I hope you and Kipling stay as in love as Jeff and me. Sure there are ups and downs in every marriage, but I would be lost without that man. And not in a way your fancy program could find me. Have a good night."

"You, too."

Destiny left the office and started home. As she walked toward home, she wondered how long she would be in love with Kipling. It had been two days since their last conversation. He'd tried to call her a couple of times, but she'd let him go to voice mail. When he'd texted, she'd asked for time. So far he was giving it to her.

She breathed in the warm air and wondered how she'd made such a mess of things. She'd fallen in love with a man who saw her as a project. Even more of a complication, she was pregnant with his child. It wasn't as if she and Kipling could simply break up. They were going to be connected for the rest of their lives.

The idea of that was both wonderful and terrifying. If she

had to stay in touch with him, how could she ever stop loving him? Because she had to stop. She saw that now.

All her life she'd been running from exactly what she found herself in now. An emotional mess. She'd been so sure she'd made all the right choices, but she hadn't made any choices at all. She'd been hiding. From life. From herself. From her heart.

She arrived at the house just as Starr was walking up to the front door. They waved at each other.

"How was your day?" Destiny asked.

"Good."

"Any more kissing?"

Her sister rolled her eyes. "You're never letting that go, are you?"

"Probably not."

They stepped into the living room and flopped onto the sofa.

"You're not the type to kiss just any guy," Destiny added. "So you must really like Carter."

Starr blushed. "I do. He's so great. I know we're young, and I don't want things to get serious, but when I'm around him…"

"Magic?"

"Yeah. Just like they talk about in songs. You know, like your feelings for Kipling."

Destiny really hoped Starr wasn't experiencing any of *those* kinds of feelings.

"But we've talked," Starr continued. "There's not going to be any more kissing. We're going to hang out with friends and stuff. Be together, but not serious."

"That's a really smart decision."

"You think? I'm trying. I thought a lot about what you said. About my parents and how they reacted instead of thinking things through."

"You still have to have fun," Destiny told her. "Be a kid."

"I know, and I will. Just not so fast with boys. See. I'm learning from you."

"You are."

But Destiny wondered how much of the lesson was a good thing. Because it seemed to her, she might have gone too far in the sensible direction. It wasn't as if her personal life had turned out so great.

Their sensible marriage was no longer so sensible. In fact, in the cold light of day, it was a ridiculous thing to have done. She was intelligent and capable. She could raise a child on her own. Not that she was trying to shut Kipling out or keep him from his baby. But marriage?

"I want to talk to you about something," she said.

"What?"

"Kipling, mostly."

Starr leaned her head against the sofa. "I wondered. He hasn't been around."

"He's called but I haven't wanted to talk to him."

"Because he hurt your feelings?"

"Yes, and because I was confused. When I was your age…"

Destiny wasn't sure how to explain something that didn't quite make sense to her.

"I was determined not to be like my parents. I wanted a stable home. A sure thing. I got that from my Grandma Nell, but when I went out on my own, I was scared. What if I fell crazy in love and ran around the country, singing at honky-tonks and living on a bus?"

Starr laughed. "That sounds fun."

"Not to me. It would have been a nightmare." She paused, mentally feeling her way as she went. "I was so afraid of what I could become, that I started to ignore who I actually was. It was safe, but now I'm thinking it might not have been the right decision."

She smiled at her sister. "I never would have let myself kiss a boy the way you did. I would have been too scared of what would happen. I ran from so many things."

"Like your music?" Starr asked softly.

"Yes. Like my music." She drew in a breath. "I guess I'm saying I'm a complete and total mess."

"You're not. You're wonderful. You took me in."

"I'm lucky you put up with me. You're my sister, and I'm so grateful we're making a life together."

"Me, too." Starr bit her lower lip. "You're not going to stay married to Kipling, are you?"

"I don't think so. We don't want the same thing. I panicked when I found out I was pregnant. That wasn't really smart of me. I still want to stay in Fool's Gold. We're still going to be a family. Just you and me."

"And the baby." Starr leaned toward her. "I'll help. I can do things around the house."

"Good. One of us should know what she's doing."

Starr laughed.

"We'll get a house," Destiny told her. "One we pick out together."

Not the one where she and Kipling made love, she thought. Those were memories she wanted to avoid.

"Are you going to get another job?" Starr asked tentatively. "Can you work with a baby?"

A really good question. Income would be required. She didn't doubt that Kipling would offer to pay child support, but that was money she would want to put away. In the meantime, she was perfectly capable and had a unique skill set.

"My mom's manager has always told me he wants to put me to work writing songs. I'm going to call him and find out if he's telling the truth." She touched Starr's arm. "In fact, I was thinking of going through what I have after dinner. Want to help me with that?"

Starr's eyes widened. "Yeah. I'd love to."

"Good. Let's check out what's thawing in the refrigerator."

They rose, and Destiny led the way into the kitchen. But her

mind was on the notebooks she'd stored in a box in her dresser.
Notebooks filled with dozens of songs she'd written over the
years. There were a few that would make beautiful duets. There
might very well be some interest in a release sung by the daughters of Jimmy Don Mills.

She wasn't willing to go on tour or anything like that, but
maybe a studio album wasn't out of the question.

"What's so funny?" Starr asked. "You're smiling."

"Am I? I was just thinking that life is nothing if not ironic.
I've spent years running away from who I am only to find out
that's the person I need to be."

For a woman who owned a business smack in the middle of
town, Jo Trellis was a difficult person to find. Kipling had been
to her bar three times, left voice mail and texts, and he'd yet
to connect with her. From what he could tell, she was avoiding him. Which seemed to be popular these days. Destiny was
avoiding him, too.

This was not how he'd planned to spend the first couple of
weeks of his marriage. Those nights had been so promising, he
thought grimly, as he walked toward Destiny's house. They'd
been all over each other. But more exciting than the physical
chemistry had been how much they'd enjoyed each other's company. Or at least he'd enjoyed hers. By the way she was avoiding
him, Destiny hadn't felt the same connection.

What he didn't get was how it had all gone to hell so quickly.
One minute they were promising until death they did part, and
the next he couldn't get her on the phone.

He knew the exact moment everything had changed with
Destiny. It had happened after the incident with Starr and Carter.
But the real trouble with everything else had begun long before that. That much he knew. But the exact when of it was
more confusing.

He walked through the center of town. The Fourth of July

festival was in full swing with booths and crafts and live music in the park. There was going to be a parade later, and fireworks. Normally, he found that kind of thing a lot of fun. But not today. Today he needed to see Destiny, and he had to figure out why he was so unsettled.

The Man Cave was part of the problem. If he couldn't fix things with Jo and his partners, then the bar wouldn't survive. Nick had shown him the books. Kipling had seen right away that while the bar could limp along for a few months, the end was inevitable. Without local support, they were doomed.

It wasn't the failure of the business that got to him, he thought. It was what that failure meant. Because The Man Cave had been his way of fitting in. Of giving back. And he'd screwed it up royally.

He paused by Brew-haha and looked toward the park. Even though it was still morning, there were crowds everywhere. The sun was warm, the sky blue.

Little more than a year ago he'd been skiing down a mountain in New Zealand, preparing to start serious training. He'd been fresh off his Olympic win and totally unstoppable. Or so he'd thought.

After the crash, he'd been more worried about whether he would walk again than thinking about the end of his career. Then Mayor Marsha had shown up, out of nowhere. She'd offered him a job and had promised to take care of Shelby.

He still remembered how he hadn't believed her. How he'd promised to follow her to hell if she would protect his sister. He still remembered exactly what she'd said.

"You don't have to be alone in this, Kipling. Nor do you have to go all the way to hell. Just come to Fool's Gold when you're able. We'll be waiting for you."

She had kept her word. He knew now that Ford Hendrix and Angel Whittaker had flown to Colorado that very day. When Shelby's mother had died, they'd brought Shelby to Fool's Gold.

Kipling had followed when he was able. In January, he'd accepted the job as the head of HERO.

When he'd realized there wasn't a place for guys to hang out, he'd thought of The Man Cave. He'd gotten several business partners together, and they'd hired Nick.

He'd been so sure it was the right thing to do. It fixed a problem. He wanted to say it was the same with Destiny, only it wasn't. Because she was more important than all the rest of them put together.

He turned away from the park and walked the last couple of blocks to her house. When her door opened and he saw her, his whole body relaxed. Being with her was right.

"Hey," he said with a smile. "I wanted to see how you're doing."

"I'm glad you came by."

She had on cut-off jeans and a T-shirt. Her hair was back in a ponytail, and she was barefoot. Not overtly sexy, but she sure got to him.

He wanted to pull her close and kiss her. He wanted to do other things, too, but mostly he wanted to hold her. They sat on the sofa, facing each other. She looked good, he thought. Maybe a little tired, but all her.

His gaze dropped to the ring on her finger. The simple gold band looked lonely. He wanted to add a nice engagement ring. A sparkly diamond. Sure it was traditional, but he was mostly a traditional kind of guy.

"I've missed you," he told her. "Is everything okay with Starr?"

She nodded. "We're getting along well. We're sorting through songs I've written. My mom's manager is going to fly in next week to talk about the music."

"Good for you. You're too talented to ignore your abilities. How are you feeling?"

"Fine. I have a gynecologist appointment next week."

"With Dr. Galloway?" he asked, hoping the answer was no.

"How did you know?"

He shrugged. "I've met her." There was no need to go into the "flowering" conversation with Destiny. "Can I come with you?"

She nodded. "I want you to be as much a part of me being pregnant as you'd like."

It struck him that everything about this was wrong. They were married. They should be holding each other and heading to the bedroom to make love. Their conversation should be easy and natural—not stilted and informational. This was Destiny—they knew each other. Only right now it felt as if they were strangers.

"What's going on?" he asked. "You wanted time, so I gave it to you. Should I have pushed harder to talk to you?"

"No. You did the right thing. I've been thinking a lot about everything." She looked at him. "Kipling, I love you."

His first reaction was to jump up and yell the happy news as loud as he could. Destiny loved him. Destiny, who was kind and funny and sexy and determined. His second thought was that if she loved him, she would need so much more than he had to offer. He'd been unable to protect his own sister from his father's fists. How could he protect anyone else? Especially Destiny?

"I didn't expect it, either," she said wryly. "I had no idea. I've tried to be rational and calm in every situation. But that's not who I am. I don't have an answer to the nurture-nature question, but what I do know is that I can't pretend anymore. I can get a little crazy. Maybe I don't throw plates, but I'm not as rational as you think. I feel things. Deeply. And I'm not going to deny that anymore."

"I like that you feel things."

She smiled. "Good. Because we're having a baby together. We have a lot to work out."

He reached for her hands. "I want that. I want us to be a family, Destiny. I meant my vows. I'm in this for the long haul."

Her smile faded. "I believe you because me being pregnant is yet another problem for you to handle."

The unfair statement had him hanging on tighter. "It's more than that."

"I don't think it is. You don't love me back. It's okay. You don't have to. You like me, and we're friends, and I've seen how you take care of your sister. You'll be a good dad. Like I said before, I want you to be as much a part of my pregnancy as you want. I won't shut you out, but I won't be married to you. Not like this. I don't need fixing. I need to be loved, and you can't or won't." She squeezed his fingers before releasing them.

"Kipling, I want a divorce."

CHAPTER NINETEEN

"You okay?" Cassidy asked.

No. I'm pregnant, getting a divorce, responsible for my teenage sister and I'm quitting my job in two weeks. Destiny told herself to breathe then smile. The phrase *fake it until you make it* had never sounded so right.

"I'm fine. Ready to get hiking."

She and Cassidy were heading out to map the last few areas on the grid. They'd already divided up the map. She figured each of the sections could be completed in less than a day. If everything went well, they would be done by the end of the week.

It was the Saturday of the July Fourth weekend, but neither she nor Cassidy had any reason not to work. Starr was with friends, and Destiny had no desire to sit home alone. Cassidy's husband was half a world away. Mapping the grid was a perfect solution.

"Radio in every couple of hours," Cassidy said as she collected her backpack. "I'll do the same." She grinned. "It would be humiliating for one of us to get lost."

"Tell me about it." Destiny picked up her own gear, and they headed for the door.

The timing of the work was perfect, she thought as she drove out of town. With everything going on, a few hours in nature were just what she needed to clear her head. She could enter data into the program and have a good cry at the same time. Because the tears were inevitable.

She could accept loving Kipling. She could accept that he didn't love her back. She was totally rational about the whole thing. The problem was, the news devastated her.

Until she'd told him she wanted a divorce, she hadn't realized how much she was hoping he was secretly in love with her, too. That he would turn to her, confess his feelings, and they would live happily ever after. But that hadn't happened. She'd said she wanted a divorce; Kipling had nodded once, said he would get his lawyer on that, and he'd left. There'd been no conversation, no whisper of emotion. Nothing. A big, fat nothing.

While she knew that staying married was a mistake, she couldn't help wishing that things had ended differently. After all those years of avoiding strong feelings, she'd finally gone and fallen in love, only to end up in an emotional face-plant. So much for acting rationally.

She pulled off the highway and into a rest area then consulted her map. When she'd confirmed she was where she was supposed to be, she got out and shrugged into her backpack then turned on the GPS tracker, along with her other equipment, and headed for the forest.

Time would heal, she reminded herself. She had a wonderful family and a baby on the way. Later, she would call her mother and tell Lacey that her wish for a grandbaby had been granted. This weekend she and Starr would continue to sort through Destiny's songs and pick the best twenty or so to play for her mom's manager. She would buy a house and get on with her life.

She had people who cared about her. She had good friends and lots of support. What she didn't have was the love of the man who had claimed her heart. That hurt, but she would survive.

For years Grandma Nell had been the benchmark by which she measured her actions. Would Grandma Nell do that? Would Grandma Nell be proud? While Destiny loved her grandmother, she knew she had to shift her thinking. Making Grandma Nell proud wasn't the point anymore. Now she had to learn to be proud of herself.

Skiing seventy miles an hour into a tree broke more bones than Destiny walking out on him, but being without her hurt a whole lot more. Kipling still couldn't figure out what to do with the information she'd clobbered him with before she'd left.

She loved him, and she was gone. Just like that. *I love you. I want a divorce.* It was the end of a bad movie. It was so extreme as to be ridiculous. But he wasn't laughing. Or sleeping or eating. In fact, it was all he could do to keep breathing.

It hurt. More than anything ever had. He who had always believed that the words didn't matter—that only actions matter—had been ripped open by what he'd been told. Words killed, he thought grimly.

Just as bad, she was gone. Oh, sure, he would see her. They were having a kid together, and he knew that whatever happened between the two of them, she would never try to cut him out of his child's life. But he didn't want to be a part-time dad. He wanted to be a family. With her.

He started out of his rental to tell her just that, only to stop by the front door and turn around. What was he to say to convince her not to divorce him? He wanted them to stay married. He wanted to live with her and have his child with her. He thought he'd shown her how much he cared by his actions. He'd been there for her, had taken care of her.

He knew there was a solution to the problem. There had to be. But whatever it was, it eluded him. He ran different scenarios in his mind. He wrote letters. He'd considered renting a billboard, but had no idea what it would say.

Don't leave me was a start. *Marry me* was out of the question. They were already married. *Let's not get a divorce* was too twisted.

What he didn't understand was what had changed. If she loved him now, she'd probably loved him for a while. So wasn't their being married a good thing?

Someone knocked on his door. He pulled it open, eager to see Destiny. But instead his sister stood on the porch.

She put her hands on her hips. "Seriously, you could at least try not to be so disappointed it's me."

"Sorry."

"Hoping it was your new bride?"

He nodded and stepped back to let his sister in. She walked past him then turned to face him when he shut the front door.

"What's up?"

He asked the question in his best casual, "I'm fine. Ignore the signs of strain and tension" voice. Apparently, it worked because Shelby didn't ask any questions. Instead she said, "I've been thinking."

"About?"

"What you said before. About the business and me and us." She sighed. "You're a good big brother, and I love you."

It was obvious she had more to say, so he waited.

"And I'm sorry."

Not what he expected. "About?"

"I've sent you mixed messages. I ask your advice then get mad when you give it. I want you to rescue me but only sometimes. It's not clear to me, so it sure can't be clear to you, either."

He relaxed a little. "Okay. So where does that leave us?"

She smiled. "I would like to borrow the money from you, but only as a loan. I'll pay you back, with interest."

"What if I don't want to give you the money anymore?"

She laughed then hugged him. "You're a funny guy."

"Not everyone thinks so."

"Then they don't know you well enough."

He didn't think that was Destiny's problem.

Shelby studied him. "Want to talk about it?"

"There's nothing. I'm fine."

"Then why are you still living here instead of with Destiny?"

She had him on that one. "It's complicated. She's…" Not mad, he thought. Disappointed? Hurt? "Upset."

"Did you try to fix things too much? You do that, Kipling. You mean well, but sometimes people want to be more than a project."

"I don't see people as projects."

She raised her eyebrows as her hands returned to her hips.

He sighed. "Sometimes I do," he admitted.

"Enough that it's hard for the rest of us to be sure where we stand and if we matter. You're my brother, and I don't always know if you're excited about helping me or taking care of the problem."

Was that what had gone wrong with Destiny? He hadn't made it clear he cared about her and the baby?

"Doesn't what I do matter more than what I say?"

"Not always." Shelby hugged him. "You're a really good guy. If Destiny isn't seeing that right now, then give her a little time. You're not wrong to care."

"Thanks." Although he knew he had to be wrong about something because Destiny didn't want to stay married to him. "You doing okay?"

"I am. I had a brief but horrible relationship with Miles, and I'm now officially over him."

"What? Miles the pilot? He's a player." And soon to be dead, Kipling thought grimly.

"Yes, I see that now." Shelby shook her head. "Don't go there. Don't take on my problem. I bought into his charm, and I learned a good lesson. I'll recover."

"You're my sister."

"Thanks for the clarification." She wrinkled her nose. "I mean it, Kipling. I have to figure this out on my own. Don't mess in my personal life, okay?"

He nodded slowly. "Sure. Come to me for money but not advice."

She flashed him a smile. "Exactly."

Not sure what to do with himself, Kipling walked through town. Just his luck, no one was getting lost on a very busy holiday weekend.

Tourists mingled with locals. The smell of barbecue mingled with the scent of lemons and fresh churros. He nodded at people he knew, stepped out of the way of unsteady toddlers and rescued a balloon that nearly got away.

All of which should have made him feel better. Connected, maybe. But it didn't, and he wasn't.

He missed Destiny. Without her, he couldn't seem to think straight. Or sleep. Or know what was going on. He could have gone to see her. He knew that she and Cassidy were out mapping the last parts of the mountain. He could have joined them. But then what?

He crossed the street and headed for the park. Live music played. Music that made him think of Destiny performing at The Man Cave and how she'd lost herself in song.

She was amazing, he thought. Powerful and talented. Beautiful. She'd claimed to love him and then told him she wanted a divorce. What was he supposed to do with that?

The truth was, he wanted her back. He missed her and—

He turned at the sound of teenage boys laughing and saw Carter standing with his friends. The second Kipling spotted him, he knew what he had to do.

He walked toward the teen. Carter saw him approaching and straightened. While the festival spun on around them, Kipling felt the afternoon grow quiet—at least in his head.

"Hey," he said, when he was in front of Carter. "I wanted to tell you I'm sorry. I don't approve of you kissing Starr, but I get why it happened. Mills women are tough to resist." He raised one shoulder. "Yelling at you wasn't my finest hour."

Carter grinned. "It's okay. Felicia explained about the protective instincts of the alpha male in the clan." The teen chuckled. "Which might not make sense to you, but it's kind of how she talks. She's supersmart. Anyway, she's right. Starr's almost like your daughter. You have to be protective. I'm glad she has someone looking out for her, you know. Because it wasn't always like that."

Kipling stared at the kid. "You're not a jerk."

"Thanks, man. Neither are you."

Kipling shook his head. "No. I mean you're a good kid."

"Always have been. Does this mean I can—"

"No," Kipling told him firmly. "My protective instincts remain intact. But I now have more respect for Starr's selection process."

"I think that's a compliment, so thanks."

"You're welcome."

Carter turned back to his friends. Kipling looked around and tried to figure out what he should do next. Suddenly, a tall, brown-haired woman stepped in front of him.

"I hear you've been looking for me."

She was close to forty, fit, with just enough attitude to make a guy think she knew how to take care of herself.

Kipling had no idea who she was.

"Ma'am?"

The woman raised her eyebrows. "Not a very good way to start, Kipling. I've heard you're charming. Don't disappoint me."

Was it him, or had it gotten a little hot in here?

"I'm Jo Trellis," the woman said. "Of Jo's Bar."

"You," he said loudly. "Finally. I've been trying to talk to you for days. You won't take my calls or return them. You're never around when I stop by."

She looked more amused than chagrined. "What can I say? I'm elusive."

"You're putting me out of business."

"Back at you."

They stared at each other.

Kipling figured it had been her town first. "I'm sure we can find a solution to this problem."

"I've heard you like fixing things. So sure. Fix this one. We all take care of each other. If you wanted to open a bar that competed directly with me, you should have talked to me first. Or someone. But you didn't. You stomped in and did your thing without considering anyone else."

"Hey, wait. It wasn't like that. The guys around here don't have anywhere to go. Your place caters to women."

Her chin rose. "Tell me how that's bad."

Oops. "It's, ah, not. Women should have a bar where they can be comfortable. But so should guys. That's all I was doing." He thought about the town and how involved everyone was. "I didn't think about talking to you. I'm not from here."

"Not much of an excuse. You should learn how to have a conversation. Words matter."

He was starting to see that. They'd mattered with Carter, they mattered with Jo. Didn't it make sense they would matter with Destiny, too? She'd told him she loved him, and what had he said in return? Not a thing.

He thought about everything that was wrong right now. "I'm sorry I didn't talk to you first. I should have. For what it's worth, you've won. My partners have pulled out, and Nick says we can't make it solely on tourist dollars."

Jo shifted from foot to foot. "Yeah, well, about that. I might have made a few phone calls. I wanted to make a little trouble, but I didn't anticipate how seriously my friends would take my concerns."

"You didn't mean to shut me down?"

"Hell, no. I was going to talk to you. Jo's does a good business, but I'm tired of working sixteen-hour days. I have a hot husband at home I'd like to spend more time with. I'm going to call off the ladies. Your partners will come slinking back. Jo's Bar is going to be open five days a week and close at seven in the evening. You can have the nights."

She held out her hand. He shook it. "Remind me never to go up against you again," he said.

"You got that right. Tell Nick to expect a crowd tonight. I'm going to make some calls."

Destiny crossed the shallow stream. On the other side, she confirmed the GPS signal was still strong. While she enjoyed a day hike as much as the next person, she didn't want to have to retrace her steps.

She paused for a drink of water. Tall trees offered shade overhead and kept the temperature comfortable, but she was in her third hour of hiking and getting a little tired.

She was out of shape, she thought. She hadn't been exercising as regularly. That was going to have to change. She had to stay healthy for two. Something she couldn't mention to Kipling, she thought with a smile. Before she finished speaking, he would have designed a program and signed her up with a trainer.

No, he wouldn't, she thought, her smile fading. Because they weren't together anymore. She'd ended things pretty abruptly, and she hadn't heard from him since.

She missed him, she admitted. A lot. There was a hole in her life and maybe in her heart. A Kipling-size one. She missed how he visibly brightened when she walked in the room. How he listened and then offered advice whether she wanted it or not. She liked how easily he'd adjusted to being a mere mortal after years spent being a ski god.

He was a good man, she thought wistfully. Funny, charming, caring. Instead of getting mad when he'd found out she'd been a virgin, he'd wanted to help her learn to enjoy sex. He was dependable and caring. If only he loved her. Because without loving her, without her being able to—

Destiny stopped in midstride. She slowly lowered her raised foot to the ground and let the swirling thoughts settle. When they did, she nearly fell over from shock.

She was still doing it. She was still running from something—just like she always had. She'd run from her parents when she'd been younger. She'd run from her emotions, her passions, her talents. She'd built up walls and hidden behind them, and she was still doing it. Right this second.

How did she know Kipling didn't love her? She hadn't asked. She hadn't given him a chance to talk or explain or even think. They'd never talked about their marriage or explored what either of them expected or needed to make the relationship work. She'd simply told him she wanted a divorce.

Running away from something wasn't the same as running to something. She'd spent so much of her life thinking about what she didn't want that she'd forgotten to figure out what was important to her. She was so worried about being unhappy that she never bothered to find what made her happy. Or who.

She loved Kipling. She knew that for sure. But did he love her? Maybe this was a good time to be asking that question. And not just of herself.

"What have I done?" she asked out loud.

There was no answer. Just the hum of insects and the call of a hawk.

She glanced down at her screen. Her exact location showed as a tiny dot. She could see the most direct route back to her car and immediately headed that way.

Men had been making fools of themselves over women for centuries, Kipling thought cheerfully. He was just one in a long line. If he was going to lose Destiny, he was going to do it in style. With everything on the table.

In the past hour he'd had a call from five of his business partners asking to be a part of The Man Cave again, and a text from
Nick saying he was expecting a big crowd. Felicia Boylan, Carter's mother, had found him and hugged him, all the while telling him how happy she was that he'd shown Carter the complete
cycle of a male exchange, from misunderstanding to threatened
violence, to apology and resolution. When he'd tried to explain
that hadn't been his intent, she'd brushed off his comments.

He stood there, in the center of the festival, surrounded by
people, and all he could think was that he wanted to tell Destiny all about it. Not just tell her, but have her share in it. He
wanted to laugh with her and touch her and take care of her.

But the telling was important, too. Talking to her. Words. It
came back to those damn words.

He got that actions were significant. Promising to be faithful
was meaningless if you went out and cheated. His father hitting
Shelby had a whole lot more meaning than the times he'd sworn
he loved her. But maybe, just maybe, he'd taken the lesson he'd
learned just a little too far. Maybe he'd dismissed the words too
quickly. And if that were the case, he just might have a chance
at winning Destiny back.

In the time it took him to jog home and grab the keys to his
Jeep, he came to several more realizations. He realized that just
because he'd never been in love before didn't mean he was necessarily flawed. He hadn't been holding back because he didn't
believe saying he loved someone made a difference—he'd been
waiting. For the right woman. The only woman.

Destiny had said she loved him, and now all he wanted was
to say it back to her. Then convince her, because action was always going to be his thing. But he would say it, too.

Destiny loved him, he loved her, and there was no way he
was going to let her go. Not without a fight. And if he made a
fool of himself because of it, so be it.

He headed out of town. A quick call to Cassidy gave him

the starting point. He had his tracking equipment and working knowledge of the STORMS program. He was supposed to be some kind of search and rescue expert. It was time he put that title to the test.

He pulled off into the rest area parking lot and pulled up next to Destiny's car. After getting out, he checked his equipment then started entering data. She was an experienced hiker, on a day trip. He knew the grid she would cover, just not which part she would be in right now.

"Looking for someone?"

He glanced up and saw Destiny heading toward him. He opened his driver's door, flung in his tablet then walked toward her.

There were so many things to say, he thought, but none of them mattered right this second. He cupped her face in his hands and kissed her on the mouth. She wrapped her arms around him and hung on as if she was never going to let go.

"I love you," he said when they came up for air.

"I had no right to say I wanted a divorce— What?" Her green eyes widened. "What did you say?"

"I love you. A lot. I have for a while. We're not getting a divorce without talking about it first. Once you agree to that, I'm going to convince you to stay with me for always."

"I do love a man with a plan." Her lips trembled. "Real love?"

"The forever kind." He kissed her again. "The kind that means I'm not leaving, so you should consider sticking around, too."

"I will. I am. I've been running away from what scared me for so long that I forgot what it was like to run to something. To you."

He held her close and breathed in the scent of her.

"Marry me," he whispered. "Not because you're pregnant or because it's the right thing to do. Marry me because you can't imagine spending another day without me. Marry me because we're a family. You, me, Starr, the baby. Marry me so we can be together always."

She looked into his eyes. "I already did, Kipling." She leaned against him. "I already did."

Kipling led her to his Jeep. She climbed inside. They would deal with her car later. They would deal with a lot of things. But the decisions would be easy, because they were together.

It wasn't flying down a mountain at seventy miles an hour, he thought as he started down the highway. It was better.

She took his hand in hers. "I'm going to write a song about this." She grinned. "After we have sex."

He was still laughing when they drove into town.

★ ★ ★ ★ ★